The Farmer's Revenge;

or,

Hunting Man-eaters.

Acknowledgement.

After publishing my first novel **It's Hauling Us**, back in 2018. I busied myself to work on another story of a different Genre. I've realized that I enjoy the field of writing stories, and thus I wanted to create my first tale of horror.

A special thank you to cover artist Brittany Wilson whose art talent had caught my eye when I was looking up the right binding to match my novel. Another special thanks to my cousin William Taggard, a dear friend who served as my prove reader and have helped me with new ideas, in placing new words and grammar into my manuscript, I couldn't have done it without him. And finally, a big thank you to my entire family for their love and support to me as I pursue my dreams to write and share my stories to the world.

Chapter 1. New Meat.

The distraught man walked out of the courthouse, in deep despair. He has been broken in every way a man could. His name is Scotfield. Nathan Scotfield, he walked on the streets of Staten Island crying and wet as the rain soaked his navy-blue dress suit. He was heartbroken after losing everything he had worked for. He made it to his hotel room and dropped in his bed sobbing completely downcast. It was midnight when he had finally calmed himself, still dressed in his damp suit.

"What am I to do now?" he thought repeatedly. As he walked back and forth across his dark room, from the entrance to the window, looking out at the city in anger.

"Well she ruined me now… I have nothing here anymore." He said to himself. "What do I do now?"

Scotfield kept thinking and thinking through the entire night, all through the coming dawn. And then it came to him, he remembered before his father passed, he'd left him a large sum of money, just enough to start a new life. And that was it. The one account his wife didn't cease from him in the divorce.

"I must start off fresh," he quoted. "I can start a new life, it's only the beginning of a new and brighter future."

Nathan checked himself out of the hotel, made for a real estate agency to find himself a new home, someplace in the upstate countryside of New York. Less than a month later they found just the place.

The hamlet of Graytown. A small group of houses, with a saloon, a meat market, a gas station, and a vast forest of pine trees. The woods stretched far out for miles, all the way to the Adirondack mountains. And at the far end of the town's dirt road was an old farmstead set on top a hill surrounded by a large green meadow.

Graytown is 40 miles north of Utica New York, at the northeastern corner of Oneida county tucked deep within the vast wilderness of the mountains. Most people from Utica and other towns of the county didn't know that such a place has ever existed. Nor did they know of the terrible dark secret its townsfolk possesses.

 A few Graytown residents were having a drink at the local bar, as a half dozen customers sat silently at the counter drinking beer, they all heard the loud noise of a truck engine. They gathered to the window watching as two heavy moving truck, being followed by a silver pickup passes by with a floppy-eared dog hanging out of the passenger's window barking at them.

At the extreme end of Graytown road sat two buildings. A small two-story, blue ranch style home with a big red barn built behind it. The place stood atop a smooth hill on an open green grassland, circled by towering pine trees.

Standing near her mailbox, at the foot of the hill of farmland, was Lidia Kess. The woman watched and observed as the moving convoy passed her home, and up the hill.

"Looks like we got ourselves a new neighbor, Mama," her little boy said holding her hand. "We sure do child, we sure do," she answered watching a man exit a silver pick up, behind the moving truck. "Let's hope he'll be easy."

Stepping off his pickup, with his trusted hound dog, was 37-year-old Nathan Scotfield. The man stood at the top of the hill where he overlooked the welcoming scenery of his ranch that he'd purchased as his new home.

The field was wide, the color of shamrock green, surrounded by an old gray wooden fence.

"Beautiful. Just as I've imagined it," he said to himself, with a smile cracking across his face, while petting his dog.

"So, Mr. Scotfield, do you like your new home so far?" the moving truck driver said as his assistant opened the back door.

"It's even better than the pictures, Ron," Nathan replied. He helped the two men unload the truck, bringing most of his furniture inside.

As this labor was going on, Nathan noticed a group of people from the house down the hill were watching him. They were his neighbors. He looked at them for a second, before waving, but they just stood idle on their front lawn and stared. It was a family of four, a man, his wife, and two kids just standing by the mailbox observing him, standing out like statues and staring as if they were studying him. Feeling slightly weirded out, Nathan just shrugged his shoulders and went back to work.

He walked into his new house. Where it consisted of a kitchen, a living room with a fireplace, a small laundry room, and a bathroom. Upstairs were only two-bedrooms, the master bedroom and a guest room.

While the two men were placing in his bed set Nathan asked them if they knew that family living next store.

"We don't know them, sir," the driver said, "I've been moving furniture for years and I never even come down this road until today. Have you Tyler?"

"No Ron, I never even knew that Graytown existed."

With all the heavy furniture off the trucks, the two assisted Nathan with his luggage.

"Oh wow, got yourself some guns here?" Tyler said holding two-gun cases.

"Yep," replied Nathan, "it's a hunting rifle and a Mossberg."

"Cool, I have Mossberg shotgun myself," the young man said.

"Are you a deer hunter, Mr. Scotfield, " Ron asked.

"Well, not exactly, I'm not a bigtime hunter," replied Scotfield, "The guns aren't just for hunting, but home and animal defense."

Later when all was finished, he tipped the two truckers, and signed the last of the delivery papers. Nathan spent the night setting up his new home and finished by setting his bed and preparing a warm dinner for himself and Tasha.

His new home was small, but it was all Nathan needed.

The next three days, Lidia was outside hanging laundry to air dry in the backyard with her two kids chasing each other. When the chore was finished, she walked to the front again and saw another truck at the farmhouse, this time offloading farm animals.

After he set up his barn with new pens, food, and water tubs, and fixed the picket fences, Nathan was ready to move his livestock into their new home.

Off the truck came a half dozen dairy cows, four dairy goats, sixteen chickens, and two giant draft horse named Dixie and Clyde,

With the livestock now moved into their new homes, Nathan couldn't be more excited to start his new life as a country farmer.

24 acres of isolated land, an open ranch surrounded by a beautiful forest was a virtual artistic portrait of country life, Nathan felt he was living in. A decent life to live until a peaceful death

For a man who had been through so much pain that nearly drove him to suicide it was his passion for the outdoors and animals, that saved him from pointing a gun to his head.

After shaking hands with the delivery, he let all his animals out of the barn to roam free out in the open field. As he watched Dixie run free along with her brother followed by the cows and the goat prancing like deer a smile shined on the man's face. It had been sometime since he felt so joyful.

Hearing a moan and felt something cuddling against his wellington boots. He looked down to find his dog Tasha a hybrid half bloodhound half ridgeback, wagging her tail and jumping on his legs, he knelt to pat her head, where she wetted them with her tongue.

"Well, Tasha my girl, our new life has begun," Nathan said hugging her.

As the day ended, Nathan and Tasha rounded up all the livestock back into the barn, to feed them their evening meals. When all where fed Nathan placed the animals in their stalls and locked the doors. The farmer and his dog went inside for dinner and then off to bed, to rest and be ready for a busy day of farming the following morning.

A few hours later as Nathan and his animals slept, the Pack rallied in the woods just beyond the fence of the ranch. Running, leaping, sniffing and stalking the property, they could sense the new life inside the red barn. The scent of cows, hens, and goats made their jaws water with the thought of fresh meat that lay just inside farm fence.

Chapter 2. Settling in.

The first two weeks went by. Nathan kept busy with his daily farming duties. Feeding the animals, cleaning out their stalls, letting them roam outside to stretch their legs, collecting eggs, and milking the cows and goats. Nathan made his profits by selling his products to grocery stores and at local farm markets.

It was hard work and doing it every day of the week alone made it no easier, but Nathan grew accustomed to his new life. He did not make much money but earns enough to pay the bills and keep the roof over his head.

Within the first month of farming, Nathan decided to plow a garden behind his barn, to make more money at the market. With the help of his two strong horses the task was much easier. In just one day they plowed a large 40 by 60-foot patch of good soil, topped it with cow manure. If all went well, he would have fresh crops by the coming fall, adding more profit to his farmer's budget.

Farming was hard work, but Nathan grew fixed to the routine, and the care of his animals. It kept him focused and the daily work gave him a renewed sense of self-worth.

He was still lonely and kept to himself, martially because the small hamlet was unwelcoming. The only times he went to town was for fuel, groceries, and beer. The Graytown gas station was run by an old man with long white hair and beady eyes. There was something strange in the man's face, whenever Nathan entered, the place he stood in from his chair, walked around the counter and followed Nathan around watching him take items off the shelves. The old man watched him with an unkindly frown, as if he thought Nathan was a shoplifter.

The old man's unfriendly manner got to him. Nathan would stay silent and just pay for the items without even saying 'have a nice day.'

Nathan never really talked with anyone, in town nor even said a simple "hello" whenever he visited the store or a fast food restaurant. Never saying a hello, a good morning afternoon or how's it going? Nathan kept pretty much to himself, quiet and shrewd.

Since the divorce, he had become a shut-in and a very antisocial person. Even at times when he would stop for a drink at the Graytown's tavern, he would sit at the far end of the bar drinking alone as the other customers would speak and whisper behind his back. The only joy he found in his new life was his animals, Tasha, and drinking.

One night after a busy day of farm work he stopped in the bar for a quick drink while he sipped a glass of scotch, he watched the bartender a ruff stocky man named Davis, chatting with two men at the other end of the counter. The trio caught the farmer staring at them.

"What are you staring at asshole?" one asked to him. Nathan just turned his head to the window and gave them the cold shoulder.

While Nathan never spoke with the unfriendly townsfolk, he did speak with his fellow farmers from the husbandry or the markets where he'd sell his products. They were far more friendly and nicer to deal with.

For many people who might think, that living such a lonely life with only animals for company would be very depressing, but Nathan was doing something he loved. He was not only working a farm as a job but living his newfound passion. He was truly happy most days as he worked with his livestock, with pure pride.

There was a time when Nathan was on 'top of the world'. He was a happy-go-lucky guy with a dozen of good friends. He was a great salesman and a machinist, who owned two furniture stores in New Jersey and Pennsylvania, and an accountant. By his mid-twenties he became very wealthy.

Nathan was so successful the he owned second home in North Carolina where he'd take his friends on hunting trips in the fall and go on deep sea fishing trips off the coast of Long Island. He also did volunteer work as fireman and raised money for children's hospitals and wounded veteran charities. Social, active, outgoing and ambitious, he really was a man of greatness.

It was when he married a narcissist it became all downhill from there, wasn't nearly a year into the marriage the woman betrayed him. She cheated on him, slandered him, humiliated him in court and as such the court ruled in the lady's favor. She destroyed him.

She took his business, his two houses and sailing boat that belonged to his late father. His ex-Candace really ruined the poor man's reputation. Through all that rotten time, it nearly rendered Nathan homeless, however, he still had enough emergency money to start over. And that's exactly he did, yet in a way it wasn't only a fresh start but also a self-exile from his friends and family.

Even though he found happiness again in rural New York, he still missed the glory days of his past and his friends, all either moved away or just forgotten about him.

The casting pain of the divorce took away his passion, for talking to people, as though he had lost all trust in everyone, and his faith in humanity. Not only to his friends but also his brother Joseph living in another state as a veterinarian.

By August, and Nathan established a strong bond with his animals, and he believed they loved him equally, especially his two giant horses and hound dog Tasha. On days when he finished his chores, he would occasionally ride his horses through the woods behind the ranch, and days when it rains, he would stay inside and drink.

One day with the rain turning from scattered showers to a thunderstorm, Nathan finished another hard day's labor and retired to his living room drinking his favorite cinnamon whiskey.

That evening when Tasha had finished her dinner bowl, she watched her master drink himself into an early sleep. An hour later it became dark outside. The dog walked up to Nathan and tried waking him up by licking his face but to no avail. So, the dog just snuggled next to the open spot of the couch and nestled near her loving master.

Late that night when the stormed passed and the moon gleamed through the clouds Clyde awoke to sounds of walking, and unfamiliar voices coming from the outside of the barn. The horse surveyed the surroundings and knew that it wasn't Nathan.

The voices of a group of people awakened the other animals. The animals sensed danger in the low pitch whispers and footsteps from outside the barn and they began to panic.

Back inside the house, Tasha awakened to the cries of horse and cows in distress. She walked to the back door in the kitchen, looked through the window and saw a pack of large carnivores stalking by the front doors of the barn and she let out a loud barking howl.

Nathan awoke nearly startled and fell off his couch, when Tasha barked loudly. He turned on the lights of the kitchen and walked to the back door where he heard the cries of his animals. Still groggy from the alcohol, he couldn't clearly see what was stalking his barn. He ran up to his room and grabbed his shotgun and some shells. He looked out the window and saw in the moonlight a dark figure standing up with a pack of what looked like wolves standing all around his backyard.

Thinking it's just a thief with his dogs, Nathan opened his bedroom window.

"What the fuck are you doing?! Get off my land!" he yelled only to get gruesome growling in reply.

Nathan loaded his weapon and ran downstairs. Tasha watched the dark figure drop down on his arms and then ran with the pack into the darkness away from the barn. She growled and when Nathan opened the door, she sniffed the ground while he held his shotgun at the ready. He turned on the backyard light only to find nothing, Nathan checked inside the farm and all animals were okay, he ordered Tasha back inside, and the animals began to calm down, he ordered Tasha into the house while he relocked his barn.

From in the darkened tree line the pack watched the human and his hound walk back into the house. they were now aware this wasn't going to be as easy like they thought, for this farmer was armed and determined to defend his property.

After locking up, Nathan went to sleep in his room and placed his shotgun under his bed, he had Tasha lying next to him and as she drifted back to sleep, Nathan petted her before lying down on his pillow.

"Thanks' Tasha, you're a good dog," before falling asleep as his hound laid still on his shins.

Nathan awoke early, around 4 am instead of 5, he quickly ran to his barn to feed and water his livestock. After they ate, he let them all out of the stalls for fresh air, then he returned to his house where he treated himself to coffee and brunch.

While eating eggs, grits, and bacon he turned to his phone where he saw the message light blinking.

"You have two old messages," the phone box stated.

"The first message sent Sunday at 1 pm."

"Mr. Scotfield? this is William Calmo, Candace Power's attorney, I'm calling you for...." Nathan pressed the button not wanting to hear the voice of the man who helped destroy his business.

"I already paid her the last alimony check!" Nathan said out loud in his house. After pressing the button again, the phone brought up the second call sent the same day and hour later.

"Nathan? It's Joe, are you there?" Nathan was shocked hearing his brother's voice, "God I hope this is the right number, I'm calling because you never said goodbye, it's been over three months since I last saw you and I'm worried if you get this message please call back and let me know you're okay. Bye now."

"Damn," Nathan said rubbing his head before going back to his breakfast. That afternoon he took a ride on Dixie and brought along his shotgun. He rode off his ranch to look around. Although he hunted in the past, he had no tracking skills and had never hunted predators before. Tasha, on the other hand, was a tracker, highly rated as a pup to track criminals for the police force.

The dog led him and the horse to the far edge of the woods, just off the highway of route 12, where Tasha discovered a large stain of blood on a patch of dead leaves. Nathan dismounted Dixie and knelt before the leaves stained red and covered with tiny pieces of brown and black fur. Then the hound led the master to a footprint, not a paw like in the dirt in front of his farm, but in the shape resembling a bare human foot.

The man stood puzzled and took a few pictures with his cell phone, Tasha followed the scent to the highway. She began to walk too close to the road, in the risk of being hit by a car. Nathan yelled and called her back.

Believing someone had been hurt, he and Tasha walked back to Dixie where he contacted the police.

Nathan road back home with Tasha, where two Utica police had arrived at his doorstep.

A captain named Francis and a female cop named Wallstone. He greeted the two, explained what he'd found, showing them the pictures of the blooded leaves and the human footprint.

Both ordered him to take them to the spot, he did so by leading them all the way through the woods to showed them what his dog found. They walked back to his house where the two cops quietly spoke to one another out of Nathan's ear range.

When the female cop left for her vehicle to make a call, captain Francis asked Nathan some more questions.

"So, tell me Mr. Scotfield, how long have you lived here?"

"I moved here about five weeks ago," Nathan answered.

"Where are you from originally?" Francis asked.

"Staten Island."

"Awe a city boy," the captain teased, "and through that time you've seen no one trespassers on your land?"

"No sir, my livestock keeps me busy, and I don't have time for searching around my woods." Nathan replied when officer Wallstone returned to the house with a clipboard.

"Now Mr. Scotfield, we've had some trouble on this highway over a month back," Wallstone said, she handed him a clipboard showing a missing person paper with two portraits of two young men named David and Drake Gracer.

"The two men are brothers. We found their vehicle crashed off the side of the road about 20 miles west of the town, right near the woods close to your land," she explained, "one the boys contact authorities because the other was seriously injured. But upon the arrival of police and paramedics they were both gone."

"So that print... you think that's one of them?" asked Nathan.

"Well we're not sure, but have you seen either of them?" asked Francis.

Nathan nodded no, "All I've seen on my property are my animals and a pack of wolves stalking my farm about two days before."

"Wolves?" Francis asked looking to the lady cop.

"That's weird," said Wallstone, "there haven't been wolves around these parts in decades."

"Wolves, coyotes, wild dogs, I have some kind of pack," Nathan said.

"Well, we're going to send some more troopers around this area to look around," Francis said. As Nathan walked the two out to their car. "Stay alert and if you see anything else let us know. Hopefully, we'll find a lead to the Gracer's disappearance."

The two police thanked him before walking to their patrol cars.

Chapter 3. Highway blood.

A week passed and Nathan spotted a dozen cops searching around the area of his backwoods. They searched up and down the sides of the road with K9 trackers and picked up the blood trail that led from across route 12 to Willow falls creek, over a mile and a half. There they discovered the bones and maggot ridden flesh of a decaying stag. No sign of human DNA, tracks or clothing or the Gracer brothers. The two men remained on the missing person lists.

In town Nathan stopped at the 'Blood Rose' Deli to buy a hot lunch. He sat down eating a cheese bratwurst with chili and fries.

The 'Bloody Rose' deli was big enough fit at least a dozen customers. The place seemed dull and stuffy without air conditioning, or music. You could hear the echoing of the stove and chatting of the cooks in the back kitchen. The only people in the dining area were Nathan an old cashier lady and a young girl whom he assumed worked as a waitress, cleaning tables, and serving him beer even though she looked to be under twenty.

He tried to be social by saying 'hello', 'please' and 'thank you' but both women treated him as if he said nothing. Even when the girl serves him beer, she wouldn't even look at him or reply to his kind greetings.

Nathan again felt a slight sting of emotional pain, from their silence and anti-social rudeness. He quickly finished his meal, left a small tip and said nothing. As he left, he felt a slight pain in his chest, for such alienation reminded him of the torment his ex-wife had put him through. Even when he tried being nice and social, he would receive nothing resentment. At times he felt like an outcast, like a deviant, in his new hometown.

While sitting in his truck, cupping his eyes, he felt someone was watching him. He looked up and was startled when he saw the deli lady staring at him through the side window.

"Can I help you?" he said when he rolled the window down.

"Aren't you that farmer? The new one now lives at the edge of the road?" she asked.

He replied. "Uh yes... that I am."

"Thought so, you got any pigs in that farm?" she asked.

"No, ma'am, I have horses, dairy cows, hens, and goats."

"No meat animals?" she asked looking disappointed.

He nodded, "sorry, the animals are not for sale, but if you'd like, I can sell you some fresh eggs and milk... if you like."

"Can I have five dozen eggs? and two gallons of goat milk?"

"Oh sure... yes, of course, thank you," Nathan said surprised that he caught a customer.

"When can I have them?"

"Um...well I'm collecting them tonight I think I'll have your order this tomorrow morning."

"Good," and the lady walked away before he can talk about the price.

He drove back home to finish his regular farm work, long hours, hard and dirty work. He finished the day milking the goats so that it would be fresh for his new costumer.

He then retired for the night, placing the order of goat milk in his fridge and began to make his dinner for him and Tasha. After supper he took a shower walked upstairs to get dressed. As he claimed the stairs Tasha stopped and picked her ears. Hearing strange voice, she walked into the laundry room that was on the side of the house.

The dog looked out the window, her ears focused on the sounds coming from outside. The hound growled at the unwelcoming trespassers who were lurking in the backyard. Then she began to bark loudly as she picked up the scent that ment danger.

Upstairs Nathan heard his dog and he rushed down dressed only in boxers and a tank top. He found Tasha standing on his washing machine growling with her hackles raised.

"Tasha? What's is it, Tasha?!" He said picking her up off the machine, Nathan looked outside but so nothing since it was pitch black.

Tasha continued to bark, and Nathan went to the kitchen to turn on the outside lights. Looking outside and found nothing either in the back or the front yard. He opened the front door and yelled.

"Who's out there?!"

No answer.

Nathan just locked up, pulled down all the shades and took his young hound upstairs in his bedroom.

"You need to settle down, my little alpha Queen, I know you dogs are smart, but everything is locked up we're safe," Nathan said laying her in his bed. After shutting off the lights he bedded down. "Now go to bed."

Nathan was awoken again by Tasha's barking. Looking his clock, he saw the time was 3 am.

"God Damn it! Shut up!" he yelled then ordered her out of the room, but Tasha stayed and stared out the window growling. Nathan saw no choice but to take her by the collar and make her sleep in the living room. When he closed his bedroom door Nathan heard loud howling from outside.

He opened his window and could hear the frightened cries of his goats, cows, and horses. The Howling was loud and sounded like it came from a large pack that was close. Nathan instead grabbed his flashlight.

He shined the light from his window, scanning his backyard. Nothing in the open, nothing near the barn, but when he shot the light on his picket fence, he caught sight of something shining.

"What the?" he said rubbing his eyes. The flashlight beam was reflecting in the eyes of several animals. The eyes of the pack.

The man yelped and jumped in sudden fear, hitting his head on the windowsill.

Nathan backed up and closed the window. The he grabbed his hunting rifle, loaded it and ran downstairs. He found Tasha up against the backdoor barking defensively.

"Down girl, get down!" Nathan turned on the backyard lights and he could see the shinning of eyes reflecting on both sides of his barn while his animals cried in fear.

In the dark flanking the farm, Nathan could see over a dozen sets of glowing eyes like ghosts. And despite the bright lights coming on the pack did not move away.

More shockingly the howling continued far beyond the farm in the woods behind the building. Nathan figured there were more than a dozen wolves. The thought of so many predators besieging his farm caused Nathan's heart to beat a million miles per hours.

He closed the back door, then opened the window with Tasha barking next to him, he aimed his rifle in the air and fired off a warning shot.

The loud gunshot made his own animals go into a panicked frenzy. But the wolves did not run or show fear. The farmer watched as the glowing eye shines disappeared into the darkness. But the howling continued far off.

That night Nathan slept fully clothed while gripping his rifle on the couch, Tasha stayed up throughout the night and listened as the howling gradually ceased.

That morning the farmer and his hound found tracks all over the mud of the backyard, and an unfinished hole dug by the wolves near the chicken coop. After patching the whole up with heavy rocks, Nathan decided to save his money to buy traps and extra ammo, and he really felt dumbstruck for the fact that there are no wolves in New York.

Chapter 4. Dinner.

The next three days, while tending his animals, Nathan notice that the goats and cows were becoming too nervous to walk outside of the barn. Despite that, he left the gates open anyway to give his animals fresh air and space.

That afternoon he went on a horse ride with Clyde, they galloped around the ranch where he spotted a kid running out of the woods just on the other side of the white fence.

He rode closer and saw that it was a little boy who was half naked only wearing shorts. When the child saw he was being watched, he stopped running and stared back at Nathan riding his giant horse.

"Hi, there!" Nathan said waving, the boy waved back, and he could see his hands were stained brown from dry mud.

"You okay kid?" he asked.

"I was playing!" he replied walking closer to the fence. "Are you a farmer?"

"Sure am, do you live in that house down the hill?" before the kid answered Nathan saw the boy turn towards the house.

"I have to go." the kid said running off. Nathan watched as the boy ran to the backyard of his neighbor's house far down the road. He wondered what made the boy look away, but he just rode on.

Upon returning, Nathan finished the last chores of his by milking the last gallon of goat's milk and finally collected enough eggs for the deli.

While having dinner in the living room with Tasha, and his rifle close in reach Nathan turned on the news channel where he learned of the bad weather coming at the end of the week. Scattered showers and thunderstorms.

After the news, he changed the channel to an old western movie, when he heard a knock at the door.

Tasha stopped eating and began growling, she watched her master walk to the door where a woman stood.

Tasha rushed up barking.

"Tasha! Down girl!" Nathan said keeping her from jumping on the visitor.

The woman at the door just stood as Nathan took the hound away, locking her in the laundry room. Nathan returned to the door.

"Sorry about that, she's not good around strangers, uh what can I do for you?" he asked.

"My name's Lidia Kess, I'm your neighbor."

The woman looked to be middle age, late thirties or early forties, wore a green blouse and blue skirt with brown work boots. Her hair was raven black with shining gray streaks running through it. Gray eyes and pale skin with wrinkles under the eye sockets and cheeks, slim but still attractive.

"Oh yeah, I saw you the day I moved here, nice to meet you finally," said Nathan putting out his hand.

"Yes... well, I talked it over with my husband, that we should get to know our new neighbor...and was wondering if you would like to have dinner with us tomorrow evening?" Lidia asked slowly, "It's our treat."

"Wow, um thank you that'll be lovely," said Nathan real touched, "So what time."

"Tomorrow at 6 pm, sharp," Lidia said shaking his hand before walking away.

Nathan felt pretty good that he finally might be making friends in his new home. He walked to the laundry room to let Tasha out who was still growling aggressively. She ran on to the front door barking and jumping.

"Shit! Tasha! Get Down!" Nathan yelled, but she didn't listen, and he had no choice but to drag her by the collar away from the door.

"Stop it! Stop it!"

Tasha became even more agitated and out of control and accidentally bit Nathan.

When her master screamed, she stopped moving and placed her head down in shame. With his bleeding hand the master grabbed Tasha by the scarf and locked her in the laundry room again where she'll sleep grounded for the night.

"Bad girl! You don't bite me!" Nathan yelled before slamming the door.

After cleaning the wound and wrapping his wrist with a bandage, he heard Tasha moaning and crying. He kept her locked in the room for the night anyway. From outside he heard the howling again, but he decided not to concern himself about it and just went off to sleep.

In the laundry room, Tasha could hear the howling, and danger that was just a wall away, she couldn't sleep but she laid down near the dryer anyway, when she heard a thump.

She stood and turned. Through the window she could see glowing eyes and a dark shadow was staring in dead at her. The Hound yelped and cowered under a table.

The creature from the outside could see and hear the hound moan in fear, he dropped off the house wall and made for the barn, sniffing the gate.

It could hear the nervous cries of the animals and heard its pack members stacking the area where they tried digging under the chicken coups.

The pack members were angry that their hole has been filled up, and all grouped the back of the farm. In the woods, the wolves killed another crossing animal off the highway, but many longed to get the farm animals in the barn. They devoured the doe and its fawn, before running off freely in the night out in the open field and back into the woods.

Nathan awoke early, before eating breakfast he let Tasha out of the laundry room. He found her shaking in fear. He walked in and took her in his arms to comfort the horse.

"It's okay sweetie, your safe," Nathan said laying the tired-out pet on his couch and thinking that he really needed to do something about the wolves stalking his home.

He packed his truck with the five dozen eggs and two jugs of fresh goat milk and drove down Graytown road to find some residents standing outside of their houses and others walking along the roadside. He arrived at Bloody Rose deli and the place was packed with truckers off the highway. When he entered the cashier informed him that the owner would meet him at the backdoor.

Nathan took the eggs and milk around back and gawked at the foul smell of the dumpster filled with rotten meat, old wasted food. He even found an old rusted fire barrel that was used to burn bones.

The back door opened, and the old lady came outside with a large man in a bloodied apron.

"You got my order?" she asked.

"Yes, ma'am," Nathan said walking up.

"Call me Edith," she said before the cook took the eggs and milk from the farmer. "Now how much do I owe you?"

"That'll be $22.50."

Edith handed him $30, thanked him and told him to keep the change before he could say thank you, and she entered the kitchen and closed the door.

While driving back home to tend his animals, Nathan listened to the radio where he learned that the body of Daniel Gracer was discovered along Willow fall creek about 12 miles from the highway. Coroners examined his mutilated body and believed it to be the work of a bear. Most of his flesh had been eaten off his bones, and only organs that weren't missing was his rectum and split open stomach. The police were still puzzled on whom they were mauled since they contacted the police, and no one claimed to have seen any black bears cross the highway. David Gracer was still missing.

Upon reaching his house he saw Mr. Kess fetching his mail and he gave Nathan a wave back with a smile.

After parking his truck, he took Tasha out of the house to help him corral the cattle and horses back in the barn.

After leaving them in the building with their food pails filled, Nathan took Tasha inside where he put on a dress shirt and took a gallon of cow milk from the fridge to give a gift to his neighbors.

He chained Tasha on the back porch before walking down the hill to the Kress' house, he was a half hour early, but he thought it wouldn't matter.

He knocked on the door, no answer, after waiting a couple of seconds he knocked again.

The door opened with the young boy staring in front of him.

"Hey there pal, is your mom home?" Nathan asked.

"One moment please," the boy said before closing the door, a moment later a young girl answered the door.

"What do want?" she asked.

"I'm...I'm Nathan I live up the hill," he said shaken by her rude tone.

"Oh right, please come inside," she said leading him inside. Nathan entered the living room where the windows were draped, the TV was playing some children show, stuffed deer heads were mounted on the wall, and a brown bear hide for a rug.

"And what's your name miss?" Nathan asked.

"I'm Erin, Lidia's daughter," she answered. The girl looked to be about 16-17 had long dark brown hair. Slim, she wore a blue shirt and tan shorts that stopped above her knees of her long legs and she was barefoot.

"I believe we saw each other before."

"Have we?" he asked puzzled.

"I work at the Bloody Rose deli."

"OH Yeah! The cashier, sorry I thought you looked familiar," Nathan said.

"Not very inquisitive, are we?" she said with a sigh then walked down the hallway. Before following Nathan observed the family pictures some were quite old shot in black and white. Nathan though they must be the family's ancestors.

"Are you coming?" she said standing by the entrance to the dining room.

"Yeah, sorry."

Nathan walked in and saw a fancy chandelier made with elk antlers. He was amazed by the decoration and he stared with his mouth opened.

"So, would you like a drink, or are you just gonna stand stiff like a dead hobo?" asked Erin.

"Uh yes, I'd like a beer if you have any," Nathan said.

"We have beer, I'll be right back."

Erin returned with two cold cans, before drinking he saw Erin open hers and began jugging it down, surprised seeing in underage girl drinking.

"Hey!"

Nathan almost jumped out of his chair, startled by the father walking in. Mr. Kess walked in and stuck his hand in front of his daughter. "Hand it over!" Erin rolled her eyes and gave her dad the half-emptied can, "Go to the kitchen and get cooking. Move it!" he barked.

When Erin left the room, Lidia came dressed only in a bathrobe.

"Nathan, glad you made it," she said shaking his hand, when Nathan touched her wet pruney hand he saw her husband giving him an evil glare.

"Well this is my husband Brad, Brad this is Nathan Scotfield our new neighbor."

"Pleased to meet you, Nat," Brad said. "Lidia go get dressed."

When the mother left in came the little boy still only dressed in shorts.

"Joey, come in here and meet Mr. Scofield," Brad ordered.

"Hey kid nice to finally be introduced properly to you," Nathan said shaking his little hand.

"Get upstairs and put a shirt on."

"Yes Pa," Joey said.

"Joey, that's what my dad called my little brother Joseph," Nathan said.

"His name's not Joseph we named him Josiah," said Brad finishing up his beer can.

"Cool, I like Josiah, it's a cool name," Nathan said, "so what are we having?"

"A special... veal," Brad answered before leaving to fetch another beer.

Lidia came down dressed in a fancy emerald vintage dress, and her son Josiah had his long brown hair combed and wore a white collared shirt.

Nathan sat patiently in the dining room as his hosts prepared dinner.

When all was ready Nathan sat with the family and everyone was silent. The veal was nice and tender, the baked potato as well, but the corn could use more cooking.

"This delicious, good cooking Erin," said Nathan, Erin just nodded.

"So, Nat, where are from?" asked Lidia.

"Staten Island New York."

"New York City?" Josiah asked.

"Well, sort of Staten Island is off the coast of the city," Nathan corrected.

"Are you Native American?" the kid asked curiously.

"No, I'm Scottish descent," said Nathan.

"Great another pure white man."

"Erin!" Lidia said firmly.

"We're half Native blood," said Josiah.

"Cool, what tribe?"

"We're Wendat-Huron," Erin said, "On Dad's side, mom's side is Irish."

"Nice, I've been to Ireland."

"So, Nathan do you have any family?" asked Lidia.

"Just my little brother Joseph, he lives in Vermont now."

"Why move up here? Of all the warm places in America, you had to choose this shithole?" Erin asked.

"Well, many reasons... I love animals, love the northern wilderness, Canada is cheaper, and other reasons," Nathan said unable to finish.

"Like what?" asked Josiah.

'Well…. uh personal troubles, that I gratefully escaped from," Nathan said.

"Escape? Are you some criminal?" Erin said in irony.

"Erin!" Lidia said.

"Ha no, I moved here to start over, I almost lost my life, when my ex took all I worked for away I was going to kill myself but instead I came up here to live on… just as a simple farmer."

Erin chuckled, followed by Brad.

"Well, that's quite a story, Nathan," Lidia said, "I'm sorry you had to go through such trouble in the past."

"There's no need to apologize, I made the decision of choosing an unworthy wife. And you know I'm happy now, living with my animals," said Nathan.

"You seem a decent fellow Nat, we like animals too," said Brad.

"Oh yeah, farm animals?" Nathan asked.

"Yep, horses, cows, goats, chickens. Dogs," said Brad.

"Ooh well… maybe I'll show you guys my animals; I'll introduce them to you."

"But we hate dogs!" said Josiah.

"Boy shut up," Brad said quietly. The quiet, and slight mean-spirited behavior made Nathan worry. He notices the strange look in the eyes of Lidia and the weird motion gesturing while sitting across the table, she whispered to herself, and stuff meat in her mouth.

Nathan didn't know what to make of it, does this family have domestic problems? Are they a broken family? Nathan tried to make it out, but since he was no expert in family psychology and failed in his first marriage, he decided to forget about it and change the subject.

"So, tell me, where do you kids go to school?" he asked.

"High school," Erin answered.

"No, we don't go to school," Josiah said with his father nudging him.

"Oh, you kids are homeschooled?"

"Yes," Brad said.

"Cool, I was homeschooled myself, me and my brother."

"Nice to have things in common, aye Nat?" said Brad. Nathan felt annoyed because he hated it when people call him Nat, but Nathan kept his calm demeanor.

"So, what do you do for a living Brad?" Nathan asked.

"I have two jobs," he answered, "I'm a mechanic and a hunting guide."

"Hunting guide? wow."

"Yep, best one in the County," Brad said.

"I'm a hunter myself," Nathan said.

"You love animals, yet you hunt?" asked Josiah.

"Well yeah, just because I hunt doesn't mean I hate deer," Nathan explained, "I respect nature and only kill what I eat."

"That's noble," said Erin.

"Well, if you come hunting with me you might get something bigger than some whitetail," Brad said. "Get you a nice moose or a grizzly."

Time passed and the people finished their dinner. Erin and Josiah went to the living room to watch TV, leaving the adults sipping wine in the dining room. Nathan checked his watch; it was 20 after 7 pm and he decided it was time to leave.

"Thank you for the meal, but I need to get home and feed Tasha."

"Oh, must you go?" asked Lidia, "we're having chocolate pudding for dessert."

"I'd love to stay longer, but as a farmer, I gotta put my animals first," Nathan said shaking their hands.

He walked out of the dining room to say farewell to the kids, only to discover the living room was empty, the TV was left on and the front door was left open.

Outside the sun was sinking down westward, it was the Golden Hour. He walked up the road to his home admiring the beauty of the final light of the day. He looked to the woods where he saw Josiah and Erin running around and thought they were playing tag.

Nathan made it home where he let his dog inside and fed her a leftover pork rib. That night it was silent with no howling, and the farmer slept in peace happy with the thought that he made new friends.

In the barn, however, Dixie and Clyde were awake, still sensing the danger of the predators that circled the building like sharks. The pack sniffed, jumped on and scratched the wood making the livestock panic again, keeping them awake throughout the night. Their master passed out in his room after drinking himself to sleep.

Chapter 5. Animal patrol.

Erin arrived late for work at the 'Bloody Rose'. She parked her bike and entered the back entrance where her apron was hung in the closet.

"Morning sweet buns," she heard and saw the sickening face of Anthony the meat cutter. He stood at the bottom of the stairs leading to the basement. He just stared at her with his mouth open. Erin flipped him off and entered the kitchen.

"Where the hell have you been young lady?!" the owner asked.

"You know damn well where I've been, Esney," Erin shot back.

"You're on garbage, mopping, and dishes today," Ester said placing her hands on her hips, "get to work!"

"What else is new," she said putting on her apron as Nathan entered the Deli.

"Good morning Erin,' he said with a jolly voice, and Erin just nodded with a smirk.

"Can I help you?"

"Hi Ms. Ester, let me have a large coffee, please," Nathan said. Ester ordered Erin to get the coffee going, Nathan sat down in a booth while waiting, and Ester walked over to order more eggs and milk.

"Sure, I get you 10 cartons of eggs and 10 gallons of milk."

"When?" Ms. Ester asked.

"Uh… well the cows haven't been feeling well, maybe 10 days," answered Nathan.

"That long?"

"Yeah… the cow's been having stomach problem, I'll have a vet take a look at them, and I'm also calling in the animal patrol."

"Animal patrol, for what?" she asked.

"Well… I'm having a wolf issue, just gonna talk to them, get some advice…maybe set up some traps," said Nathan.

"Erin hurry up with the coffee!" she said walking behind the counter. Erin walked up and served him his coffee.

"Keep the change as your tip," Nathan winked paying her 20 bucks in cash.

"Oh… thank you," she said with a grateful smile. As Nathan poured milk and sugar, he heard Ms. Ester talking down to Erin, in a cruel and harsh tone. He listened to the verbal abuse, and heard the lady calling the girl 'useless'. Nathan got off his seat and walked to the counter.

He saw Ester took the $17 in change that was supposed to be Erin's tip.

"Go to the back now."

"Wait! you took her tip money," Nathan said, feeling angered at the way she treated Erin.

"This is not hers," Ester said.

"Yes, it is." He repeated.

"No."

"Yes, it cost 2 bucks for a coffee I paid Erin $20, and told her to keep the change as her tip, it's hers," he said.

"Well she doesn't deserve it; Erin get out of my sight!" The teenager looked battered by the cruel woman and went into the kitchen. Nathan felt terrible. As a former store manager, he knew he had to give orders and sometimes pushed employees to work hard, but he would never call them useless, talk down at them or take their money.

After seeing the way Ester treated her employees Nathan had one final thing to say to Ms. Ester.

"Well, in that case, seeing how you run your business here, I'm not giving you any eggs or milk, of mine," Nathan said calling off the deal and the lady looked shocked, "find someone else...you're a real cold person."

As Nathan walked out the door, the old bitter lady Ester came out yelling.

"And stay out! You're banned from my deli!" Nathan just shrugged and walked to his truck. He restrained himself from giving her the finger.

Nathan parked in front of the Kess house, he saw the family vehicle parked outside so someone had to be home. He walked up and knocked on the front door. Brad answered.

"Morning."

"Morning Brad… listen I just came from the Bloody Rose and… uh, Miss. Ester was mistreating your daughter," Nathan said.

"What happened?" Brad asked.

"Well I can't repeat everything she said, but some of it was really nasty. She was abusing her, and she stole the tip I paid her. I know it's not my concern, but Erin's a young girl and I used, to be a grocery store manager. I think Erin shouldn't work there anymore."

"Thanks for informing me, I know what my daughter's been through working there, but it's just a Summer job," said Brad, "and she won't be there long."

"Okay good, just wanted you to know that."

"I know exactly what Miss. Ester is," said Brad.

Nathan said goodbye, walked to his truck and went home.

Later that day the vet came to check on the cows and told Nathan that one has a common sickness of scours and prescribed neomycin fluid for the animals.

While doing this the animal patrol cop Claude Toussaint was tracking the woods behind the barn where he traced signs of wolf feces and tracks.

After the Vet drove off, he met Toussaint on his tilled soil.

"Well Scotfield, you have without a doubt got yourself a wolf problem."

"I knew it," Nathan said while shaking his head.

"Really strange though because I haven't had wolf cases around here in ages," Toussaint said, "and this pack...it's a pretty big one."

Nathan followed the man in the woods where the patrolmen showed him the area.

"How big is it?"

"Probably over 12; there are tracks of all sizes from omegas to the large alphas in the woods. There are feces, fur, the works. And they definitely want your animals." The man warned.

"So, how should I deal with this? Can I trap them?" asked Nathan.

"Well, you're a farmer, do what you gotta do to protect your animals, so yes. But first, you must pass a trapping management course for fur-bearing animals. After that you get the license from the game warden."

"Gee and I thought New Jersey had tough hunting and trapping laws," Nathan said.

"Laws are laws sir, but if the wolves continue to harass your animals and try to attack them you have the right to shoot em," Toussaint said, "That's what I'd do if I were you. And also, I would take the course now if you really want to rid yourself of this pack. With fall on the way they're gonna get hungry."

"Great, thanks officer," Nathan said leading him to his van.

"You got a very nice farm going, I gotta admit. Hate to see it destroyed… Like last time," Toussaint said enter his vehicle.

"Last time? What do mean?" Nathan asked.

"Oh, the real estate people didn't tell you about the man who lived here before you?"

Nathan mind numbed with confusion. "No, they didn't, all I know is that no one has lived here in over 30 years," he said, "what happened?"

"Well… it happened about 36 years ago, back in 1982. I was a young EPA patrolman, but my brother was in the state police and he told me the farmer… can't remember what his name was, but he was found… mauled in his own farm with all his animals."

"Mauled?"

"Yep, the poor old man was eaten alive, by…. Had to be a bear, it had been something big and powerful to break through a farm door and rip him and over 20 cows to pieces in a single night. And when I saw the crime photos… Christ, it kept me awake for weeks."

Nathan eyes bulged out; his mind was completely shocked for what the real estate lady didn't tell him about his farm's past.

"Well, since you're gonna take up trapping, and you seem like a guy that really care for his animals," the patrolmen said, "I think you'll be alright. Take care now."

That night sitting in his kitchen, Nathan placed a call to book an appointment with the local game warden's office to set up his course for the trapping license. After making the call he went to the fridge to grab his whiskey.

While pouring himself a shot the phone rang, but he decided to ignore.

'Hello no one is here to take your call, please leave a message.'

"Mr. Scotfield this is Mr. Calmo attorney at law, just calling to inform we have received your alimony, but Mrs. Powers…."

"Oh, fuck you and Mrs. Powers!" Nathan yelled.

Tasha nearly jumped at her master's shouting. After the call ended, she looked up to Nathan with a sighing gasp. The man smiled and rubbed his hound's head.

"Sorry, girl… come on let's go to bed." The dog followed him upstairs. Outside there was a rainstorm brewing. After drifting off to sleep, Tasha was awoken by her master's yelping and moans.

Nathan was having a nightmare. In his mind he was in his barn, trapped in the large dark building. He could hear the agonizing cries, of his animals being devoured. He was helpless and frightened and when the cries died down, howling grew all around, then from the wooden walls, gate door, and ceiling the wolf pack broke through. The last image was of a wolf's open jaws, the razorlike teeth glistening, closing on his face.

Nathan awoke covered in a sweat, his heart beating like a paint mixer. Tasha crawled up and licked his face.

"Oh Tasha," Nathan hugged her, "You're the only girl who understands me."

Outside in the rainy night, the pack alpha scouted out in the open field. Lightning flashed in the sky, the beast snarled, waking the animals in the barn. The alpha walked through the mud of the garden and bounced on the back wall testing how weak the wood was, slowly it left deep scratch marks. Despite the rain, it could sense the fear of the livestock inside. All that was left was to rid the farmer, break in, and she and the whole pack could feast.

Inside Clyde could hear the scratching, and growls. He broke from his dene and whinnied, kicking his hind legs. Telling the trespassing animal to go away and hoping to wake the master, but the thunder was too loud.

The next morning the farmer found Clyde had broken his pen gate. After fixing it he decided to restrain the horses with a harness every night. One the cows was still feeling sicker not because of the food or water, but constantly being afraid. Scared of was keeps stalking them outside.

Chapter 6. Run away.

It was Nathan's day to meet the game warden at his office in the town of Boonville.

He stopped at the Graytown gas station to fill up. As Nathan filled his truck with feed, he saw the old attendant staring at him from the window, Nathan smiled and waved to the man, only to get a grumpy frown in return.

When walking back inside the place to buy a lighter the man looked at Nathan as though he wanted to beat him with a bat.

"How much?" Nathan asked.

"$4.99."

"Keep the change," said Nathan handing over a five.

"I don't want your eggs or milk," the attendant said. Puzzled, Nathan said nothing, and walked out. He drove off still puzzled by the attitude.

Hours later, he returned home from the warden's office, Nathan had to attend a five-hour trapping class the following week, so he contacted the animal vet to hire a part-time farmhand to look after his animals.

The next Monday Nathan was to start his class. A young farmer related to the owner of the vet, Josh Jacobs, was hired to look after his livestock. Nathan instructed him to feed the cows their medicine twice daily, once in the morning and once at night. Nathan informed Josh to always let them out to stretch their legs and to always bring them inside before dark.

"Can you manage?"

"Yeah, I can manage," said the young man.

"Alright make sure you always lock up the place before leaving, make sure you count them and leave nothing outside."

"Right everyone inside. I get it!" the man said really shrewd while, Nathan handed him the barn's key. Tasha barked from the window.

"Are there any important things I have to do for your dog?" Jacobs asked.

"No, just take care of the livestock," Nathan said before leaving.

On the third day, another storm came, while the animals were getting wet and dirty, Jacobs was occupied texting his girlfriend and drinking beer. He neglected to feed the cows their morning medicine and even though the storm was getting worse he kept the animals out in the cold.

Jacobs' got a call on his smartphone.

"Yeah?"

"Josh it's Nathan."

"What's up?"

"Well, I'm gonna be late tonight. I should be home around 6pm, but I'll pay extra if you stay overtime."

"Okay, no problem," said Jacobs.

"And I hear it's gonna rain all night and temperatures gonna drop. I would like it if you put blankets on the horses, alright?"

"God! Yes, I'll take care of it…. Anything else?" gasped the young man.

"No, just make sure you get all the animals inside and locked up. Okay?" said Nathan before hanging up.

"Idiot!" Jacobs yelled. As he walked out of the barn in the pouring rain Tasha barked at him.

"Oh, shut up!" he yelled annoyed. Tasha growled at the young farmhand.

After rallying the goats, and taking in the horses, Jacobs struggled to get the cows inside. When he tried to haul the last of the six cows inside, one Holstein refused to budge making Jacobs slip in the mud. The angry young man kicked the animal and the cow turned and bit his thigh.

"Ow fuck!" Jacobs back off and ran to the woods where he returned with a stick. He beat the cow on the side and rump making it run in panic.

It broke straight through the wooden fence, running into the neighbor's backyard, Jacobs dropped the stick and ran after the frightened cow. He slipped in the mud again, and the cow escaped into the woods.

While taking his quiz Nathan felt the vibration of his phone. He walked out of class and answered.

"Lost?! What do mean by lost?!" asked Mike.

"One of your cows broke the fence and ran away, I lost it," Jacobs said standing on the outskirts of the woods.

"Thanks! Well I'll coming home now, I'm gonna give you your payment, but don't ever come back to my farm. Understood?!"

"I'm sorry..." Nathan hug up and told the game warden he had to go home due to an emergency and left for his truck.

On the highway, a car slid off the road, holding up traffic. While stuck in a long line of cars Nathan called up the animal breeder Jun DeGroot, Jacobs' employer, to inform what had happened.

"Oh, I'm really sorry Nathan, I'll talk to Josh and make sure he'll be more responsible from now on," DeGroot said. "Would you like me to call Toussaint to help you search for your cow?"

"Sounds like the best thing to do, but I might be held up quite late, you can tell him to come tomorrow to help me find it."

"Okay Nathan, again I'm sorry one of my boys lost your cow."

"We all make mistakes, goodbye now," Nathan calmly replied. But inside he was already pissed, and his anger only increased as the traffic slowly began to move on.

Far off deep in the woods, the cow slowed down realizing it was too far out from the barn and was in dangerous territory. Disoriented, cold and scared, from its ear it heard a twig snap. It found itself encircled; 14 large wolves trapped the cow.

The beast shivered in horror as they closed in on her. And then came the alpha walking upright on its hind legs. The wolf approached the helpless cow, and with a cold clean strike of its paw, cut deep into the cow's throat.

The forest echoed with the cries of death from cow, and then the noises of the pack tearing flesh from the cow's body, eating her alive.

Nathan made it home after 8pm. Jacobs had already left. Nathan went to the barn to find that the idiot forgot to lock it and left the keys in a bucket of water, he counted his animals, then went out to find his missing Holstein.

Bringing Tasha on a leash and they found the broken part of the fence. The storm was getting worse, so he reluctantly went back to his home.

That night the angry farmer spent the night drinking until he passed out.

The next morning Nathan woke up with Tasha licking his face. After vomiting in the bathroom, he went about to feed the dog when there came a knock on the door. Upon answering Nathan saw it was game warden Wayne Vetter and officer Toussaint.

The two men began the search on the highway with Tasha. The wet ground and rough terrain made it hard for the dog to track the cow, so the two men wandered the woods, and returned to the house late in the day.

"I'm sorry Mr. Scotfield, I can gather more help tomorrow, for the search."

"$800 bucks lost!" Nathan said slapping his forehead.

"It's wasn't your fault, these things happen."

"The more help the better, I need to sell more of my product," said Nathan.

"I understand. We'll do our best."

After the animal patrol man departed. Nathan fixed the fence and returned in his house. He received another call from his ex's attorney, in a fit of rage he smashed an empty bottle on it. The man was on the brink of his breaking point, overwhelmed from all the stress and pressure. Nathan couldn't think straight as his mind was wrapped with sadness, anger and pain. He went into a rampage through another glass bottle at the wall, throwing over his dinner table. He even struck Tasha.

The dog ran upstairs barley escaping her master's rage. The heated farmer blinded by rage, he never realized that he was being watched from the window as the alpha sneered and laughed at the sight of the human slowly beginning to lose his mind.

Chapter 7. Trespasser.

It was late September, over two weeks after losing a cow, Nathan was able to calm himself and went back into taking care of his beloved livestock and made up with his friend Tasha, but his alcoholism was building up.

Whenever he buys beer at the Graytown gas station the mean attendant treats him like an outcast, by insulting his roots back in America, calling his life as a farmer a waste of time, and go as far in calling him a failure.

Nathan kept his cool in not retaliating, but he does take words like that real personnel at heart, words can really hurt people even a fully-grown man. Nathan went back to the trapping course and past high score, but he still has to wait for the season.

At the end of the course, Nathan decided to eat out at a truck stop. He sat on the counter having a simple breakfast burger, peameal bacon and fries.

"Enjoying the burger?" Nathan heard a voice and saw it came from a cop.

"Oh yeah it's great," said Nathan, "Especially the bacon."

"Oh yeah, it's the best," the woman said sitting next to him.

"You look familiar," said Nathan.

"I'm officer Wallstone, we met when you found that blood patch."

"Oh right, yeah, how's it going?"

"Busy as always," she said after ordering coffee and steak. "Heard you lost a cow."

"Yep, ran away," Nathan answered.

"Well it's not our job to look for animals but I'll call you if we see anything," the cop said, "Overall how's living up here doing for you?"

"I love it up here," he said. "Do you like it?"

"I've been living in these backwoods ever since I was born, but I always wanted to go to the states."

"Well, I hope you'll get the change."

"So, you met Lidia," said Wallstone.

"I'm Sorry?" asked Nathan.

"Lidia, she lives next to you, she's my sister."

"Oh, Lidia Kess is your sister?"

"Yep."

"Huh… yeah, nice family, they invited me over for supper a few weeks back, quite odd she never mentioned you," said Nathan.

"I expected she didn't, and I'm surprised she invited you over for dinner."

"Why is that?"

"Because they're shut ins, quiet folk who keep to themselves," she said. "Ever since she married Brad, Lidia distance herself from me."

"That's ... sad."

"I know, doesn't call or invite me over on holidays, and she wouldn't tell me why," hearing this made Nathan think about his brother and he realized he was doing the same thing.

"Well I... hope you'll get the chance to hang out with your sister," Nathan said calling the waiter to give him his check, "I really must get going."

"I Know how busy farmers are," said Lizzy raising her mug, "just like us cops."

"Take care now," Nathan said and left out the door after leaving his tip.

Lizzy finished up her dinner and went to her cruiser, to get on the road for the station.

"Station of Wallstone, Station to Wallstone do you read? Over." a call from her radio.

"This Wallstone I read you, over," she replied.

"We got an emergency up in Camp-Mercier, we got a report of public intoxication, a drunken man assaulting a camper and the park rangers need some backup, over."

"Okay I'm on it, over and out," Lizzy drove north to the campground, and the Rangers led her to the campsite, all a mess with the suspect throwing rocks at a person's car.

She approached the man and informed he was under arrest when the man swung his fist to punch her, Lizzy swiftly ducked and rushed behind the man where she knocked him on his stomach, and she retained him in a basket hold.

"Calm down buddy!"

"Get off me bitch!" the man yelled, and Lizzy pulled his arms tight.

"Ow, ow, ow, okay, okay stop!"

"Will you calm down while I put the cuffs on?!" Lizzy said firmly.

"Yes, just, please… it hurts!"

Lizzy singled handedly cuffed the man and walked him to her cruiser. The amazed rangers and campers thanked her then she drove the suspect to the station.

After arriving at the station around 10pm, she booked the man and placed him in a cell. Then she walked up to where the chief informed her another situation.

"What happened?"

"We got a 911 call, need you to meet officer Merv to Graytown," hearing that Lizzy heart dropped with fear.

"I spoke with Scotfield a few hours ago, what happened," Lizzy asked.

"He called and said he'd shot a person who attacked his chickens, you need to head there now!" her captained replied, and she quickly got to her car and drove off to the house of Nathan Scotfield.

The two police officers found the man sitting on his back porch holding his shotgun and crying like a toddler in time out.

"Mr. Scotfield? Merv said gripping his sidearm, the farmer looked up, his face was red and wet with tears, shocked to see Lizzy again who took his shotgun.

"What happened?"

"I... I... killed him."

"What?" said Lizzy turning to the other cop and Nathan pointed to his farm with the front gate opened.

 Merv walked in shining his flashlight to find the animals shaken in fear, the chicken pens were destroyed as if they were ripped open. Then he found a dead naked man with a large bullet wound to his chest. Next to the man was a dead chicken in his bloodstained hands. There was blood, and feathers all over the hay covered floor.

Merv walked back to his car to call an ambulance and then went to question the weeping Nathan.

After explaining what happened Lizzy and Merv didn't arrest the man but Nathan still had to come to court when summoned. He went the following week to tell a judge and jury what had happened. For Nathan it was not only redoing the experiences he had in his divorce, but he had to explain a half-truth story and leave out the giant wolf part.

In the Utica city court, Nathan was brought before the judge, with the local police, and Nathan's brother Joseph came to hear the case. All were informed that the naked man was identified as David Gracer, for reasons unknown had broken into a farm and ate a live chicken. The coroner's report showed no traces of drugs, alcohol or any abnormal symptoms in his brain.

"So, tell us Mr. Scotfield, what happened that night on September the 5th, 2018?" the attorney asked.

"I came home from a diner around 9:30 pm, then I went to home to check on my livestock...."

"Was David Gracer in there?" the judge interrupted.

"No ma'am, when I entered, and fed the animals, I saw no sign of an intruder. Then after locking up like I always do, I went back inside to call my brother Joseph."

"When were you on the phone and how long was the call?"

"I think it was near 10:00 or between 10:30 at night," Nathan answered, "and we were talking for quite a while."

"Okay, and then what?"

"I was talking to Joseph when I heard my dog barking," he said, "I went to the back door and saw the barn door wide open, which was strange because I always lock it every night. I know I had locked it."

"Go on," said the judge.

"I suspected it to be a trespasser or some animal like a bear, so I first yelled from my house, "Get out of my barn! I'm calling the cops!' but then I heard my animals going off in a crazed frenzy, so I quickly dropped the phone and ran to my bedroom to get my shotgun."

"So, you decided to fetch your shotgun first before calling the police?" the prosecuting attorney interrupted.

"Yes, because of the sounds I thought it was an animal. I ran outside, Tasha rushed into the barn first, then when I entered, I saw her fighting…." Nathan paused with him breaking eye contact with the judge.

"What happened?"

"The… I mean Mr. Gracer was hitting my dog, I called her back and I told the man to back off."

"Did he cooperate? From your point of view, how did this man look and act?"

"He wasn't cooperative at all," said Nathan. "I didn't know he was the missing trucker, he looked really sick, yet dangerous. Then he lunged at me, I yelled for him to stay where he was, but he didn't, and I was afraid for my life and the life of my animals."

"Jesus! I object your honor," the town attorney interrupted. "This is so one-sided, trespassing and attacking livestock is one thing. But shooting a young man stark naked, helpless weak and scared, this sound more like cold-blooded murder than self-defense."

"It's not like I wanted to kill him if I'd known he was hum… I mean if he'd stopped attacking my animals and had attempt to attack me, I wouldn't have pulled the trigger!"

"I agree!" Nathan's attorney stood up, "I know that every death is tragic, but this was not a cold-blooded murder Mr. Caldwell!"

"David Gracer went missing a month back, he was a loving son, a college graduate, only to be found shot dead, he's the victim!"

"Let me remind you and all of the court that my client was the one who called the police, and he was in total disarray and tears from going through what he had done," the lawyer said, "It was not murder! Mr. Scotfield feels deep regret for what has happened. And as a farmer, it's his job is to protect his property, land, livestock and himself. It's his living and he did what he had to do!"

"Now! Now you listen here!"

"Alright order! Order! Order in the court!" the judge said slamming the hammer on her deck. "Mr. Scotfield please tell us all what happened before you pulled the trigger."

Sitting on the stand, with misty eyes, Nathan took a deep breath, then looked out to the rows of people sitting in the courtroom. All eyes were on him.

"When… when I ordered Tasha to go back in the house, I saw the boy holding one of my chickens by the neck, it was dead. I ordered him to put it down…."

"Then what?"

"He didn't, he wouldn't comply, instead he pulled a handful of feathers off the hen. And then I thought he was gonna attack me... so I shot him," Nathan said as he broke down crying. Lizzy watched at the benches and saw Joseph sitting on the other side, he was also crying worried that his brother would now end up in jail for this.

After both attorneys finished questioning Scotfield, it was now left for the jury to deliberate.

The case went on for another two long hours before the jury ruled Nathan Scotfield not guilty. All charges were dismissed and the whole thing was ruled as self-defense against a depraved trespasser after the judge dismissed everyone Lizzy

and Joseph tried to talk to Nathan, but the weeping man rushed out of the courthouse where he followed David Gracer's parents.

"Mrs. Gracer?! Mrs. Gracer?!" he said in the lobby and was stopped by a trooper, the sad mother turned with her husband and daughter standing beside her.

"Look, I'm really sorry, you gotta believe me. I didn't want to if I had known it was him!" Nathan broke down crying again and the Gracer family just walked out to their cars to avoid him.

Joseph came from behind, he helped his brother on his feet and walked him to his car, the two ignored the cameras and reporters. Joe took the wheel and drove his brother home.

"Lord, Joey I'm so glad you came."

"I'm always here for you Nathan," Joe said giving the man a hug.

"Can't believe this happened," sniffed Nathan covering his soaked eyes.

"You didn't murder him, Nathan," said Joseph. "It could have happened to any other farmer."

"Just when I wanted to rebuild my life... this shit happens... I'm forced into courtroom again, scared of almost losing everything, including my own freedom."

"No Nathan, the charges were dismissed, and this is not be the same as with Candace. Let's just get home and settle down."

Joseph came all the wat from Vermont, a hadn't seen his brother in over a year, to make sure his big brother didn't end up in jail. And he did confirm that Nathan did call him that time before his farm was attacked. One of the many testimonies and evidence that proved Nathan was innocent of murder.

He moved into the guest room of Nathan's home to stay for a month. After a couple of days, Joseph still saw how depressed Nathan was, with the same sad expression he had when his marriage failed. He helped Nathan care for the animals, go out for drinks and spend time hiking and horseback riding. Nathan still looked as though he was going into someplace dark though.

Chapter 8. The town's outcast.

It wasn't long after the shooting, before Mr. Scotfield became real unpopular in his neighborhood. It all began in the Bloody Rose deli with Miss. Ester holding a public meeting of town residents urging them to shun Nathan, to reject and make him feel unwelcomed in any way possible.

One night when the brothers entered Davis' bar to buy whiskey, the bar keeper just spat on Nathan and told the two to "fuck off! And Go elsewhere for a drink!"

And it kept getting worse. When the Scotfield bros stopped at the hamlet's gas station they were refused service and ordered out by the attendant.

"I don't want no murderer in my station! You bastard! Get gas somewhere else! You sick Human mother fucker!"

Joseph was speechless by the harsh tone, Nathan grabbed him and the two stormed right out. Nathan drove to another station not saying a single word, he just filled his tank, stopped inside to buy a case of beer and got back in to drive Joe home.

The next morning the brothers boarded Nathan's truck to go out and purchase fresh hay, they drove past what looked like a rally of people numbering over a dozen men and women all standing outside the deli with chanting and shouting curses and threats at Nathan.

"Murderer! Leave our town! Monster!" they all yelled standing just off the road near his truck. The two struggled not to look at them even when one mob member through a pebble at Nathan's windshield.

"This is bad," said Joseph as his brother drove on.

"I know," Nathan replied lighting a cigarette.

"Nathan, I thought you'd quit?"

"Well now I'm doing it again," he simply replied uncaringly, Joseph rolled down his window, took the cigarette from Nathan's mouth and flicked it out on the road.

"Come on brother, stopped beating yourself up!"

"I'm not beating myself..." Nathan interrupted.

"Nathan, your drinking heavily, not eating right, back to smoking, your isolated, and alone, yet you still have friends and me back in the states. Maybe you should come back."

"I don't want to go back to New York!" said Nathan with a plainly annoyed tone.

"You don't have to go back to Rochester, come with me to Vermont, or back down to North Carolina. You can start a farm there," Joe said, "Not up here in this backwood hillbilly town, just come home."

"Joey, I'm happy here! I like being a farmer, I love my animals, and I love being up here away from my past troubles, I step one foot back in New York City Candace, her new rich husband and lawyer will come after me," said Nathan.

"Oh Nathan, they're not still bothering…"

"Yes, they are! Almost twice a week to be precise. I get a call from that Calmer, Camo or Clamo whatever he's called, saying she wants more money.

More money, more pain, more of my blood, sweat, and tears like the gold digger she is! Even when I've sent the last of the alimony, she and her attorney will want me to pay her more."

After giving that explanation, the stricken Nathan Carefully parked his truck off on the side of the road, "So you see Joe? Up here her lawyer may hit me with calls, but no legal action. She can't force me in a courthouse as she did back in the city."

"It's just that… I really miss you," Joseph said patting his shoulder,

"Joey… dad raised us to be strong, and successful, that's what you are now, a doctor who saves animals," Nathan said looking him in the eyes, "Me… I fucked up, I can only rebuild my life here, in the country, I need to do this. So, go back to Vermont to make a living, buy a good home. I hope you'll find the right woman to start a family. My advice to you, is doesn't make my mistakes. Don't let someone or something take control of you like that gold digger did with me."

"Oh, Nathan…"

"I'm a 38-year-old man, I've used but the last of my savings so I can't move back... And if I do Carmella will lock me up and that's how it is. This conversation is over," Nathan said staring up the vehicle, "now let's go get the horses some fresh hay."

Late that afternoon the old gas station attendant exited the deli when he saw the Scotfield brothers drive past and he flipped them his middle finger.

"I can't imagine living in a town with people like this," said Joseph disturbed by the hand gesture.

"Fuck them!" Nathan replied.

After placing the fresh hay in the horse, goat and cow pens, the brothers relaxed on the back porch drinking beer. When Joseph couldn't drink any more, he went inside with Tasha to prepare dinner. Nathan, on the other hand, went upstairs brought and down his hunting rifle, and loaded it. He then took out a fresh bottle of whiskey and sat down back outside as the sun set on the western tree canopy.

Night came and Joseph finished cooking a pot of chicken and rice soup. Before he went to call his brother, Nathan fired a shot in the sky. Joseph walked to the door and Nathan fired another round into the open air, aiming above the farm's roof.

"What the hell are you shooting at?!" he asked.

"Nothing. Just warning shots," Nathan answered. Joseph rolled his eyes and didn't question him. He took the rifle and brought his intoxicated brother in to have supper.

At the dinner table with Tasha eating next to Joseph's chair, Nathan gulped down another can of beer.

"Wanna know why I fired off warning shots?" Nathan asked out of nowhere, Joe nodded.

"I was warning them."

Joe immediately got confused, "Warning who? Your animals? Your Neighbors?"

"NO, No, No dummy the pack!" Nathan yelled.

"Pack?"

"Yep, I've been having a pack of wolves stalking my farm. The bushy tailed Bastards are scaring my livestock!" Nathan said his saliva splatting on the table, "And that's what broke into my barn."

"What?" Joe asked fearfully.

"I didn't know it was Gracer...I didn't, I wouldn't hurt any goddamn person unless I had to," Nathan said in a Scottish accent.

"Nathan, what are you talking about?"

"I couldn't tell the people in court, my lawyer or the judge. They never would've believed me...you wouldn't believe me either," said Nathan drinking the soup from the bowl.

"Believe what Nathan?... you're scaring me!"

"The pack of wolves stalking my farm and trying to get my animals, like the old farmer who lived here before me. One broke in, ripped on the lock. Tasha went in I followed only to find… a fucking wolf on two feet," said Nathan. "Two feet!" Joseph thought he had to be drunk out of his mind. "So, the beast killed one of my hens, almost killed my dog, but I shot it in the heart. The gunshot rumpled the barn, my ears rang, and the thing dropped like a fallen branch. In one blink of an eye, it was a 6-foot wolf with pure yellow eyes, sharp-clawed paws with fucking thumbs, only to see it turn in that kid who went missing. I thought I was crazy but when I touch the man, I realized I killed a half man half wolf...wolfman... a werewolf."

Nathan started smiling, with a few chuckles.

"Let's get to bed brother," Joe said helping him upstairs.

"Pretty soon I'm not gonna get much sleep because that pack is gonna eat all my livestock and then come after me!" Nathan smirked before taking another gulp.

"Okay, okay, let's go, you had a little too much to drink," said Joe leading Nathan to his bedroom.

"I love you, Joey," Nathan said as his brother placed the blanket on him.

"Yep you too, Nathan."

"Tasha? Go share the room with Joey, he needs your protection," Nathan said before turning out his lamp, the hound followed Joey and as he pulled the blanket over his shoulder Tasha jumped up and laid next to him.

Joe woke up the next morning with the hound sleeping by his side. He got up to dress. When the dog got up and went downstairs, Joe checked to find Nathan still passed out.

While in the kitchen cooking pancakes, he heard Tasha growling in the living room. When Joe walked to the front window, he saw a group of several town's people standing by Nathan's mailbox with his trash cans knocked over.

"God damn it!" Joe said walking to the door, "Tasha? Stay!"

Joe walked down to the small crowd of people with one woman who had a familiar face.

"Something you all want?!" Joe asked.

"Yeah, that monster Scotfield! He should be hanged for murder!" said one of the men.

"Leave my brother alone, he's had enough trouble."

"Brother? Trouble is what your brother is to this community! A drunk, and a thief, he stole food from my deli," Ester said lying.

"Go away! Get the hell away from here!" yelled Joe. "Leave my brother alone!"

"You're telling us to leave?" Ester asked.

"Listen here! If you don't get out of here and put those cans back up, I'm calling the cops," Joe threatened.

"He's crazier than his brother!" the gas station owner said, "We ought to maul him! Maul them both."

"That's it! I'm calling the police!" Joe ran up where he contacted authorities.

Officer Wallstone responded to the call and chased the small group of residents away from Scotfield's home. She then got out of her car and stood the trash cans up.

"Oh, thank you," Joe said walking down, "You didn't have to do that I just wanted those people to leave my brother alone."

"No problem. You're Nathan's brother? Is he okay?"

"Yeah, I'm Joseph by the way," he said shaking her hand. "Dr. Joseph Scotfield."

"Lizzy Wallstone Utica police. Doctor huh?" she asked amazed.

"Yes, a Veterinarian actually. Thanks for the help... I was surprised cause I thought New York cops don't interfere with petty protest issues."

"Well we usually don't, since my sister lives here, I wouldn't want those people bothering her either," Lizzy said.

"Well I thank you again... things have been quite crazy, from what my brother's going through."

"Ha, I feel it. We had another major accident on the highway, a missing camper, and now an angry mob led by a crazy deli woman."

"Who is she anyway?" asked Joseph.

"Oh, that was Edith Ester... just a cranky old crone who owns the deli," Lizzy said rolling her eyes.

"Does she always do stuff like that?"

"Not really, but my niece works for her and Miss. Ester is not a welcoming person," Wallstone advised. "Don't eat there."

"Every town has to have at least one psycho," Joseph said. He thanked the officer again and walked back inside. Lizzy boarded her cruiser, and as she drove past her sister's house, she saw Lidia standing on the side of the road.

"Lidy hey!"

"What's going on? I Heard your sirens, and people were running down the road," Lidia asked in a curious voice.

"Public dispense, nuisance and trespassing. They littered Mr. Scotfield's lawn, and threatened to hurt him," Lizzy said. "So, how's Josiah and Erin?"

"Why are you helping him?" Lidia said ignoring her sister's question, "Scotfield killed one of us."

"Us?" said Lizzy.

"Scotfield killed that boy, he's a murderer."

"No, he's not. He was protecting himself and his animals," Lizzy said.

"Some cop you are," said Lidia. "Letting men like him live in peaceful towns like this and chasing away nonviolent protesters. Disgraceful."

"What is with you?" Lizzy said upset by her sister's words.

"What's with you? First, you can't find a man, and have a family, now you can't perform your job properly..." before Lidia continued, Lizzy drove off in despair by her sister's alienation.

Chapter 9. Traps.

It was the first week of October, and Joseph had to leave for Vermont in three days. Nathan's behavior made him worry. After Nathan received his trapping and fur-bearing permit for the season, he brought numerous leg traps, piano wire, female wolf urine, deer blood, and large boxes of ammunition specially made.

He also noticed Nathan was becoming increasingly paranoid. The locals of Graytown began filling his mailbox with anonymous hate letters. Not only treating him as the outcast of the town but as though he was some kind of deviant. On the evening before Joseph's last day Nathan spent most of the time in the woods and made him care for the animals, he walked off the ranch and found his brother setting the first trap.

Nathan was atop a thin maple tree; small but flexible, tying up a line.

"So, you're gonna snare the wolves?"

"I'm going to snatch them by the neck, leg trap them and even use a deadfall," Nathan said securing the stainless-steel neck wire.

"Neck snares? Sounds ...pretty inhumane," Joe said.

"I hate trapping as much as you do," said Nathan climbing down, "but I must. For all the problems forced upon me, I'm forced to take precautions."

"Nathan? You really don't have to go through this," Joseph said.

"Yes, I have to!" Nathan replied, "if I don't deal with this fucking pack they'll stick around and eventually snatch more of my animals."

"That's not what I meant," said Joe.

"Oh Christ! Joey, no," Nathan said realizing what Joseph was bringing up. "Not this again!"

"Nathan, I spoke with your attorneys last night, they discovered a fraud scheme that your ex pulled during your divorce," Joseph said. "And with all the slander and harassment you've received, you might have a good change in striking back and..."

"Joseph listen here!" Nathan cut in throwing down his hatchet, "I went through all the court shit once, I had to go to court again with that Gracer kid business, I'm done! I don't want to go back to New York City! I'm done with that place, I'm done with my life as a businessman, and that's the end of it! Now leave me alone!"

Nathan went back to work. And Joseph was shaken by his brother's tone. He walked back to the barn followed by Tasha.

Joseph again made dinner, it was a surprise dish, Nathan's favorite, chicken Marengo. But hours passed and Nathan remained outside. When dark came Nathan still did not return to the house. Instead he went into the barn to work on something.

Hearing the loud noise of power tools Joseph peeked through the door and saw Nathan barricading the barn's window hatches and the back entrance. Drilling in heavy thick lumber and blocking it was water barrels, haystacks and equipment tools.

Joseph wanted to ask if he could give his brother a hand. But fearing it would only annoy Nathan he just returned to the house. Joseph finished up his plate and left a warm plate of food out for Nathan on the table. While reading himself to sleep Joseph heard glass breaking and Tasha yelping.

The man rushed down to find that Nathan, who was again, very drunk.

"You don't bounce on me you little bitch!" Nathan yelled at Tasha.

"Jesus Nat, don't hit your dog!"

"Don't fucking call me Nat!" Nathan almost tripped to the floor, but Joseph grabbed him. The drunken Nathan shoved his brother away.

"Yeah I got dad's smarts but mom's gentleness...." said Nathan reaching for another can of beer.

"You're a rotten drunk, and this will only make you worse," said Joseph taking the half-filled box of cans.

"Oh really, you don't know shit on how alive I am. Being a farmer is less stressful and less difficult than you think...Mr. I Polk fingers in animal anuses."

Joseph just nodded his head and dropped the pack of beer cans. "Alright brother, I tried, but if this is what you want, then I guess you don't need me."

"I never said I needed you!" Nathan spat out harshly.

"Good riddance Nat!" Joseph said walking upstairs and began to pack his bag.

Nathan passed out only to awake by to rising sun and Tasha sniffing his face.

"God...ow... my head," Nathan said bringing himself on his feet, after stretching his back, the farmer retreated to the bathroom to throw up. As he returned to the kitchen to feed his dog, he called on Joseph but got no response. After cleaning the mess in the kitchen, he went upstairs to find the guest room neatly cleaned and emptied.

"God damn!" Nathan said banging his wrist to the wall. Now alone the farmer had two tasks: tending to his farm and setting up more traps around the property.

In a couple of days, Nathan set up a half a dozen necks snares, and leg traps around his property. But still had not finished the deadfall. As the weather became colder, the leaves covered soil became harder to dig up.

Nathan returned to the barn to bring all the animals in, and after feeding them treats of apples and carrots he heard Tasha Barking in the house.

"What is it, Tasha?" Nathan said walking up the front door where he heard knocking.

"Hello, Mr. Scotfield," Erin said walking to him. Tasha suddenly advanced on the girl, growling as though to attack.

"Tasha Stop!" Nathan quickly grabbed her by floppy ear and dragged her back inside by the collar into the laundry room.

"Oh Erin, I'm so sorry," Nathan said finding the young girl had walked into his living room.

"It's all fine," she replied sitting on his couch crossing her long legs on his coffee table.

"Uh… so what can I do for you?" he asked, "would you like a drink?"

"Sure, got any beer?" she asked.

"Um… no," he lied, "but I have soda or tea?"

"I'll take a soda," Erin replied.

After serving her drink, Nathan asked how her family was and her job at the deli.

"I'm not working there anymore?" said Erin. "Essy laid me off."

"Oh, I'm sorry," Nathan said.

"Don't be! Anyhoo the reason why I'm here is that, mom and dad wish to invite you over for dinner again."

"Wow, well thank you, about what time?"

"5pm tomorrow, don't be late."

"Okay great, would you like me to bring a dessert?" Nathan asked but Erin didn't answer and stormed out the door leaving it wide open, the man walked up and saw the girl jog down the hill but didn't go to her house and ran into the woods instead.

Nathan spent the evening baking a simple chocolate cake to give to his neighbors and planned to stop at a liquor store to buy wine. While in the kitchen the phone rang, and he decided to just pick it up. Without looking at the caller I.D.

"Farmer Scotfield."

"Bonsoir Mr. Scotfield, it's Toussaint."

"Oh hi..." before he finished the animal cop interrupted.

"We found your cow," said Toussaint.

"You found her?"

"Yes...but I'm afraid the cow is dead," Toussaint said.

"Dead? What happened?" Nathan said shocked.

Toussaint let out a sigh, "a bear, tore it to pieces. We found the remains four miles north of your property, you can meet me at the truck stop on the highway tomorrow morning, and I'll take you straight to it. You must see this for yourself."

"Okay, I'll see you then," Nathan said goodbye and hung up. He stood in his kitchen for a moment too upset to think clearly.

Meanwhile, Toussaint was standing outside his van off the highway about to drive back to his station. Until he heard a rustle coming from the thick forest at first, he thought it was nothing then boarded his vehicle.

"Hey, you!" he heard.

"What the?" Toussaint opened his door and looked to the dark woods.

"Over here!" said the voice coming from the forest, Toussaint took out his flashlight but found nothing.

"Who's there?" he said drawing his sidearm. Slowly he walked about three yards from his van to the edge of the woods. He heard the sounds of bare footsteps, twigs snapping and light-voiced whispers, the animal control officer had a bad feeling growing in his nerve.

"Who's there?!" he yelled, again. In response from the woods only came the growls of something big and dangerous. "Oh god." The man said, slowly walking back to his van; unaware that a being was just standing at the entrance of his van.   Upon bumping into it the man, Toussaint screamed and turned to the tall, furry figure staring dead into its glowing yellow eyes.

The beast lunged at him, and with its footlong jaws bit the man's left hand and dragged him into the misty woods. With the pain in one hand, Toussaint lost his pistol the man screamed in horror, yelling and crying for someone to help. As it dragged him deeper and deeper into the woods the last source of light, he saw upon dropping his flashlight.

The beast dragged its human pray to the center of the forest and ripped his left arm right out of his socket, dying Toussaint screamed again and felt his other arm being torn by another wolf like creature. Another wolf came, then another, and the entire pack of giant wolves encircled the helpless human, they bit into his large form, and slowly ate him alive. Upon finishing the meal all howled at the moon with the human blood-stained snouts and they licked their jaws for more blood.

Miles away in the Scotfield barn, the sleeping horses and cows awoke to the horrific wolf cries. And inside the house locked in the laundry room, Tasha growled out to the window, staring at the woods illuminated by the moon.

Nathan awakened to the cries of his animals. But he went back to sleep on his bed gripping his rifle, with his shotgun under the bed, and his pistol tucked under his mattress.

Chapter 10. The Bones.

Nathan drove to the truck stop where Toussaint said he'd meet him, but after an hour the man was nowhere to be found. Frustrated and confused Nathan boarded his truck and drove couple miles north and spotted Toussaint's van off the side of the highway.

Nathan parked behind the van and walked up but saw no sign of the officer. He walked around and found the back-passenger door left wide open.

"Hello? Toussaint?" Nathan called out.

Nathan continued to look around before trying to contact the patrolman on his cellphone. But got no answer. The farmer then decided to investigate in the woods. Where he found a trail of some sort. It didn't look like a hiking trail. Instead it looked as though something was forcibly dragged through or out of the woods.

As he followed the dragged marks it into the deep pine woods, Nathan called out for Toussaint. The woods were all silent, with only the noise of wind blowing through the tree's with moist dripping off the needles and leaves. Nathan continued walking, starting to feel nervous, when he smelled something awful.

As he walked off the trail to follow the foul odor, he came across a dying flashlight. He picked off the ground and knew that it had to belong to Toussaint. Nathan walked on until he found an opening where the bones and decaying flesh of the cow lay up against a tree stump.

Nathan stood devastated at the sight; the poor cow was half eaten with a puddle of blood all around it like a moat. He ran with all his might back to the vehicles, tripping and falling until he hit the road surface.

"Toussaint!" he yelled; Nathan stood by the animal control van for over an hour shouting and screaming for the man, but Toussaint never showed up. Something was very wrong. He tried to call the man by phone again but still couldn't reach him. Shaken with dread and frustrated Nathan had no other alternative but to call the police.

A cop showed up, and it was officer Merv.

"You?" Merv said surprised.

"I need your help, I can't find Toussaint anywhere!" the concerned, wet and dirty Nathan said. The officer stared at the man with suspicion before following him to the tree line.

"So, you never saw him in the woods?" Merv asked as they walked back in the forest.

"No, I just followed this trail and only found the dead remains of my cow," said Nathan while leading the way. "and I found this dead flashlight."

"Okay show me," demanded Merv, Nathan handed him the flashlight before leading the officer straight back to the cow's carcass.

"Gross," said Merv struck by the horrid smell, "So, you found this, but Toussaint wasn't here?"

"He called me last night and said he would meet me here, but he was nowhere to be found. I tried calling him twice by his cell phone but he never answered or texted. I'm not liking this."

"Well, that is strange," Merv said shaking his head, "because last night he never returned to the animal shelter either."

As the two men walked back to the road, Nathan looked at the time and it was a quarter after 4 pm.

"So, officer what are we going to do? I would love to stay and help search but I have to get home and…"

"Well, I'm afraid you'll have to wait!" Merv said, before calling for backup on the radio. As he waited for more cops to arrive on the scene, Nathan tried to contact the Kess family to let them know, he's going to be late, but they never answered the phone.

Two police cruisers arrived with Captain Francis and two other policemen. The sun began to set, with rain clouds floating over. Nathan had to fill out them a police statement on when he last heard from the patrolmen.

"Alright Mr. Scotfield, you can go on home now, and we'll call you if we find him," the captain said. As the cop watched Nathan board his truck and drove off, Merv walked up to his superior.

"You know sir? I don't like to be all suspicious or anything… but I think that farmer is up to no good."

"What the hell are talking about?" asked Francis.

"Think about it sir, a strange dude from the city comes up here for whatever reasons, only to kill a young man and now a missing animal control officer…"

"Oh what? Are you saying Scotfield killed Toussaint?"

"Well, no not exactly," Merv said, "What I'm saying is… I think he knows something we don't."

"Ollie, shut up," said Francis walking to his car, "the man is just a farmer trying to make a living, and the he's got too many problems to commit a crime. Besides he reported to us"

Upon Nathan's arrived at the home of his neighbors, very late. It was 6:300 and already dark.

He knocked on the door and rang the doorbell but no answered, he believed someone had to be home since the lights were left on.

"Lidia?! Brad?! Erin?! Is anyone home?!" he shouted, after a couple more knocks, he decided to walk over to the back door. There he found back entrance left open and saw plates on the kitchen table.

"Anybody?!" he said walking in. There were five untouched plates on the table and four pairs of shoes were left by the back door.

"What the hell?" Nathan said to himself confused by the empty house with food left on the table. "What? Did they go out somewhere?"

Nathan tried calling out to them again, but the house was completely empty. No one was home. He felt terrible being so late and was afraid his neighbors would be mad at him. He placed his cake in their refrigerator and left a note.

"Hello Lidia and Brad, I'm so sorry I didn't show up for dinner, I had an emergency. I entered your house because your back door was open. I left a cake I made in your fridge so yall can have it for dessert. Hopefully, we can do dinner some other time. Mr. Scotfield."

Nathan turned out the kitchen light locked the door and closed it behind him, as he walked off the steps, he heard snarling.

"What is that?!" Nathan paused and stood perfectly still. Unable to see since the night was pitch black with no moon. The man slowly retreated to the house.

Nathan walked back one of the porches and didn't know where else to go since he'd locked the door and his truck was parked around the front. When he tried to walk down again, but after less than two steps away, the growling return and it was coming closer.

He paused again standing perfectly still, and touched the side of the house, staring out into the darkness. He was not afraid but stayed cautious and calm. He stuck his back to the wall of the house, slowly stepping around the corner, then he made for his truck.

Nathan entered the passenger side of the truck and crawled over to the driver side, and upon turning on the headlight, there 'It' stood.

Nathan saw it, standing on its two hind legs like a bear. It was tall, 7 feet from the pointed ears on its head to clawed paws. He couldn't believe what he was seeing.

"No… no not real!" he said to himself. The beast had a human feminine figure with brown fur covering over the head shoulders and breasts. It's over long arms with sharp claws and stared back at the man. Its eyes glowing yellow, with the tail wagging behind her and from its long snout she showed her sharp white fangs. Then its tongue licked her black nose. The creature stood in a position hunched over and growling at the truck.

With their eyes locked, Nathan's heart was pumping faster. Sweat soaked his hair and forehead. And his fear only increased when a second werewolf walked into the lights of his car.

"You've gotta be freaking kidding me!" he said seeing that there was a third one followed flanking the tall standing wolf.

The second werewolf slowly walked from the neighbor's lawn, on four legs, though small they all had similar physical appearances.

He couldn't take it any longer. Nathan started the ignition, the wolf trio let out loud thundering barks that rang in the man's ears.

He quickly shifted into reverse. The truck drove backward knocking down the Kess' trash cans. Nathan then speeded forward to his house so fast he'd almost crashing into his front porch.

He quickly shut off his truck and rushed through the front door. Tasha came up and could hear the danger coming outside. As Nathan closed and locked the front door, she jumped up barking. Nathan took her by the collar.

Outside the three wolves came up to the front door, with the larger female banging against it.

"Oh shit!" Nathan said, he retreated with Tasha to the kitchen where he grabbed a butcher knife, then locked himself in the laundry room with his hound. He heard a fracturing noise from the living room. The werewolf has broken into his house. Quickly with all his might Nathan single-handedly shoved his heavy freezer against the door to barricade it.

Tasha by his side growled in anger as the intruders stalked around the house.

The trio of creatures could hear Nathan and Tasha behind the door; could smell the hound and its master in the room. Instead of trying to break the door, the two young werewolves rummaged through the farmer's food pantry.

The alpha female sniffed at the door. Inside Nathan slowly backed up to the washing machines on the far side of the room. The man was by all accounts scared out of his mind. He held the knife up and began to cry. Tasha, on the other hand, stood firm, Nathan watched his hound bark and growl at the monsters just outside, telling them to go away.

Seeing how brave his dog was, that Tasha was going to protect him no matter how strong and powerful these werewolves were. With this Nathan began to calm himself and fought back his fear as his hound loudly barked at the animals.

Outside the alpha wolf decided against breaching the door and just left with the other two wolves. The trio ran out and Nathan could hear them howling from his front yard.

"They're gone," he whispered, getting back on his feet he flicked to his lights but didn't want to leave the room.

"Good girl, Tasha, good girl," he said rubbing her head as she licked his hand.

From the dryer Nathan took out a sheet he rolled up in a pillow for his dog lay on, he then took out another bedsheet for him and upon standing, he saw through the window pure yellow eyes glittering and a snarling sound.

Surprised, Nathan screamed and fell on his back, bumping his head on the metal boiler, knocking himself unconscious.

Chapter 11. A hunting trip.

Nathan awoke, that morning with Tasha licking his face. He got up and saw it was daylight, his watch read 8:45 am. He opened the door to find his kitchen a disaster, with no signs of the wolves and his back door was left wide open. The farmer stood with his head aching and throbbing as he went to the bathroom to wash up. He went back downstairs to the kitchen freezer, took out and frozen blue pack to rest it on the side of his skull. He knew he was late in feeding the animals, but he just couldn't think straight after what had happened last night. He didn't know what to do, he didn't know who to go to or how to handle this situation.

As all these thoughts burned in his head, adding pain to his sore headache. Then suddenly he heard a voice calling.

"Nathan?!" he heard a voice yell, Tasha stood from her laying down and began barking.

"Tasha, hush! Shut up!" he said grabbing her collar, then a knock came on the door.

"Who is it?!" yelled Nathan annoyed while restraining his hound.

"Nathan? It's Brad, Brad Kess are you alright?"

"Ahh! Hang on a moment!" Nathan said, he walked up and pushed the freezer out of the way and opened the door with Tasha trying to get through.

"Tasha stop!" Nathan pushed her back and got out of the room leaving her inside violently growling and yelping.

"Are you okay man?" Brad asked.

Nathan nodded no still holding the frozen pack upon his head, he leads Brad to the living room and sat down on his couch.

"What the hell happened man?" said Brad.

"I...I found my missing cow, she's dead," Nathan answered, "I arrived late at your home for supper… no one answered."

"Oh yeah, Lidia uh had an accident… I had to… take her to the doctor. Sorry I was so worried that forgot to call you and…"

"Then I saw three wolves!" Nathan interrupted.

"Wolves?" Brad asked.

"Big wolves, chased me… broke my door, they tried to kill me!" Nathan said panicking, trying to stand but Brad pushed him back on the chair.

"Ok, ok just stay seated, everything's going to be alright,"

"No, it won't!" he yelled.

"I'll get you a drink," Brad went to the kitchen to fetch some milk.

Nathan saw his broken front door laying against his coat hanger. From afar he saw someone running down his yard… totally naked.

"What the fuck?" Nathan muttered then Brad walked up handing him a glass of cold milk.

"Here just relax," Barad said standing in his view.

Nathan took a sip then pointed, "there's someone outside!"

Brad turned and looked but only saw his wife entering their house down the hill.

"It's okay Nat, don't stress yourself."

Nathan wanted to object and tell him what he saw, but with his head wracked with pain he felt dizzier, Brad laid him on the couch.

Nathan woke again this time the clock showed 12 o'clock noon. He saw Brad drilling in new hinges for his front door and heard Tasha barking back in the washroom.

"You're fixing my door?" Nathan said getting up.

"Take it easy buddy. The door was old, and I took the liberty of getting you a brand new one."

"A new door?" he asked.

"Yeah, I have plenty of lumber in my shed," said Brad as he began working on the doorknob. "It must've been a pretty angry momma bear, willing to break through solid oak.

"No...no Brad, it was no bear!"

"Nat, there's no way a wolf can break a door down," Brad said.

"Maybe a wolf 7 feet tall!" Nathan yelled, with Brad still working. The man rubbed his palm over his head and sat back down.

Brad signed and walked up, "Look, man, how about after I fix the door, come by my house for lunch, have some company."

"I... I can't my animals."

"Nat, you need some time off, I'll feed the livestock. You just go take a shower, take some ibuprofen and come on over for a meal, we insist."

Nathan agreed. Brad finished the new door, solid cedar with iron smelted hinges and two-barrel bolts screwed on both the top and bottom.

In the laundry room the barking Tasha smelled the man walk up, with one hand Brad pushed up the door, moving the freezer aside and saw the growling hound.

"Hello, you little bitch."

Nathan came out of the shower, and saw Tasha chained outside. With Brad doing the farm work, the farmer walked upstairs to get dressed. When he returned and saw that Brad had also cleaned his pantry and mopped the floor.

Inside the barn, Nathan found all the animals frightened out of their wits. Brad was gone but their food and water tanks were filled up because they've never touched it.

Nathan decided not to let the animals out since it was getting colder outside. After mucking out of the stalls, he walked to his neighbors' home for lunch.

At the Kess table, Nathan wanted to tell them all what he saw last night but thought they'll never believe him, so he just kept it to himself.

"So, Lidia's at the hospital?" he asked after Erin served him a burger.

"Oh, no the accident wasn't really bad," said Brad. "She accidentally burned her arm. The doc gave her some pain relievers, some bandaged over the blisters. She's okay."

"Then, where is she?"

"Visiting her sister," Erin cut in, sitting next to him.

"Oh... that's nice," said Nathan.

"How are things going Mr. Scotfield?" Josiah asked.

The man looked at the kid and gave him and sad look, "Not good I'm afraid... things have been... weird."

"Like what?" the kid asked.

"I don't wish to talk about it... I'm sorry," he replied.

"Seems you got a lot of stress weighing on you, Nat."

"You have no idea," Nathan said.

The three stared at the man before Brad spoke up.

"You know, Nat I… I own a hunting lodge up in Apica woodlands, I plan to go up next week for moose. Would you like to join me?"

"Moose hunting?"

"Yes, on this last week of October. Maybe it'll be nice for you to get out and have some free time."

Nathan thought for a minute, before shaking his head, "I can't, my farm, I would need someone to care for the animals and check my traps."

"Well, my wife and kids can manage," said Brad. "And it'll just be for the weekend."

"They can do farm work?"

"Sure, they can. Right kids?"

"Yeah, I love animals!" said Josiah.

"Well, I can't pay you guys, my tax time is coming soon and…"

"Nat you don't have to pay them," Brad said.

"Oh, I can't have your kids do manual labor…. For free."

"I'll put it in their allowance," Brad said, Nathan thought again, and maybe he's right a little time off the farm might be good for him.

"Well, I have… "

"We're not afraid of wolves, Nathan," Erin said. "We can handle it."

Nathan took a deep breath and shook his head, "Well, I shouldn't. But very well, I'll go hunting."

"Great."

"But just for two days!" Nathan said. "So, when Lidia is home come by my house and I'll show you guys what to do while I'm gone."

While making his way back home, Nathan wanted to punch himself. He felt he shouldn't have two kids tend his farm, especially with the traps he set in the woods. But again, he thought it would help him keep away from the booze and perhaps a weekend of peace was just what he needed.

That evening Lidia showed up with her two kids. As Nathan showed them around the barn, he notices. Lidia showed no sign of injury or had any markings on her forearm. The moment he opened the doors, to show them his animals, Clyde and Dixie went ballistic, kicking and whining like they were wild rodeo bulls.

"Do they always act like that?" Erin asked as Nathan walked to their stalls to calm them down.

"No, I have never seen them so frightened."

"Do we still have to let them out of the barn?" Lidia asked worriedly.

"Hmm, I think not," Nathan replied bringing them outside. "Best keep the animals inside for the weekend. So make sure you feed them twice a day, including Tasha my dog. Always give the fresh clean water, and milk the cows three times a day, check the chicken coops for eggs and shovel out the stalls to keep the place clean. Any questions?"

"Do we really have to shovel the shit?" asked Erin.

"Oh, stop complaining you sissy, it's only two days," Lidia said in.

"Now here's the key, both to the barn and my house," Nathan said handing him his spare set. "If Tasha doesn't listen just keep her chained outside. But always bring her inside before dark. And again, keep the animals inside the barn."

"Why? Are there wolves?" asked Josiah.

"Yes, I'm really not liking this pack; their dangerous. So, if you three want you can spend the night in my house, and I have a shotgun in my closet."

"We don't kill wolves," said Josiah.

"But we promise to take care of everything," Lidia said.

"Thanks, guys... and if you want you can keep the milk and eggs you collect. And of course, you can use my kitchen and TV," Nathan said.

"You're too kind," said Lidia smiling.

"Too open," said Erin.

"Well, you guys are willing to give you're the time and energy. I really appreciate this."

"That's what good neighbors are for," Lidia said.

Friday, October 26th, Nathan packed his pickup with some extra clothes, his old hunting gear, and his savage 99 hunting rifle, and followed Brad to this hunting lodge.

They arrive, 30 miles north in the Apica forest just west of Woodgate on the border of Herkimer county. The hunting cabin was a small single room with a moss-covered roof, a fireplace made of stone, two beds and a bunk bed. It had no electricity and an outhouse next to a giant firewood pile.

"Nice little set up you got here Brad," said Nathan.

"Pleased you like it."

"So, you take customers up here hunting?"

"All my grown-up life, I've hunted up here. I take customers on trips as far as New England and Canada," Brad replied, showing Nathan some old photos pinned to the wooden wall over the fireplace mantel. Each showed Brad with a hunter and a large buck, black bear, bobcats and even moose.

There was also one picture showing Brad, his wife and their two kids when they were much younger standing over what looked a reindeer.

"Wow, you took your family up here too?"

"Yeah, we used to live here before we moved to Graytown."

"You lived here? Really?" Nathan asked, surprised.

"Yeah, when I married Lidia, we had nothing but this cabin. When her drunk, abusive father passed and her sister Lizzy stayed with us, I worked double shift at a factory. When I saved enough, I helped put Lizzy through school and brought a new home."

"That's quite a story. My father did the same thing," Nathan said.

"You guys were poor?" Brad asked.

"Not only poor, we were homeless," Nathan said, "My mom got sick and dad had to cash in to try and save her, but sadly the cancer won, and the medical bills render us penniless. But my dad, being a great man, never let anything or anyone stop him. He worked day and night at two jobs until he put a roof over our heads again. He raised both of us to be successful, but I let him down."

"Let him down?"

"I became careless. And now I'm drinking turning myself into a loser," Nathan said.

"You shouldn't give up, but perhaps you should go back... to New York and rebuild yourself."

After thinking, Nathan decided to change the subject, "so, are we going hunting?"

"Oh right! we're wasting daylight." So, the two men took their weapons, hike through the woods straight to their hunting stand.

Back at the farm, the horrified animals were being cared by Erin and Josiah. Inside Nathan's house Lidia was vacuuming the floor ignoring Tasha whining pitifully from the closet. When she finished, Josiah walked in with a basket full of fresh eggs.

"Good job sweetie, I'll use some eggs to make a large batch of brownies."

"But mom, Nathan made us a cake we didn't finish," the boy said.

"I know, the brownies are not for us it's for Nathan," Lidia said now mopping the kitchen floor. "I'll also make a batch for Miss. Ester."

"I don't like her."

"Shut your mouth Josiah Kess, you need to watch your mouth!" Lidia said, with slight regret, "you're starting to talk like your sister."

That afternoon after feeding the animals, the three people left them animals with their stalls dirty deliberately neglecting to clean out the waste.

Tasha barked up a storm when the three opened the closet. Erin and Josiah pulled the dog out by her floppy ears and dragged her through the kitchen and out the door where Lidia chained the dog up.

Tasha continued to violently bark at the family, almost biting Erin's hand when she lashed out.

At the cabin, the two hunters sat quietly on a hunting stand overlooking a giant gorge full of mud and shrubs. Both waited patiently, for any sign of prey.

Nathan admired the beauty of the woods with the rays of sunlight shining through the branches of the pine trees, shadowing forest floor.

He sat firm and silent as a statue but noticed some gesturing movements of Brad sitting a yard away from him. Nathan could hear the man tap his foot, whispering quietly. Nathan looked to him to ask if he was alright.

"See anything?" Nathan said softly, but the man did not reply and just continued to stare out into the thick woods. After another two hours passed with no sign of moose or deer the men noticed it was getting late and decided to head back to the cabin.

"So, what are we gonna have for dinner?" Nathan asked.

"I brought some canned goods, I'll whip us up some a pot of beef, potatoes, and gravy," Brad said.

 "Sounds great. I'm gonna call your wife, would you like a beer?"

"No thank you."

From his pocket, Nathan felt his silent feel his cell phone vibrating, he answered the call and it was Lidia. She told Nathan they have done all the tasks he instructed them about. That all the animals were okay, and the farm was locked up and secured. But did not mention they had left Tasha chained outside.

As the two men ate their stew, Nathan saw rad was down in the dumps as though something bad has happened.

"Hey, are you okay buddy?" he asked Brad.

"Huh? Oh yeah, I'm fine," Brad said. But Nathan noticed something was unsettling his host. Yet Nathan didn't question him again.

Chapter 12. Trap accident.

That evening after supper, the two went to bed. But Nathan awoke sometime around midnight. He got up and went outside to use the outhouse. When he returned inside, he discovered Brad's bed was empty.

"What the hell?" Nathan felt, he knew Brad wasn't at the outhouse or the truck since he'd passed by it. He then notices that Brad had left his parka and his boots were under his bed. "The important things a man would need on a cold night like this and he's not wearing them?" thought Nathan. He then walked back to the door to call on Brad.

"Brad?! Brad Kess?! Are you out there?!" Nathan yelled but got no response. When he looked around outside the cabin with a flashlight, he heard the start of an engine. Nathan rsued to the front door and found Brad's truck was gone. Nathan thought that Brad will be back soon and decided to go back to sleep.

The night became colder with a frost of rime growing on small trees, windows, walls and freezing the ground solid.

At the farm, the cows, horses, and goats slept close to one another to stay warm, while outside poor Tasha laid in her doghouse cuddled as best, she could with only a ragged towel to lay on. She survived through the night and upon the sunrise melting the frost covered lawn, the hound saw three naked humans enter her master's house.

At the cabin, Nathan awoke with Brad still gone.

"Damn where did you go?!" Nathan took out his cell to call his wife.

"Hello, Nathan."

"Hi Lidia, have you seen Brad?"

"I thought he was with you?" she asked.

"No, I woke up to find him gone. He left his boots, cell phone, and parka but his truck is gone," Nathan said.

"He must've gone out, for gas or coffee or something."

"In the snow, barefoot?" Nathan said concerned and dumbfounded.

"Look, I'm sure he's fine. Just wait a while and if he's not backs in over an hour call me. I can't talk right now, I'm headed to your farm," and before Nathan could speak, she hung up on him.

Lidia called on the kids who came downstairs, they walked out the back door, where Tasha came storming out of her doghouse. She bit Josiah in the shin, Erin kicked her and grab a stick to keep her at bay. When the child screamed, Lidia ran up and kicked the poor dog again with steel-toed boots. Tasha yelped and tried to bite the lady, but she and her kids stayed out of her reach.

"Dog's a smart one," Erin said.

"Don't feed this bitch and leave her outside again!" her mother said angrily while rubbing her boy's shoulder.

Far north in the lodge Nathan got dressed but stayed by the cabin. He was beginning to get a bad feeling in his stomach, and not from the stew or beer. His mind was now burning with strong anxieties, he knew something was horribly wrong.

Just as he took out his cell phone to call Lidia again, Brad drove up. Nathan walked out and saw the man coming out of his vehicle dressed only in jeans, and a t-shirt not wearing any footwear or jacket in the 40-degree weather.

"Hey Nat, come on over here and give me a hand!" he called out, Nathan walked up and found a large dead eight pointer in back of the truck, "Isn't he a beauty?" asked Brad with a smirk.

"Brad where were you last night?"

"I was… out," Brad answered stuttering.

"Out where?"

"I had a call from my garage, one of my coworkers called out and I had to make a car inspection."

"With no shoes on?" Nathan asked.

"I have a pair of work boots in my truck, okay!" he yelled causing Nathan step back. After a moment of hesitation Nathan helped Brad carry the dressed-out deer from truck to the tree next to the woodshed. And hanged it up to let it dry.

"Well, that's done. Now let see if we can find you a deer," Brad said walking in the cabin. Nathan though, felt angry and puzzled by the man's hash tone and weird attitude. He began to think that he should leave. He didn't even wanna question where Brad got the buck and thought he should just call it a day and go home, but he didn't. He followed Brad back into the woods, without saying anything.

Brad took the farmer deeper into the forest and they settled near a small running stream on top a moss-covered boulder. Three hours passed and Brad took out a moose mating call. He made several calls but had no luck. Another hour went by and they still had no luck. By the afternoon Nathan began to lose patience.

"I think we should go now," whispered Nathan, but Brad just ignored him.

"Don't move," said Brad and slowly pointed out ahead, Nathan turned and from a thicket came a pair of gigantic antlers attached to a 6-foot high bull moose.

"There you go Nat, ready yourself."

His blood paused with excitement, Nathan quietly and slowly positioned himself to a kneeling pose, the bull casually walked out of the thick exposing his huge body, sniffing the bank of the running water.

And just before the mammal was about to take a drink of water, Nathan shot it through the lungs. The giant dropped and made one last move to stand up before collapsing again in the stream, dead.

"Woohoo! nice shooting Nat!" Brad patted his shoulder. The hunters walked up, to the dead giant, dragged it out of the stream and, Brad took out his knife to begin the field dressing. As the day turned late a flurry of light snow began to fall from the sky. After removing the moose's entrails, the two men tried to carry the fully-grown moose by the legs, but it didn't work. So, for the next couple of hours they used their knives to cut it into four large pieces.

It was around 4 pm when they finally made it to the cabin and Nathan felt his cell phone vibrating.

"Wait a sec Brad. I've got a call from my house," Nathan said dropping the branch.

"Hello?"

"Nathan, it's Erin!"

"Hi Erin, is everything okay?" he asked.

"No, I'm afraid we had a bit of an accident…"

"What! An accident? what happened?"

"Josiah and Mom stupidly left the barn doors open. When he went to milk your goats, they went berserk and ran out the farm," Erin explained.

"Christ, okay, you guys think you can corral them back inside?"

"That the other problem. They ran off the ranch and into the woods…"

"What?! Oh God Damn it!"

"What the problem?" Brad said, but Nathan waved him off.

"Okay well, I have to come home right away, don't let your mom or brother go after them I have legs traps out there," Nathan said, "Just stay by the house and I'll get home as soon as I can."

Nathan ended the call and gathered his duffle bag.

"What's the matter?!" asked Brad.

"Your son and wife lost my goats," he answered, "I have to go and get them."

"What about the moose?"

"I'm sorry Brad this is an emergency I'll come back to pick it up later!" Nathan got in his truck and drove off. As he drove down the highway more snow began to fall, and Nathan began to worry that his goats would get snared or injured by the bear traps, and that he would have to put them down.

He made it home about 15 after 6. He first entered his house, but no one was there. He called on Lidia but got no answer, not even on her cell phone that he found up in the guest room. When he walked to his room, he saw from the window that they've left his barn doors wide open and Tasha was left chained outside.

He ran down with his rifle, to let Tasha loose.

"Tasha girl!" he said calming her down, "Oh God you're so cold."

He led her back inside to warm up by his furnace and draped her with a blanket. Then he ran back out to the barn.

Inside the barn the goat stall was empty, and the spare keys were left hanging on a chain hook.

"Shit, Lidia!" he cursed. It was getting dark quickly, but Nathan had to find them. He saddled Dixie and rode out to the woods.

The snow and wind began to pick up, but he heard the agonizing bleat of one of his goats. He rode along using a flashlight until he found one horribly wounded, its right hind leg snapped off from the leg trap.

He got off Dixie and tied her to a tree. He walked up while the goat limped against the trunk of another tree. He brought up his rifle and shot it in the head, putting it out of its misery.

Then something yelped, Nathan looked out to the snowy woods. Dixie began whining in fear. The man walked up to calm her as the sound of growls caught his ears.

"Ah shit!" He exclaimed as the panicked horse tried to retreat. As the horse turned a wolf pounced, scratching her by the throat.

Dixie let out a horrid sound and fell to her side, breaking Nathan's leg.

He screamed with pain as the weight pressed against his right leg, Dixie stood herself up, Nathan turned on his stomach to push himself up, but the injured and shakily horse, mistakenly stomped on her master's back, breaking his left shoulder blade.

Nathan screamed again, his cry echoing through the woods. The wolf pack replied by howling. Losing more blood from its neck the horse tried to run off but got caught in a snare pulling the giant off her feet.

Then the pack attacked the house. The farmer watched helpless as six big wolves tore into the draft horse. Now Nathan thought that this was the end as more and more snow began to blanket him. The wounded man just laid and waited for the wolves to finish, hoping they'll give him a quick death. Then he blacked out from the pain.

The alpha walked behind the unconscious human sniffing him, with the dead goat in its jaws. Two of her lead hunters came up.

It dropped the dead goat then ordered the pack to storm the barn, with the farmer out no one could save the animals now.

"We have it now," the alpha said, "the meat is ours and we will not go hungry this winter. Kill this human but eat him not."

"Kill him?" the female huntress asked.

"Just rip open his throat and leave him to waste like the worthless human he is," after giving the order the alpha picked up the goat and ran for the open barn.

In the house, Tasha watched helplessly from the kitchen window as the pack, chased down and killed the cows, the chickens and chased Clyde away. She howled and called for help, but no one came, and the pack gorged themselves on the meat.

Nathan was left, injured in the woods the wolf pair though did not kill him but sat him against a tree, ad brushed the powered snow off him.

The next morning at the police station, Captain Francis taking the calls at the deck, received an anonymous phone call.

"There's an injured man in the woods, behind the old farm of Graytown."

Though there was no answer to who or where the call came from, officer Francis, Merv and Wallstone immediately drove down to Scotfield's farm where they discovered the gruesome carnage of blood, guts and the remains of dead animals lying everywhere all over the snow-covered lawn. In the snow the officers followed huge blood tracks leading to the woods, where they found a dead horse and Nathan Scotfield... barely alive.

Chapter 13. Babysitting.

Two days later, in Burlington Vermont, Dr. Joe Scotfield was tending a sick German Shepherd, when suddenly he was interrupted by one of the nurses.

"Dr. Scotfield, we just got a call from New York!"

"Is this important?" he asked rolling his eyes.

"It's your brother, Joseph," the old nurse replied.

Joseph instantly stopped his operation and walked out of the room, "What? Is he okay? is he in trouble again?"

"No, he's hurt, we just got a call from the hospital. Your brother was in a horrible accident."

Hearing that the man dropped everything he was doing and left the patient in the care of his colleague. He went to the office and took the phone where he learned that his brother had broken his leg, shoulder and back, and had caught pneumonia. Without a moment's hesitation, Joseph left work, packed some clothes and drove all the way to Utica, to be by Nathan's bed side.

He arrived at the hospital where he was greeted by doctors, who led him to Nathan's room. The injured man laid passed out, all pale a drugged up on his bed, with his leg wrapped in a cast and a cervical collar around his neck.

"We drugged him before we operated his leg," the doctor explained. "He's been out for over 24 hours now."

"Is he going to be okay?"

"Well, his back and leg will heal, but he must stay warm, and in bed until he recovers from the fever. He'll die if he's not cared for."

Waking from his coma, Nathan slowly open his eyes and discovered he was lying in a hospital room. Puzzled and disorientated he yelped and called out for someone. A nurse rushed in.

"Oh Mr. Scotfield you're awake!" she said laying him back on his pillow.

"Where am I?" He felt so lightheaded and very puzzled. He found his right leg mummified in a cast and tried to sit up but then discovered his left shoulder and arm were restrained in a brace.

"No sir, please you mustn't stress yourself." The nurse said. "Look Nathan you're in Mohawk Hospital, and your brother's coming today."

"How long have I been out?"

"About four days now."

Unable to pull himself up with causing pain, he laid back down in the pillow and with his good arm, he felt the facial hair on his chin has grown into a beard. Unable to move due for the pain, he began to drift back to sleep.

Joseph arrived at the hospital and entered Nathan's room. His big brother awoke, real pleased to see him again. Three more days in the hospital, Nathan wanted to go hom. So, they check him out of the hospital and took him to his farm.

As Joseph is brother home, Nathan stared out the window. And asked.

"My animals … are they okay? "he turned to Joey.

As happy and relieved Joey was that Nathan was okay, he wasn't prepared to inform tell his brother that his livestock had been slaughtered. When informed of the tragic death of his animals, the Scotfield brothers returned home in silence.

The first morning home, Joseph was downstairs, preparing breakfast when he heard Nathan, scream upstairs. Barging Tasha rushed up by her master's bedside and began kissing Nathan's cheek, with her tail wagging like a flag.

"Down girl! Tasha get down!" Joseph said pulling her collar.

"Joseph?"

"Hi Nathan, are you okay," Joe said taking Tasha out of the room.

"Joey... Yeah... just hit my elbow."

"Nathan, please you need to stay in bed, you're sick and can't move around so much."

"Will, I ever use my arm again?"

"The doctor said you shoulder blade injury wasn't so bad, with some physical therapy, you'll be fine," Joe said handing him some painkillers.

"Wh... what about my leg?"

"Well, the doc supplied us with crutches, but you're still gonna have to stay in bed for a couple of weeks."

"Shit!" Nathan said in a whining tone falling back on the pillows.

"Just get some rest. Don't stress out."

When Nathan had finally calm down and started to rest, staring out his window at the falling swirling snow flurries all, Joseph left him alone to feed Tasha.

Downstairs he found the dog eating with officer Lizzy Wallstone standing next to her.

"Oh, you fed her. Thank you," he said.

"How is he?" Lizzy asked.

"Well he's finally awake, I think he'll pull through, would you like some hot tea?"

"Yes, thank you."

Lizzy was off duty for the weekend and came to visit the Scotfield farm after checking up on her sister. After serving Nathan tea and soup she sat with his brother in the living room. The two relaxed not watching TV but observing the snow falling outside.

"It's really peaceful here?" said Joseph.

"Yeah it is, it's a nice place."

"You know Officer Wallstone... thank you for saving my brother."

"It's part of my job, besides whoever gave us the anonymous call should be thanked. If he or she didn't tip us off your brother would've frozen to death."

"Still it was you who found him, and got him to the hospital," he said touching her shoulder.

"So, did you tell Nathan about his animals?"

"I did. He'd was pretty sad, and I don't think that depression is gonna go away anytime soon."

The officer sighed and looked down with sorrow, "It was my stupid sister's fault, making her kids tend the animals."

"I'm sorry?"

"Lidia told me, when her husband took Nathan hunting, she volunteered to look after his animals, but instead she made her kids do the work..."

"She makes her kids do farm work?"

"Manual labor, and chores. She makes her daughter work a regular job even though she's under 18. I'm so disgusted with her," Lizzy said. "And making her eight-year-old milk cows and goats."

"So, she lost my brothers animals."

"I swear ever since she married that loser Kess she became weak and stupid… like a 1950s style housewife. She never calls me. And when I visit, she treats me like a stranger and barely makes eye contact with me."

"You think she might have marital problems?" Joseph asked.

"Oh, no question!" Lizzy said with a sigh, "Brad's a tight neck, smudged bitch, never lets his kids go to school, holds them back from the world and would act up if I ask any questions…. Of course, I tried to help Lidia and told her she should leave that looser, but she won't," Lizzy said. She took a deep breath and apologized.

"My brother went through the same thing with his ex. She held him back had him alienate his friends," Joe said. "She cheated on him, stole from him, and divorced him… it was horrible."

"And your brother moved up here to be a farmer?"

"Yeah… he always loved animals, for as long as I could remember. We were most happy when we had pets and went to zoos."

"My sister and I loved animals before our father kicked us out in the streets, we had a German terrier," Lizzy recalled with a sad expression, "And in a drunken frenzy our dad shot her right in front of me."

"My God… I'm so sorry," Joseph said tapping her hand.

"Shame there is so much evil in this world… that's why I joined the force to try to fight it."

"And you do a good job of it. You're a good cop. And don't worry hopefully one day you'll save your sister, niece, and nephew."

"I need to get going… thanks for lunch Joe," She said taking his hand and he walked her to the door.

"By the way, you should inform Nathan, that we disarmed all his traps and placed them in his barn, and also we'll keep an eye out for his missing horse," she said putting her coat on.

"You think that horse made it?"

"Probably. Francis followed the tracks all the way across the highway, it might have a chance."

"I just can't believe it, I mean as an animal healthcare professional, I never heard of a wolf pack that could ever tear apart a whole farm livestock in a single night," Joe said crossing his arms.

"Neither have I. It looked like something out of a horror movie. Like they were torn like… never mind. But to be honest if I were Nathan, I would just move somewhere else."

Lizzy walked down the porch to her car and drove away.

Joseph stood at the front door as the snow continued falling. Then looked to Tasha sitting at his feet. He then walked up to Nathan's room where he found the wounded man was twisting and turning, moaning and sweating. Like he was having another nightmare.

Joe walked up and touched his head; Nathan awoke with a yelp.

"Oh Joey…" he whispered.

"Just relax bro… you'll be fine…" he said rubbing his head and shoulder. Nathan fell back to sleep and began dreaming about his animals and the simple peaceful life that he wanted.

A Week into the month November. And Joseph became his brother's home nurse, driving Nathan to and from Utica for physical therapy. Joseph would cook, clean, help Nathan get in the shower, sort his medicine, shovel the snow, gather firewood, and take care of his dog. He was in truth, the only thing keeping his big brother alive.

It wasn't long before Nathan could get out of bed and walk around with his crutches. Joe didn't allow him outside since he was still running with a fever.

"Joey have you seen my Jack Daniels? And where's all my beer?"

"It's all gone Nathan," Joe answered.

"What the hell do you mean, it's all gone?!"

"I threw it out. You're not having a sip of alcohol until you fully recover," Joe said plainly, "and there will be no arguing with that point."

"Shit," said Nathan.

"Oh, stop it!" his little brother replied.

One night while the brothers relaxed in the living room watching hockey, Nathan said he ordered them a pizza and gave his brother the money to go pick it up.

"Here take another $20 for gas," said Nathan, "but don't go to that local station."

"Okay, thanks Nathan, you really don't have to lend me anything have I have money," Joe said.

"Oh, shut up, you've turned yourself into my butler, nurse and chauffeur. I owe you."

"You protected me when I was a little guy, saved me from bullies plenty of times. I owe you," Joe said trying to hand the money back, but Nathan refused to take it and told him to get the pizza.

Joseph drove down to the truck stop where they had a pizzeria. He picked up their dinner and drove back to Graytown. While driving the snow became a storm. But luckily Joseph had placed chains over his tires, so he had no trouble driving. While making his way to the end of Graytown he discovered someone walking the side of the road. It was Mrs. Kess.

"What the fuck?" Joseph said aloud. He slowed down and rolled down his passenger window, "hey are you alright? What are you doing out in this storm?!"

The woman looked at him truly scared. She looked so pale, wearing only a robe as a coat and rubber Wellington boots.

"I'm being punished," she said sniffing.

"What? Hey I...I... I know you. I know your sister, Elizabeth. You shouldn't be out here dressed like that. You'll freeze to death," Joe said unlocking his door, "Please come in my car I'll take you home!"

"I can't. This is my punishment!" Lidia yelled.

"Punishment?" Joe unpickled got out of the car and took the lady by the hand, he leads her in his car and drove off.

"What the hell were you doing out there?" Joey asked again.

"She punished me," Lidia said crying.

"Who punished you? Your husband?!" Joe said angrily.

"No, I can't... she punished me, because I didn't kill him!"

He stopped the truck in the road and asked, "Who's she? What are talking about?" Lidia just ran to her house without replying.

"Wait!" he yelled. He got out to try and stop her, but she was gone into the dark house, He stood there for a moment as the snowing continued to fall. Then he just drove to his brother's house. When he made his way inside the power was out and Nathan had started a fire in his fireplace, gripping a pistol.

Nathan turned to him with a sterned face, "make yourself warm Joey, it's gonna be really cold with the power gone."

He sat with Nathan eating chicken pizza and hot cocoa, with Tasha laying by Joseph's side staring into the flame.

"So why the gun?" Joe asked.

"Oh... uh... nothing," he replied.

"Nathan... did you see anyone or anything outside?"

"No... but I know something is out there."

"When I was driving back, I saw your neighbor, Lidia walking out in the snow almost naked," said Joe, "something is wrong."

"Who cares, screw them," Nathan said derisively, "They're just crazy, they got all my animals killed, left me the keys and didn't bother to stay and help me. They run around naked in the for all I care, so let freeze to death."

"She said someone was punishing her... like making her walk out in the cold."

"That's what people get when they chose the wrong spouse brother, I would know," he said sipping his chocolate.

That night the two decided to sleep in the living room, by the fire Joe notices his brother stayed awake to keep the fire going. After he drifted to sleep Nathan limped to the back window, where he looked out into the dark forest behind his barn.

Farther outside in the snowy woods the alpha could see the human watching from the dark house armed with a gun. She growled before running back deeper in the woods.

She met with the rest of her pack.

"Children, this human's anger is strong, and he will hunt for us. He must die!"

"Kill him? do we have to?" her lead hunter asked.

"Yes! A task you and your mate failed at," she said snarling angrily, before slapping his face so hard, he shed a tooth. "And if you fail again, I will kill you!"

She led her pack to the top a large rocky hill overlooking the closed highway. She let out a wolf howl, with a mix of human sketching. In the darkened house, Nathan heard their howls and gripped his pistol tighter.

Chapter 14. Kidnapped.

Two days passed and the snow finally died down, Nathan got his power back and he began to do things with his left arm again and began practicing the physical therapy at home. When Joseph went out to buy groceries, Nathan gave him money and a list of ammo he wanted to buy, upon returning with two dozen boxes of .303. Caliber, .357 magnum caliber bullets, and 12-gauge double buckshot shells.

"What do you need all this ammo for?"

"I'm an American, I love the Second amendment, and I was hunting," Nathan said taking the boxes up to his room.

"You know you're gonna miss the hunting season, don't you?" Joey said following him.

"I know that, but it's not just for hunting, it's for home defense."

"Why? Are the neighbors bothering you again? Are they trespassing?"

"I think there's something more dangerous out there than just weird town's people," Nathan said quietly while staring out the window.

"What?" Joe said.

"Nothing forgets it. I just like to have the extra ammo," he said, "It matters not how many guns you have but the shells and bullets you need for them. Now let's have some lunch."

A few miles south, while on patrol near Tewkesbury, officer Wallstone received a call from the station to head down to Floyd a small Hamlet east of Rome for a neglected animal roaming around the area.

She arrived to find two animal control officers, hauling in a large, sickly looking Draft horse.

After helping the horse get into the trailer, she informed the animal patrol that she knew the owner and took them to the Scotfield farm. When the two vehicles arrived at the farm, Officer Wallstone went up and knocked on Nathan's front door.

Upon hearing the knock Nathan used his crutches to answer the door.

"Hello Mr. Scotfield, it's officer Wallstone. Listen I have good news! We've found one of your animals!"

"Really?! Which one?"

"It's one of your gentle giants," she said cheerfully.

"Clyde? He's alive?"

"Yes, he looks really poor though. He needs a vet," she said giving him the address to the animal hospital they would take the horse to.

The brothers drove to the local animal hospital, where Clyde was. The poor steed looked very sickly, cold and starving.

"The poor horse was found at Floyd hamlet under a brigde," said the doctor, "He's been wondering in the snow for days and needs good care."

"If I may sir, I'm a veterinarian and Nathan and I can nurse him back." Said Joseph.

"If so, I'll let him back into your custody," said the doctor. After checking Joe's certification, he said "let's go to the office and fill out some papers."

Clyde was shipped back to Nathan's empty farm the next day. The two-brother tended to him diligently. Joseph took the lead in looking after the animal and soon the horse was able to walk, he would take the horse out on walks around the ranch. Though Clyde made a good recovery, regaining his strength and speed. Joseph still had another burden to care for.

Nathan offered to assist, but Joseph still made him stay inside the house and in bed.

On a light snowy day of November 15th while cooking supper in the kitchen Nathan heard a knock at his door. Tasha rushed up barking at the visitor. Nathan limped on one crutch to the door and ordered Tasha down. He opened the door and saw Lidia running back to her home.

"Jesus Christ, I walk in pain to answer the freaking door, and she runs off!" he exclaimed. Looking down he saw an envelope. He picked it up and went to his couch. He opened it and took out a note written in crayon.

"Dear Nathan, for your safety, don't go outside at night, the danger is lurking near your home, and She wants to kill you. Leave now, if you have the chance."

"Fucks sake! I move to a peaceful corner of the world, only to have psychos for neighbors!" he said throwing the note in the fire.

Inside the barn, Joseph laid a soft wool blanket over Clyde. As he readied to leave, he heard someone outside.

"Hey you!" someone shouted.

Joseph walked around the corner and saw an elderly woman, who looked slightly familiar.

"Uh… can I help you, ma'am?" Joe asked.

"Yes, I'm in trouble, you must come! Come quickly!" she said distressed, the lady walked behind the barn with the puzzled Joseph following her.

"Wait a minute, hold it!" said Joey while he followed.

From the kitchen window, Nathan saw his brother walk around the red building, the man just shrugged his shoulders and went back to fixing dinner.

A half hour past, dinner was ready, but Nathan saw no sign of Joseph. He began to worry about his brother as it got more and more dark outside. He walked on the back porch and called out for Joe.

"Where the hell did you go, Joey?" he cried. Nathan pulled on his coat and limped through the snow to his barn. He peeked inside to find his only surviving horse laying in a new bale of hay and a trail of footprints leading to the woods.

Nathan followed the trail to the edge of the woods, where he hollered out for Joey again. He heard no reply or sign of life, only hearing the whistling of the wind. Nathan felt an aching, and a pain in his gut, that worsened as he waited.

"Oh God…" he whispered.

He began breathing heavily in gasps as panic began to set in. Nathan quickly made for his house and slipped in the snow. He screamed after landing on his bad leg, but he picked himself back up and made it into his house where he called the cops.

Once again, the three Utica patrol officers, Captain Francis, officer Merv and Lizzy Wallstone arrived at the Scotfield farm. He told him his brother went outside and never came back. They followed Joseph's footprints through the woods and discovered signs of a savage struggle.

"He must've fallen on his face," said Merv examining the footprints, and bodily shapes in the thick snow.

They then came across a stain of blood on the ground, with the shape in the snow depicting at though he was being dragged by something and that there was a violent struggle.

"A bear perhaps?" Merv suggested.

"Maybe…," Francis said pointing to a trail looking as the man was dragged off. "I'm gonna call for back up, you two follow the tracks. If it's a bear use force."

"Can't we let animal control deal with…"

"That was not a request Merv!" Francis said jogging back to the house.

"Come on, we have no time to lose," Lizzy said holding her flashlight.

Francis first entered the house.

"Did you find anything?!" said Nathan.

"We picked up a strange trail leading in the woods. He couldn't have gone far, and I'm calling for help and more backup!" the captain answered

"Wait, officer wait, where's Wallstone and other…"

"They're following the trail, as I said!"

"Oh No! No, no, no, you gotta call them back!" cried Nathan.

"What?"

"There are some creatures out there!" Nathan said limping to the back door.

"What the hell are you talking about?" the bewildered captain asked, "What's the matter? was it a bear or what?!"

"You gotta call them back here now! They're not safe!"

"Not safe from what? Answer my question!" Francis demanded and before Nathan replied the two men heard howling from the woods.

"That, that's what's out there!" said Nathan drawing his pistol.

"Wolves?"

"Captain listen to me! Listen to me, you gotta call those two back now!" said Nathan shaking with anger and fear. "I know you'll think I'm crazy, but these wolves are not what you think... they're werewolves."

"What?!"

"These creatures... I saw them, they're huge and strong. Please sir you must call...."

The pack sprung from the woods and attacked the house. Seeing the gigantic wolf faces up against the windows both men screamed like children and fell back into the living room.

"What the fuck?!" Francis yelled. The captain tried to grab Nathan to pull him away from the nearest beast. The farmer aimed his .357 magnum revolver and fired a shot at the werewolf. The beast yelped as the force knocked it down.

"Let's get the hell out of here!" Francis took him by his bad shoulder with Tasha barking crazy. When they got to the front door Francis looked to the window and saw four wolves tearing the two police cruisers apart. Pushing the vehicle upside down and with their bladelike claws they tore the rubbed tires clean off the rims.

As the wolves began to destroy Nathan's truck, Francis drew his gun and fired three well aimed shots at one of them. His 9mm bullets only seemed to have enraged the creature and the four werewolves turned their attention to the humans in the house.

"Oh shit," Francis said.

"Upstairs! Come on!" Nathan yelled. The two men and hound bolted upstairs, first blocking the staircase with the recliner and ducked into his bedroom.

Nathan handed the captain his shotgun and Nathan loaded his rifle. He could see two werewolves standing beside his barn. Without opening the window, he shot one of them in the shoulder.

"Call for help!" Nathan yelled.

"No, Oh no, oh fuck!" Francis yelled, as he just realized he'd dropped his radio back in the kitchen.

"What about your cell phone?!"

"I left it in my car!" Francis said slapping himself.

From downstairs the werewolves broke through the front doors and windows with ease. The two wounded werewolves broke into the kitchen, smashing tables, chairs, and anything that stood in their way.

Hearing the ruckus downstairs, the two men quickly blocked the bedroom with Nathan's heavy bed, end tables and dresser. Despite the pain, Nathan worked all his might to block the entrance while holding his firearm to defend himself.

The six wolves emerged from the house and leaped up on the walls and began to claim up to the window. The first wolf that reached the pane of glass peaked through and saw the two humans aiming their guns. The two men opened fire point blank range hitting the werewolf in the chest making it fall from the roof.

The beast fell flat in the snow, and the five others who were inside ripped the recliner out of the way and began to make their way to the bedroom. They scratched and clawed through the wood, and both men opened fire.

Far off in the woods, Merv heard the gunshots.

"You hear that?"

"I sure did," Lizzy replied. "Let's get back to the farm!"

But from out of the shadows a beast pounced on Merv. The six-foot tall fur covered wolf humanoid creature, savagely bit out his stomach. Merv scream, as Lizzy fire six shot in the werewolf but the monster didn't budge. As she was reloading Merv's flashlight shined on another wolf standing on its hind legs. Realizing she could not help Merv she ran to a pine tree and began claiming.

As Wallstone claimed the wolf came behind and bit her on her left boot. She held tight to the trunk and reached one hand down to untie her boot and the werewolf pulled it off. While climbing she watched the two giant wolves haul Merv's body away. As they disappeared into thew darkness, Liz heard more gunshots coming from the farmhouse.

 They shot another beast and the wolves fell back.

"Let's get up on the roof!" said Nathan, he took Tasha and the men claimed out his broken window. On Top of the house, they saw the five wolves running out of the house and in the forest.

"Where the hell are they going?!" Francis said.

"They probably got Lizzy and the other cop," said Nathan.

"We gotta get help!" said the captain.

"It's too late sir, they'll be dead before anyone gets to them.

"We can't just sit up here and do nothing. I'm getting your phone!" Francis carefully walked down the snow-covered roof to the window where he saw a young man, more of a child laying naked and dead in the blanket of snow.

Francis was shaken, disturbed and downright dumbstruck from what'd just happening. This was unreal. He was unsure what he was doing and felt like a little boy lost in a nightmare.

Nathan tried to follow the man, but almost slipped off the ice-covered gutters. Francis broke through the bedroom door and entered the kitchen, only to find the phone smashed into pieces on the floor.

"Need to call somebody?" said a female voice. Francis almost jumped to the ceiling, and upon turning he saw an old woman.

"Who the hell are you?" he said. And in a flash of an eye the lady-shaped shifted and began to grow taller and taller. Towering over him with pointed ears growing on the side of her head and her sadistic smile turned into a long grinning snout with sharp fangs.

The police captain cried in fear and disbelief. Before he could make a move to fire Nathan's shotgun the werewolf with her six-inch-long claws ripped into the man's face, slashing out one of his eyes.

Ripping off his cheeks, ears, eye and the bottom part of his jaw, the poor officer slowly perished he was being eaten alive.

On the roof near his window, the sickened Nathan watched as the Alpha dragged away from the dead body of Francis into the dark woods.

Beside him, Tasha moaned sadly, and even Nathan broke down crying thinking that the pack of monsters have killed Joseph. They've killed his own brother.

Chapter 15. The chamber.

Hearing the sound of dripping water, with the feel of heat and moisture all around him. Poor Joseph awoke and discovered that he was locked in small a dog cage, locked with heavy chains. The man examined all around in a large barley lit room from a Kerosene lantern that was hung to the ceiling. He could only see what he could describe were meat hooks hanging over a large wooden table with the stench of something have rotted.

He tried to move only to feel pain in his shin and back. He soon recalls his latest memory, he followed some woman in distress, who led him deep within the woods when something jumped on him.

To the end of the room, Joe heard heavy footsteps, and a jiggle to a door knobbed.

The swung wide open and what had entered the room came a large stocky man wearing only blue overalls, boots, and a bloody apron. He stumped through the room while dragging a dead man in a police uniform. When he flicked on the lights, he saw the prisoner has awakened.

"Who the hell are you? Where am I?" the disoriented Joe asked, frightened to see a dead cop.

The man came up and kicked Joe's cage with his steel toe boots, "Shut up meat!"

Joseph kept silence and watched the butcher lay the dead police on the table. The table was laced with tools, knives, an iron face, and a long row of human head skulls patterned with animal skulls.

Anthony the butcher grabbed a huge trench knife and gutted into the poor cop's abdomen.

"Yes, oh yes, he's still fresh…" Anthony chuckled. The man took a taste of the victim's blood, stared at Joey for several minutes then just walked out of the room leaving the lights on.

Joe looked around to find bloodstains on the concrete floor, there were pentagrams with goat heads painted on the walls. What was more frighten he discovered the cop on the table was not dead.

 Merv twisted in pain and fell off the table, with blood bleeding from his skull, Joe tried to get his attention, but he notices the man was hurt worse than him. With a piece of his skull hanging off his head exposing a corner of his brain. His right hand was gone, and a large chunk of flesh was ripped off his right thigh. Joseph nearly vomited at the sight and shouted for help.

The man returned with a lady.

"I told you to shut up!" he yelled.

"I'll handle this Anthony," the woman said, who Joe recognizes as Ms. Ester.

"You?" he said.

"Hello young man, it's nice to have a new face in the pack."

Ad before Joe could ask questions, she sprayed him with chloroform seducing him into sleep.

"You're one of us now."

Far deep in the woods, Lizzy Wallstone claimed down the tree with his right barefoot freezing in the snow. She looked around only to find a trail of blood, she first wrapped her foot with a torn cloth from her jacket and made followed the path where her partner was taken.

She attempted to contact for backup but was unable to reach Francis or her station as another snowstorm rolled in.

Meanwhile, on the other side of town, farmer Scotfield and his dog looked down to the dead boy that he identified as little Josiah Kess.

The child laid dead in the snow with his upper head blown off by the gunshots.

Nathan carried the boy in his messy house and wrapped him in a blanket. He then dressed in his warm hunting clothes, grabbed his bowie knife, the shotgun Captain Francis dropped and gathered all his ammunition.

The farmer walked in his farm to find Clyde prancing freely around the building.

He and Tasha stopped the horse happy to see he was back on his feet and was the prod strong beast he was after a few pats and rubs on the neck Nathan said to his two animals.

"Well, guys we're going move again."

All of confused and depressed believing he had lost his brother; Nathan really didn't know what to think when suddenly Tasha sensed something. She walked to the doors of the barn and began growling.

Nathan drew his rifle and slowly opened them to fine Brad outside.

"Nat is that you?" he said. Nathan opened the door and lowered his weapon.

"Brad?"

"Christ Nat, what happened to your house?"

Hearing the man that question, Nathan smelled a rat, a father wouldn't ask that question when his son is missing. Giving no answers Nathan raised his 99 savages at the man.

"Nat? What are you…"?

Nathan cut him off, "Get in the barn!" Brad began to walk back.

"Hey, get in the barn! now! I want to talk to you!" Brad just walked back and before he tried to run off Tasha ran up and bit him in the leg.

The man screamed and punched the dog, which made her angry master shoot him in the knee.

When Brad dropped to the ground, he cursed and let out an agonizing scream. the man tried to run but with the butt end of his rifle, he swung it at his head knocking him out.

In the chamber under under deli market, Joseph was still trapped in the dog cage where he watched poor Merv die slowly of his injuries leaving a stream of blood dripping from his arm, flowing down into the floor drain.

Joey began to cry in a total panic, he couldn't believe that all of this was happening and from the bite wounds on his leg began to sore again. The scratches on his back made him get hot flashes, feeling as if he was in a giant oven slowly being baked alive.

Anthony the butcher walked in with another man; it was the old gas station attendant.

"So, this is him?"

"No idiot it's his brother," Anthony said walking up with a key.

"Oh, even better."

"Shut up Curtis and come give me a hand," the two flanked the cage and unlocked the chain, when they dragged Joseph out, he tried to fight back but the two men overpowered him and dragged him to the other side of the room.

They chained his neck that was attached to a wall of cement and the two began beating him with their fist and kicking him in the gut with their boots.

"We're gonna have ourselves a good time turning you into our omega," Curtis said laughing. "The pet of the pack."

After the two left upstairs and out the back door, hiding behind the dumpsters, Lizzy followed the snow trail that leads right to the deli.

She waited for the two men to leave and snuck in through the backdoor and down the stars.

The snowstorm built up with power outages closed roads, the province was in a state of emergency Graytown was cut off and isolated.

It was now late in the afternoon and Nathan woke up his prisoner.

"What means this Nat?!" Brad said.

"Don't fucking call me Nat, I'm asking the questions here!"

"Untie right now!"

"Not until you give me answers," said Nathan with Tasha growling as his face.

"Answers to what I come to help you and I get this…."

"Cut the shit you fur-bearing smug bitch I know what you are!" hearing that Brad's face turned shakenly pale, he trembled with his eyes bugged out like red golf balls.

"You, I, I don't, you don't know what you're getting into…"

"I yes I do, I do now!" Nathan said restraining himself from giving him a kick of his boot.

"Look, look Nathan just leave this place, take your truck and drive as from…"

"Don't dodge the questions, have you notice what has happened the night before? Saw the three messed up vehicles in my parking lot, or my house all destroyed?!" Nathan yelled and Brad began to sob.

"It was all a set up was it?" Nathan said. "Tanking me hunting, so the pack can steal my animals, was it? Answer me damn it!"

Brad looked up with red teary eyes, "Yes… you killed my son."

Nathan lowered his gun and took off his hat. "It was not like I wanted to."

Brad continued to cry, for the loss of his boy and confessing the secret, he was supposed to keep. He thought Nathan was going to kill him but instead Nathan, still restrained with a leg cast and shoulder brace was struggling to put a saddle on Clyde.

"Wh… where are you going?" he asked.

"I killed your son, your pack killed my brother and I'm leaving, spend the rest of my days running."

"No, no, Nathan your brother's alive."

"What did you say?" he said turning to him.

"Nathan, it' true we are not human, though we were this whole town was cursed by Miss. Ester, I don't know how I don't know why but, in our beast, forms she can control us and…"

"I don't wanna hear your story! Tell me where my brother is?!" Nathan cut in.

"He's alive, he's held captive under the Deli, but I fear he'll be one of us when the moon comes," he answered with regret, with Nathan's brain burning in worry, "but please Nathan, just promise me this?"

"What?"

"There's no cure to this curse, only death. The least you can do… is kill my wife, my girl and me. I know I deserve no favors but… Nathan, please understand if I wasn't a mindless werewolf, I wouldn't have tried hurt you, your animals, nor your brother. I wouldn't have done any harm, not my Lidia, or my kids Erin and Josiah… please, Nathan… free us all."

Nathan again felt a sick feeling and began to feel a bit sorry for the poor man. When his hate slowly disappeared, he nodded in agreement, "I will."

When the man held his rifle to Brad's head, he had one more word of advice.

"You must kill Edith Ester, the other Graytown folk may be the pack, but she pulls the strings, kill her so she won't harm anyone again."

"I promise."

"Thank you... May God have mercy on me," Brad said for his last words thinking of his son. And then Nathan pulled the trigger, making Clyde jump off his front legs, before leaving for the woods Nathan dragged the corps of Josiah to lay him next to his father. He took the horse and hound outside then set the barn ablaze. He gathered last minutes supplies, food, his crutches, a sleeping bag with extra wool blankets and some of his traps, before setting his house on fire. He claimed on Clyde and road into the forest followed by Tasha.

Officer Wallstone made it down to the chamber door, and came across a foul smell, slowly she creaked open the door.

Laying in pain on the floor with the tight cuff around his neck Joseph saw the officer walk in with her gun drawn.

"Joseph?!" she said rushing to him.

"Elizabeth!" replied Joe. The woman came to his side and helped him sit against the wall, "Where? How?"

"I don't know! One minute we were out looking for you then giant wolves come..."

"Shh, they'll hear you," Joe interrupted.

"Is there a key? Do you know where the key is?" she asked then turned to find her dead partner. Lizzy also screamed out loud, but Joe grabbed her mouth.

"The butcher Anthony has is."

"Okay, I'll go get it," she said taking her gun out and checked the magazine.

"Can't you call for help?"

Lizzy nodded with a sniff, "the storms getting worse I can't get any fucking signal."

"Lizzy doesn't go after them alone,"

"Well I can't stand around and do nothing!" she said taking the shoes of Merv and right when she walked to the door, Edith, Anthony, and Lidia were standing right outside.

"Lidia?" Lizzy said really shocked while holding her gun in the old lady's face. "You all stand back and give me the key to the chain!"

The two laughed with Lidia beginning to cry. The three just shut the heavy door and locked her inside with Joseph.

"Well Joseph we'll give you a little supper for your first transformation," Anthony yelled.

As Lizzy banged and fired a shot at the iron door, Lidia dropped to her knees sobbing in regret.

"Get over it bitch!" Edith talking down on her, "you failed me one too many times, I should kill you, but instead, your sister will pay your price... now upstairs."

Lidia obeyed by crawling on her hands and knees, Erin stood at the top crying as Edith forced Lidia to undress and stand out in the freezing cold.

Chapter 16. Revenge begins.

Late in the afternoon with darkness rolling in, old man Curtis sat on his counter drinking beer in his dark empty gas station.

When suddenly he smelled smoke and coming from outside. He walked to the front entrance and saw a fire building up near his pumps. Quickly the man jolted from the building and rushed out the back exit with a fire extinguisher.

"Hey old bastard!" he heard and saw that it was Nathan aiming a rifle at him.

"How do you do?!"

The man attempted to attack Nathan, only to get shot in his chest and Curtis dropped in the snowy driveway and fire built up near the gas pumps. As the gas station attendant laid dying in the snow, Nathan retreated to a safe distance as the station exploded into a massive blaze, burning the old man to ashes.

Neighbors of the seven nearby homes heard the blast, including the two prisoners, locked down in the Deli's basement.

"Lizzy? Lizzy listen to me?" he said as she attempted opened the door. "Elizabeth!"

"What?"

"I... I don't think you can open that and, you need to lock yourself in that cage."

"What? Why?"

"You saw those things...last night? did you?" she looked at him and saw the bite marks on his legs.

"Oh God, what are we gonna do?" she asked.

"I told you to lock yourself in that cage, so you'll be safe, you have the gun..." then Lizzy interrupted.

"No, I mean you, there's gotta be a way to help you..."

"We have no time, there's nothing you can do for me, just keep yourself safe."

Seeing him still bleeding at the legs, Lizzy searched around the room only to find, bones in boxes, butcher knives, rope and buckets of animal blood. She then had no choice but to rip off the shirt of her dead friend to wrap it around Joe's bitten legs.

He thanked her real kindly as she touched her shoulder. From her watch, she saw it was a quarter to 6.

Outside where Edith investigate the fire of the gas station, she could sense danger and the smell of a horse.

"Tracks lead from the station to the highway, my lady," said Davis, the town's bartender.

"It's Scotfield," she said turning to her followers, "take him."

They bowed to her will and shapeshifted into their beast forms.

"Lidia? I send you on this task... kill that pathetic soul, fail at this and your daughter will die."

Lidia kneels to her master in the snow before transformed into her wolf physic.

"You know you can't trust her," Anthony said.

"That's why I let you have Erin, have her as your bitch mate, do her for as long as you like my loyal Zeta, time to increase our ranks."

The five wolf giants vastly sprinted through the pine forest in the same area they found that cow and animal patrolmen. The bartender leading the way caught a sound in his ear and halted his party.

"Horse, I hear the horse," he said in the chilling echoing voice. The hunting pack spread to a distance, slowly and quietly moving through the dead bushes.

In a far safe distance under a wool blanket covered in snow with Tasha next to him, Nathan aimed his rifle, eyeing one of the werewolves.

The pack saw the gentle giant between to tree, Clyde was hopping and twitching in fear as they came closer and closer unknown it's all a ploy.

The bartender rushed out into the open to attack the horse, only to get a nasty surprise, he made it to about a yard to the frightened horse to have his front right paw caught in a bear trap.

The beast let out a painful wolf yelp mixed with human screaming.

The pack stopped, and Nathan opened fire shooting another werewolf in the shoulder and it dropped dead. Nathan stood from his hiding place took out his bowie and in one swipe he cut loose a rope where he snared the third wolf to the legs lifting it off the ground.

Tasha ran out to fight the bartender wolf who was still restrained by the trap. Though smaller compared to the beast's huge muscle body, gave the hound no fear and she managed to get her sharp jaws of the monster's throat.

Tasha bit deep, tarring into the flesh. The beast swung its free paw and dug the claws of his free paw in the hound's rips. But the pain only made her bite down harder like a pit bull and she tore out the neck an exposing the werewolf's windpipe.

As the bartender slowly dropped dead, as he turned back into his human form. As Nathan approached the dead bodies, he saw the struggling of the third wolf, hanging upside down in a metal cable. The beast struggled, kick, howl and moan, Nathan, aimed his rifle and shot it in the head. Then in a matter of seconds, the wolf hanging by the leg turned back into the human form of a woman who he did not recognize. Nathan walked closer with Tasha, staring at the dead nude person, feeling all regret for this action. And as he looked into the woman's eyes and saw the innocence, only added more guilt to his conscience.

The fourth wolf took cover behind thick trees, and as he watched the hunter pull his dead sister down from the trap, he took this opportunity to attack.

He ran and leaped in the air to attack Nathan, only to get a horse kick from Clyde the horse. The kick was so powerful, it pushed the wolf hard against a tree trunk.

Nathan grabbed his gun, but the werewolf got up and retreated out of sight, Clyde though caught up to it and began crushing the beast with his heavy iron hove shoes. He stumped and stumped until the dead wolf turned back into a human with an unrecognizable face.

Both Nathan and Tasha watched as the loyal horse returned.

The hunter feeling pain in his shoulder decided not to pursue the last one and quickly laid the four dead bodies in the spot where he hid. He covered all of them with dry twigs and branches to set the bodies on fire, so the other wolves wouldn't eat them.

As he watched the fire grow, Tasha smelled a predator she turned to a werewolf peek behind a tree. She barked and her master turned to find a beast with a similar female figure with brown fur. The first werewolf he saw in front of the Kess home.

He took the safety off his hunting rifle and ordered Tasha to stay still with Clyde behind her. With his rifle at the ready, he waited patiently for the beast to sprung out, but instead of springing from the tree to attack. The werewolf slowly walked from the tree on two legs with her two arms up in the air, as a surrender pose.

"Stay exactly where you are!" he yelled, feeling a bit stupid, thinking it can't possibly understand him, but felt like she wants to communicate. Nathan lowered his rifle, but the hound kept barking aggressively. She attempts to step forward but got pulled back by Nathan. But when the she-wolf attempted to walk closer, he got scared and fired a warning shot.

In fear of her life Lidia decided to transform back into a human, she stood, exposed before the man and his animals with her arms still in the air.

"So, it was you?" Nathan said keeping his eyes glued to hers, Lidia shaking both in humility and cold she again tried to walk up but Nathan warned her to stay still. He tied his dog to the horse and took out his last wool blanket, then tossed it to the naked woman.

"Nathan… I know why you're doing this; I saw what happened to my son, but I want to help," Lidia said with the blanket wrapped around her.

"Yeah… waited all this time to tell me," Nathan said still holding his weapon up as the snow covered the shoulders of his coat, "And now my farm is gone, I'm homeless and, your son and husband are dead because of it… why?"

"We were forced to keep it a secret…"

"I know that one! Brad told me! What I meant was why should I trust you, or anyone here?!"

"Oh, Nathan..."

"Shut up with the sorry thing and get to the point!"

"They have my sister now with your brother!" Lidia screamed. "Their gonna kill them, and I know they're going to kill my girl Erin I know it! I can help you."

"You help save my brother, I'll help save your daughter and sister," said Nathan, he claimed on Clyde's back and Lidia turned back into her wolf form.

Chapter 17. The end of the Kess family.

Sudden darkness rolled in with Edith practicing her Satanist rituals, the clock struck 7, the time for Joseph's change was close, as she read through a forbidden text of Santan lore.

Erin was laid against a cut table, with the middle age Anthony touching her sensitive area in the dark the kitchen.

"Finally, I have a bitch of my own," he said laughing while licking her ear.

Erin wanted to just grab a knife and stab the bastard in the face, but for the fact she had lost her little brother and frightened that she'll put her mother and aunt's life at risk, she just let the man take advantage of her.

In the Deli's lobby with the tables and chairs pushed aside. The Satan Priestess stood in a candle ring surrounded with the last six residences of Graytown. Pressing her gospel of the evil supernatural from the Sermon of the Devil.

From outside came another cult follower, Brad's co mechanics Lewis DeRose.

"My Lady… Lidia returns," he said breathing heavily from the cold.

"Lidia? Alone?" she asked slightly annoyed for the interruption.

"With the body of Scotfield!"

Rushed out with excitement the two came out of the deli, where wolf Lidia walked up in the snow with a corpse in her mouth.

Hiding far back into the pine woods, Nathan followed Lidia's plane to shoot and kill the alpha first. Both the horse and hound stood behind as Nathan laid cold and still like a sniper aiming for the head of Ester.

Lidia stopped in front of her master and dropped the body before the two people with the other members looking out of the windows.

Edith walked up and saw the corps had burned flesh and a broken face.

"What happened did you try cooking him?"

"No," Lidia answered.

"And where's Davis and rest of the hunting party?" Edith asked suspiciously.

"He's dead, the human set his traps Davis got shot, along with the Lobaine siblings and Dueset."

"He killed all but you?" DeRose asked.

"This human was stronger than we thought, but a promise he's dead."

"Go fetch Anthony, Lewis," Edith said.

As Anthony began to take advantage of his new mate, Lewis interrupted and ordered him to come and help with the corps.

"Great timing," Anthony said pulling his pants up. "Stay in that position little bitch."

When the man left the kitchen, he also left the keys next to Erin.

The girl stood herself up feeling despaired by the horrid cruelty. And for that Erin decided to follow her mother's steps, in rebelling agaist Ester's curse. She grabbed the keys and made her way downstairs.

Outside with more snow covering him, Nathan awaited the signal from Lidia to take the shot, but as it got colder and cold, he grew restless. Then in a strange notion he saw Edith through his rifle scope. The woman turned her head looking past wolf Lidia, directly at Nathan… dead into his eye.

Nathan looked back for a second, slightly creeped out from the strange grin she gave him. When he looked back into the scope two men came outside and looking down on the dead body they took from the fire.

"So… the farmer's dead?" Anthony said, Edith shook her head.

"No, this is Jack Dueset, and Lidia has betrayed us again," she said, and Lidia's eyes widened. "Boys killer her."

"Jesus Christ!" he said in a horrific shock, Nathan watched the two men transform into wolves, they pounced on Lidia, tearing her to pieces.

Erin unlocked the iron door, then heard a gunshot from outside.

Upon entering the basement Joseph was on his hands and legs, over a puddle of his own vomit.

"Erin?!" Lizzy said near the dog cage.

"Come on we gotta get out of here!" she took her aunt's hand, but Lizzy pulled out and went for Joseph.

"What are doing go!" said Joseph.

"We're not leaving you," she replied as Erin came with the key to his chain. Lizzy heard another shot from outside, she rushed to the door two find two pack members on top the staircase with a knife.

"Drop the weapons or I'll shoot!" she said with her pistol at hand, but instead the two walked down, armed with knives. Lizzy shot one man twice in the chest and, but he had made absolutely effect on him. The horrified cop fell back.

After getting Joseph's neck freed, she told Lizzy to take him and run.

The teenage transformed into her beast and mauled one of the men, while the second one was stabbing her in the face, Lizzy took Joseph by the hand and made their way upstairs.

As the two ran out the back, Nathan was retracting the opposite direction.

After shooting Lewis dead, Anthony and other chased pack members were after him. Clyde ran with all his might carrying his injured master through the woods and across the shutdown highway, followed by Tasha.

Down in the chamber, Erin killed the second man, she transformed into her human form, crying for the loss of her whole family. Edith walked down laughing.

"Well, well, well, guess you can fight," Edith said with a sadist grin.

"Fuck you!" she said cupping the knife wound to her right eye.

"Oh, Erin you, your brother was so, young, should have spared you both for pup bearing, but instead you force me to do you like your mother, then...your aunt."

Erin just sat in the corner as Edith transformed into her monstrous Wendigo, with tight skin over her bones, horns grew out behind her ears, eyes turned fiery red, and arms grew almost longer than her.

Erin decided to go down fighting, she turned back into her wolf form and charged at the monster. Only to end with the sounds of painful screams, and ripping.

Chapter 18. Lost.

Lizzy ran with Joseph through the dark forest unknown where they were going, just tried to get away from the deli as far as possible, the time on her watch read 11:55 pm.

Joseph fell face down in the snow, and Lizzy helped her up.

"Please, Lizzy doesn't worry about me, just run and get away."

"We're gonna freeze to death, we got to find shelter!" she said putting his right arm over her shoulder.

As they made their way in the snow cold woods, Joe's body began cramping and worst still he felt himself burning up, Lizzy looked to him in shock and felt the pain of scratching to her neck and back.

She grunted and let the man go, then suddenly as the clock struck twelve, she felt the same pains.

"Oh no, oh shit!" Joe said with a scream. He rolled around in the snow trying to cool off, but his transformation was just building up.

Lizzy felt light-headed, dropped to her knees, he undid her belt and felt stretch pains all through her entire body.

"Oh Christ...heaven no!" he said as she felt her flat teeth turning sharp and pointy.

"Lizabeth run...hurry!" Joe said getting out of the snow as his face grew out into a snout. But then he saw that he had infected her as well, she began to grow bigger and bigger by the moment. Lizzy's entire body and limbs stretched out of her sleeves. Her skin, blood, and bones boiled with heat, she stared at him in tears showering out from her sockets from the torturous transformation.

Joseph!" she said as her police uniform ripped to pieces right off her fur covered body. In less than a minute the two were all in the form of wolves. They stood on four legs, over seven feet long from snout to tail and four foot in height.

The two werewolves walked in a circle observing each other and themselves in their fur covered muscular bodies.

Wolf Joseph had dark gray fur, with blackness to the shoulders and head mixed with his human hair. Lizzy's fur was dark brown like her short brunette hair, with white fur paws.

Both were frightened, and disorientated beyond believe, lost most memory to what happened as the untamed wolves just stood a distance apart. When a sudden noise caught their ears and the smell of danger caught their sent.

Something, bigger and dangerous was approaching them and the two werewolves took off running through the woods.

Holding a lantern looming over the tracks, and the scattered shredded clothing in the snow, Edith glanced around, watching, smelling and hearing the panic jogging of the two wolves.

"So, two new wolves we lost," Edith said annoyed holding up the severed head of Erin. The Lady placed the lantern down, her two arms grew into the long claw bony limbs, and it one squeeze, she smashed her head like an egg, and partaken her brains, licking it like jam.

Miles off Clyde road faster with all his might, Nathan was unable to make a stand to shoot since the pack was still after him. Chasing him north across the Willow Creek deeper and deeper in the middle of nowhere.

Behind the running horse, Tasha heard the pack gaining up in hot pursuit. She decided to try and draw the wolves off by going in the opposite direction.

The night rolled in and Clyde kept going breathing clouds of mist from his cold nostrils When Nathan decided to slow down, he noticed he was no longer being followed and Tasha was gone.

Nathan pulled Clyde the other way and shouted her name, snow began to build up, so Nathan had no choice but ride on to find shelter for him and the horse. It was 2 am with a full moon and he found an abandoned cabin. The man broke in and pulled the horse inside to rest.

Nathan laid the horse on the floor and started a fire in the fireplace.

The cabin was a small summer cottage, no electric or a bathroom with two beds with the old mattress. The man ripped off the covering to give it to his horse as a blanket. As the cold tired horse drifted to sleep his master stayed awake by the door with his rifle.

As he stood guard Nathan began to sob a little. About all that has happened, killing wolves who turned out to be people.

"What have I'd done?" he thought to himself, "how could all this happen?"

As these questions went through his mind, he only felt worst thinking he had failed his brother. When Nathan tried to stand up pain sparked in his leg making him drop to the floor screaming the name Joseph.

Chapter 19. Spirits.

Running through the realm of the Adirondack forest, the two wolves slowed their escape upon discovering they were not being chased. Both Joseph and Elizabeth tried to coup with what has happened to them and what they have turned into. Yet with a sniff in the air, they smelled prey and they felt their large stomach growl with hunger. All their human thought was gone when the werewolf pair decided to go hunting together.

Peacefully asleep and cuddled up next to its mother among the rest of the heard. None could hear the danger that was silently approaching them in their bedding area.

And like a murder in the night when the victim sleeps in bed, the two wolves lounged forward and attacked, killing a mother deer and injuring her fawn, who escaped with the rest of his heard.

The two werewolves ripped the creature in half, savagely devouring its flesh off the bones. They ate the hide, organs, and even the snow that was stained in its blood. Joe and Lizzy felt proud of one another after such a successful kill and enjoying the fact that they've caught their food together. It did not end since they were still ravaged with hunger, thus they've decided to go after the heard and hunt for more.

The duo quickly caught up with wounded fawn, running in lighting speed, Lizzy leaped like a cheetah and picked it up in her mouth smashing its neck between her jaws.

Running faster ahead out in an opening meadow, Joe chased down a fully-grown buck, taking it by the legs dragging it off to its doom. After cutting the buck's neck with his knife sized claws he dragged to his partner to share the extra meat with her.

Barley regaining memory of their humanity, the pair again felt proud of their hunting and together they howled up to the moon.

At the cottage where the fire died down and the master sleeping against his stomach for warmth. Clyde sniffed Nathan's injured leg before kissing his face with a lick. The giant saw the man twist and turn, moaning and grunting, having tears drip from his eyes. Nathan was having a nightmare. After falling on his leg again, Nathan took to many painkillers knocking himself out.

His dream depicted a true sadness sight his father looked down at him like a lame pet, he turned giving the boy the cold shoulder, due to his failure in life and taking care of his little brother. And no matter how much he pleads for forgiveness all the father gave was a cruel silence.

Another site shows him a true horror, where his brother is hanged by his feet and dressed out like a deer. Nathan watched as the corps of Joseph turned to him and looked straight in his eyes and in a weak voice, he heard Joseph saying his name.

"Nathan? Nathan?"

He awoke with Clyde standing by the corner and when he looked up, and he saw a glowing figure. Nervously picking himself up with his pistol at the ready, the glow formed in the shape of a man.

"Brad?" he said walking back to his horse. The man was gray color, skin, and clothes with a bright white optical around the entire body.

Hello Nathan," Brad said in a light voice, then came his wife Lidia, daughter Erin holding little Josiah by the hand.

"Have I gone crazy?" he said.

"No, Nathan we're here talking to you," Lidia said.

"You're… you're all dead," Nathan said shaking along with Clyde.

"We're lost spirits," Josiah corrected.

"Lost?"

"I'm afraid this curse is more powerful," said Lidia laying her head on her husband. "Not just on us, but Mr. Arthur, the Gracer brothers and all pack members of Graytown were cursed to wander the earth in misery."

"Is this Ester's work?" Nathan asked and the Kess family nodded.

"I will help… but… my brother."

"He's alive Nathan," Erin said. "He escaped with Lizzy… but… he's a werewolf now."

"A werewolf?!... what should I do?" Nathan said confused and frustrated.

"Sorry to say, but we must ask you for another favor," said Brad. "you must kill Edith and we will all be free."

"Will it cure my brother from the werewolf curse?"

"We're not sure," said Brad.

"Do you know where Joseph is now?" Brad and the kids nodded no.

"For all, we know Nathan, is that your brother and my sister Lizzy is alive, and Edith is on the loose," Lidia said placing her ghostly hand in his bad shoulder, but Nathan felt no pain. "Please Nathan, you must stop her, she'll hurt more people. And we know you can do it."

Nathan looked to the other ghosts of the pack members he killed, standing behind Brad and his kids, he shook his head.

"I'll do it," Nathan said, with that, he saddled the horse, loaded his gun and brought it outside. He mounted and saw the sun rising. As he looked to the group of a ghost floating off their feet, they gave him a grateful smile and the road back to the hamlet.

With the morning sun shining the snow warming the treetops. The remaining pack members returned to the deli.

Entering the cold cooler room, Anthony approached Edith laying in a metal tub of animal blood bathing with joy.

"My alpha," he said bowing. Edith just looked at him with odds and rolled her eyes.

"Uh, I'm afraid we lost track of them…"

"I know, I always know when you fail," Edith cut in.

"Forgive me, madam, he gave us a slip past the creek…."

"And instead of results you give me excuses," she interrupted again biting a small bone.

"I'm a sorry madam, the hound tricked us, we'll go out after him again."

Edith stood out of the cold tub and step on the frozen cobbled floor she walked into the kitchen and grabbed a butcher knife and took him by the left forearm.

"Just know this Anthony, the Scotfield's predecessor failed us, Lidia betrayed me, and you know how I get when I starve. It's not even winter and my deli's half empty. I send you and the remaining out one last time," She said cutting his hand. He yelled and with her long snake-like tongue she licked it like a bat. "Bring me that man, I want his corps roasted on a spit…and if you fail… well, I guess I'll have to make another pack. And of course, for your own sake."

Anthony trembled and slowly walked back bowing. When he and the five others a back into the woods. Edith dressed and decided it was time to move on.

Chapter 20. Awakening.

It was when the pare stalked a teenage coming home from a late-night party, Joe and Lizzy attacked. They killed a young skier, dragging his body into his rented house on the resort. Though the house was human territory the two half-wolves claimed it as their own as they mindlessly ate the young man.

When the sun raised up in the skies, both turned back into human forms. In just a minute the past out monsters, shrunk back into their normal size, fur disappeared from their pale skin and their long snouts turned back into the human faces.

Lizzy awoke first cold and disorientated. She was naked with blood on her hands, ears, neck, and face. She realized she was in a hallway of a house.

With only her hands to cover herself, she walked into a bathroom in shock to her state. At first, she was in self-denial, but upon crossing Joseph equally naked and blood covered. He crawled on his hands and knees and looked up at Lizzy.

And before anything was said they turned to find the mauled corpse of the man they attack last night.

A horrid feeling went into Lizzy's stomach as she ran into the bathroom too through up. Joseph stood to see the carnage. The man had no face it looked like it was ripped off, his torso had no skin, a leg was missing, blood and tatters were all over the room.

Joe began to cry and went after Lizzy who was now crying on the floor.

"Liz?" he knelt.

"Don't touch me!" she hissed. Seeing how sad, scared, and confused he was, she took the robe from the weak behind the door and lay on the toilet near he, he then covered himself with a towel and closed the door to give her privacy.

Joe walked back to the living room, where he closed the door that was left open, letting the heat out, he walked in the kitchen where he washed the blood off him. He then explored further into the house and found a bag of spare clothes belonging to the victim. Lucky they were just about the same size, he dressed, Lizzy came in with a blanket she took off the bed and drape it over the mutilated corpse. Joe handed her some clothes and she got dressed.

"I can't believe this happened," Joe said palming his head and Lizzy began to cry.

"We're monsters now..." she sniffed morning to poor boy's death, Joe dropped to his knees again sobbing uncontrollably. Lizzy walked beside him and told them they had to leave.

"Oh, Lizz I'm sorry," cried Joe, she picked him up on his feet and gave him and hug.

"Joseph, it wasn't your fault, they did this to us," she reminded him. "Now we have to leave this place and find Nathan."

Before leaving Lizzy found boots in the closet that was three sizes too big for her but because the snow was deep outside, she put them on and tied them as tightly as she could. They exited the house to find out where they were.

It was 7 am and people in nearby condos were still asleep, the two walked down a blown road until they came across a billboard.

"Stoneham condos," she read.

"Where are we?" he asked.

"Stoneham ski resort," Lizzy answered, "I know where we are, we're still in Oneida county, my home isn't far from here!"

"Wait I thought we were looking for Nathan!"

"Joe, we don't have all day!" she argued, "we need to think this through before we turn tonight, we don't know where he is or he's still alive!"

Joe had a frightened look to his face, and Lizzy dragged him by the hand.

As the couple was making their way home. Anthony was on the hunt for the farmer.

Riding off the cottage ground and to the woods back to Graytown, Clyde stopped on his tracks, nervously scanning his surroundings.

"Steady boy," Nathan whispered. He dismounted the giant took out his rifle and brought the horse to an old cedar tree.

Though he could hear or smell as good as an animal can, Nathan trusted his steed's judgment and decided to sit and wait for whatever is coming.

Anthony spread his hunting party apart, he can smell the human with his horse far ahead.

The hunter felt branches to the tree were strong enough to claim on, thus Nathan hops up Clyde's back and made his way up the tree, overlooking the open white covered woods.

Anthony held his ground, to sense the grounds ahead, he sniffed and glanced around the surroundings, and knew the human was somewhere in a tree.

He barked for the others to stop. Realizing they were in a dangerous position, hunting during the day, they knew with the human up high will easily spot them. Not wanting to risk it he ordered his party to sit and wait him out.

When an hour past in the quiet woods, Nathan still stayed up in the tree with Clyde laying against the trunk. The snow of the cedar needles melted off by the shining sun, but the cool wind stung the man's face, drying up his lips. Nathan cared not and was determined to wait for the predators out until he realized he still had the last of his traps.

Chapter 21. The return.

After three hours walking down the streets in the cold with only snowblower riding on the roads, Lizzy and Joe finally made it to her house in the town of Shannon.

It was now 12 o'clock noon, Liz offered Joe a drink or something to eat but he turned it down. She noticed Joseph was really depressed when she said him down on the couch, she asked what was bothering him.

Joe broke down crying, "Sorry Lizabeth… I'm so sorry…"

She rolled her eyes and patted his shoulder. "Joseph, please, this won't help!"

"So, what are we gonna do? Call the police?" asked Joe.

"Really?!" she replied frustrated, then walked into her room where she got out a duffle bag and began packing some of her clothes.

"What I mean is we should at least inform them about Merv and Captain Francis!" Joseph said.

"Oh, and what are we to tell them? they were eaten werewolves, now we're infected by them, so do something about it!"

"So, you don't want to inform them about the death of your superior? Or your partner? You're a cop!"

"Not anymore!" she replied real upset.

"Hey! I said I was sorry for turning you..."

"Damn it! Stop apologizing!" she interrupted.

"So, what do you propose?"

"I'm leaving..."

"Leaving you're not gonna help!" Joe asked startled.

"No! Listen to me!" Lizzy banged her fist on her bag. "I'll help you find your brother, but because we're...werewolves now, we're dangerous, we have to leave this place. I have to leave here, and I don't even think I can be in the force anymore!"

"Guess you're right," he said. Joseph helped Lizzy pack more belongings and got into her spare car. She left her keys and spare badge in her house and locked it up. And before making their way to Graytown Lizzy stopped at a payphone and made an anonymous phone call to provincial police about the deaths of Francis, Merv, Toussaint and the Kess family.

Hours waiting in the woods, with all silence Anthony decided to send one wolf out ahead to scout the area.

The werewolf followed the scent of the horse, with the smell of blood. The blood made the beast's mouth water and stomach rumble for a taste. It was drawn in like a shark.

The wolf came up to the cedar tree where he saw Nathan sitting against the trunk. He stood up and could see the monster standing from a distance. He stood perfectly still and didn't reach for his rifle. Instead, he stood up and ripped off the cast of his bad leg, making him scream painfully.

The werewolf saw the man drop in the ground and with no hesitation, it eagerly leaped from the bush to charge at Clyde.

The giant horse whimpered, and Nathan watched from the snow as the monster came close and poked the horse with a stick and off, he went running.

Upon leaping over the human, the wolf got its neck snared by a swivel lock wire tied over a branch and to the saddle of the running horse.

Quickly Nathan crawled away as the werewolf was being pulled up.

The beast tried to grab the wire, but it pulled tightly and tightly through its fur and to its skin, squeezing the neck. The hanging beast kicked, howled and wheezed like a grampus. The long pink tongue sucks out like a slab of bacon and the monster slowly choked to death by the snare wire.

Nathan stood up and grabbed his rifle but was too late to put a bullet in the wolf turned human's head.

The werewolf was dead and turned back into a young man. Looked to be in his twenties, blonde hair and very lean. The sight of a man that young, hanging dead in the air, made Nathan sick to his stomach. He ran Limped back to Clyde to untie the wire, dropping the dead boy down, he took some painkiller meds to ease his leg gathered his equipment and road off to a different position, leaving the strangled body in the frozen snow.

Anthony and the four remaining members of his party found the body.

"Alright he is not far away, let get going," he said.

"No," one werewolf said.

"Say what?!" Anthony stood on his hind legs overlooking his pack.

"You heard me Zeta!" the Iota stood firm. "You carelessly sacrifice one of our young members!"

"Stand down this instance!"

"Or?!" the Iota growled showing her white fangs. Anthony smacked the she-wolf in the face and thus leading the last five werewolves to engaged in a violent struggle. Fighting and killing each other.

 From afar, Nathan could hear the shouts, howls, and scream but he kept riding on to distance himself to set another ambush.

With the day turning late in the afternoon, four dead naked humans laid in the snow with only Zeta Anthony surviving with his right ear bitten off his head. He ate two of the dead members. Upon finishing his inhumane meal, the butcher realized he had failed his task in catching the farmer. Not wanting to return to his Alpha Anthony decided to omega himself and not return to Edith. Unknown to him Edith was aware of the event.

After meditating another satanic ritual in the Kitchen, the Wendigo treated herself with the last of the meat in the deli freezer including the half carcass of captain Francis.

From behind came Elizabeth and Joseph armed with two of her spare pistols.

"Hand up bitch!" Lizzy yelled pointing her 44 magnums at the lady's head.

Edith took a big chump of a cold rack of lamb meat and turned slowly with a smug on her face.

"I said put your fucking hands up!" Lizzy yelled with Joe by her side. Edith nudges her head and put her boney hands up in the air.

"Fine work officer Wallstone, you've got me," Edith said with irony. "So, did you two have a good night out in the snow? Did you enjoy the blood and flesh of the young skier?"

"Shut up!" Joseph said. "Let's just kill her. Lizzy!"

"Not until we get answers," she replied. Edith walked out of the cooler, but the couple stood a distance from the lady.

"You can't arrest me," Edith said laughing. "And you cannot even kill me with bullets."

Joe and Liz looked two one another.

"Then… then you better clear off before night come and will tear you apart in so many pieces the crows won't find you!" Lizzy said in a heated voice.

"Oooh, brave, cunning, strong hearted…I hate bitches like you," Edith said. "Guess you're not simple-minded and stupid like your sister."

Hearing that mockery Liz lost it and opened fire. She shot in Edith's face, making her fall back down on the floor. The policewoman exhaled with a tear streaming her face, and Joseph standing horrified.

Edith raised back up on her feet, giving the startled couple a sadistic smile with a bullet hole underneath her left eyes.

"Guess you are stupid like her, I told you-you can't kill me, lead or even silver," Edith laughed. Joseph grabbed Lizzy by the hand and ran her out to her car.

Yet before they could enter to get away, they felt a severe pain through their whole body.

"Oh no…" said Joseph seeing fur growing on his hands.

"You two wanted to act like animals, then be animals," she said turning the couple into their wolf forms early in the afternoon sun.

When Lizzy was in her werewolf body, she decided to attack the woman. Edith stood in front of her deli, perfectly still as the brunette wolf leaped for the attack and at the last minute, she ducked and grabbed Lizzy by the and back.

She picked off the ground and through her hard at her car. Joe watched in horror when Lizz moan in pain, he turned to see Edith laughing, he ran and bit the woman by the leg. Pulling her off her feet, Joseph twisted the lady's foot and Edith transformed into her monster form and dug her knifelike claws into Joe's side.

The pain made him let go and the lady transformed into the Wendigo, towering over him. She growled and swung her long arms at him, Lizzy got up off her damager car and rushed to help Joe. She bit Edith by the left-hand biting off the toe of her fingers. Edith yelled and screeched like an owl. So loud it hurt the ears of the two werewolves.

Both backed off and decided to run off before escaping to the woods, Lizzy graded a duffle bag from her car.

The Wendigo ran after them, but the two managed to outrun her. Frustrated and wounded, Edith went back to her layer to finish up the meat before moving on.

Upon making it across the icebound Willow Creek the two werewolves stopped to catch a breath.

"Are you alright, Liz?" Joseph asked sniffing her.

"I'm...I'm fine nothing's broken," she said placing the bag in her mouth on the ground. With the thumbs on her padded wolf hands, she opened the bag that had to pairs of female pants, four pairs of socks, three pairs of panties and two sweaters, there were also two towels and tampons. She took out one towel.

"How about you dose the wound hurt?" she said. Joseph laid on his left side and saw the large cut into his rib cage.

He sighed and nodded.

"Listen to me Liz I know what you have to do, I'm a vet."

"Oh, thank God," she sighed with relief. First, he told her to place the towel in water to clean out his injury.

As she down this Joe grabbed a branch to bite down on, as Liz wiped out the fur, dirt and broken claws.

"She didn't break a rib, did she?"

"No," Joe answered with pain, "Good thing it's not deep, she could've punctured my lung. Ow!"

"Sorry," she said. She cleaned the wound then took out one of her sweaters and another towel. She used the elastic fabric of the pink sweater to tie the towel around Joe's torso.

"How does it feel?"

"I can breathe, but it'll come loose if I run," Joseph answered feeling the self-made rib bandage. "Thank you, Liz."

"Just so unbelievable huh?"

"What is?" he asked.

"Us, werewolves, and a Satanist Wendigo with powers. ... just so unreal," Liz said in a voice mixed with irony and sadness.

"You said it," Joe said standing on four legs and the two followed the icy creek upward hoping they'll find their way around and wait till they turn back human and search for Nathan again.

While making their way the two north, with Lizzy by his side to keep him from falling the two werewolves, heard something ringing into their long ears.

"You hear that barking?" Joe said.

"Yes, it's a dog. A hound," they looked around and saw Nathan's hound Tasha standing on the other side.

"It is Tasha! Where did she come from?" asked Joe. As the dog approached over the ice with her tail wagging happily, she knew the two were Joseph and Elizabeth. She circled around them sniffing their butts before licking their faces.

"She must've got separated from Nathan," Lizzy said listening to the tone of her yelping, "and she wants us to follow her."

Chapter 22. Night Warming.

After making a long distance from the hunting spot, Nathan realized he was lost and without a map, he hadn't the slightest clue to where he was, the man decided to build a fire and shelter for the night.

Before darkness came Nathan dug in a snow cave, big enough to maneuver around and lay in his wool sleeping bag. It was still challenging due for his bad leg and shoulder, but it was good enough to rest on and aim out his rifle. Outside the shelter, Clyde was tied to a tree with the last blanket draped over him to keep warm.

With a small campfire, roasting a pork loin he took from his fridge, Nathan did a supply count of all the stuff he took with him before burning his house.

He had three weeks' worth of painkillers, 29 prescription pills, two spare elastic bandages, three boxes of wood matches, his Zippo with a flask of lighter fluid, his toothbrush and paste, four boxes containing 20 .303 savage Silvertips bullets, two boxes of buckshot shells, his gun cleaning kit, his spare boots and wool socks, and his aluminum crutches. He also bought a spare set of horseshoes for Clyde, one sack of horse feed, 20 nails and a hammer.

He then searched his hunting coat to search his pockets and pulled out his near emptied wallet with an old Polaroid in his driver's license pack. His food supplies contain a bag of jerky, two cans of soup and a half-empty bottle of whiskey.

He took it out the old picture taken many years ago. the photo depicted his father Patrick Scotfield with Nathan standing by one side and little brother Joseph on the other, dressed in his high school graduation robe.

Seeing the smile and pride in his father's eyes, how happy he was with his two sons. Nathan blinked a tear from the corner of his eye, as he goes in a flashback. Nathan remembered he and Joseph were on their father's bedside. It was over seven years ago, and their father was done after a massive stroke, Patrick struggled with walking and talking and before the past, he took his firstborn by the hand.

"Protect your brother Nathan."

Those words were his father's last; it was his last request and last drawn of breath before passing in the hospital. And it was that last request, burned into his memory.

Back to reality, Nathan recalled how he promised him, only now realizing he had failed miserably. Through the night with a clear sky with bright stars and the lunar moon. The distressed man shivered in the cold and his mind wrapped depression as he leaned on his giant horse by his side, nibbling on his supper. The man checked his watch, it was 10 after 6 and it was already too dark and too cold. His fire began to die out, Nathan finished his pork, eating the grizzle and fat, before crawling into his snow cave.

Nathan wanted to stay alert, to protect his horse, but because he hasn't slept in three days, he was too exhausted and dropped into a deep sleep.

Strolling through the Luna lit forest, the two werewolves were following the Tasha. It pained Joe to walk since it pinched his side wound but he was certain that Tasha was leading him to his brother. The three left a track trail mile from the creek and farther north into another county.

While Joseph was focused on finding Nathan, Lizzy began to wonder what Edith had really done to them, changing them into their wolf forms much earlier before the sun went down. She also began to think a bad feeling, that she and Joseph might kill Nathan. And just before she could inform her friend. Tasha paused into a halt.

"What is it a girl?" asked Joe looking towards the distance.

The canine and the lycanthropes couple stopped where they stood glancing all around their surroundings in the dense forest, watching, waiting, smelling and listening.

"Someone's out there," he said and before Lizzy asked what. Tasha began growling and out came another werewolf. It was Anthony.

"I know you," Joseph said recognizing the smell, lust in the eyes and his sadistic grin, he dropped his head growling alongside the hound. The wounded Zeta towered on his hind legs eyeing Lizzy. He stuck his long tongue out at her and began wagging it.

Joseph barked along with the dog.

"What's a matter Scotfield? Gonna keep the bitches to yourself?" Anthony said in a snarling laugh.

Hearing that made Joe explode in rage and without thinking, he leaped at the beast. Joe pounced and missed Anthony, he picked Joe up by his ear and flesh wound, raised him high over his head and just before he was about to slam him against a tree, Lizzy and Tasha bit him by his legs, making him tumble.

The ragged Zeta dropped Joseph in the snow, Tasha lost grip to Anthony's shin, while Lizzy bit with all her mite twisting his foot from the joint, nearly dislocating the metatarsal bone.

Anthony let out a painful howl and bit down on Lizzy's neck. As he tried to wrestle her down and shift into a position where he can mounter her, Tasha attacked again by biting his tail.

He let Lizzy lose giving her the opportunity to get free. Tasha bit down and ripped the Zeta's tail right off, only angering the monster more. He slapped the dog down on her side, he turned back to Lizzy to attempt a rape her, and then came Joseph tackling him by his side, knocking him face down in the ground.

Anthony was pushed down in the snow and Joe dug his teeth into his abdomen, Lizzy came and when the scent of blood caught her nose, she came alongside her partner Joe and the together they ate Anthony alive.

Tasha frightened by the gore, backed away and disappeared into the woods as the two werewolves lost their human senses, and gorged on Anthony's human corps, eating everything, his flesh, fat, organs, even the bones.

From the other side of the woods, miles away Clyde the horse could hear howling. He stood on his legs, whimpering, but his master Nathan lead passed out and heard nothing.

Back to the spot where the couple shared the joyful howling of battle victory, the two began to cuddle up closer together and began licking the blood off each other fur. Realizing he had killed a bigger wolf; werewolf Joe took this opportunity to make it with a mate.

After more lick and nip kisses, snuggling closer and closer to one another wolf Lizzy was equally feeling sexual needs. She shifts herself for him to mount behind her he, wrapped his paws around her stomach and soon the silent woods echoed with their moans. When the amorous werewolves finished, they drifted into sleep. They laid down together in their bedding area, warmed up with their bodies brushing together sealing their new lives together.

Chapter 23. Torment.

The sun came up shining on the forest, melting frost of the branches. Nathan awoke and clawed out of his shelter with Clyde standing at the ready. After covering the ashes of his dead campfire and crushing his shelter, Nathan tied a splint to his leg as a brace took his relieve pills and road on to continue the hunt.

Far off in a different spot of the forest, waking up with a heavy yawn, Joseph found Lizzy laying asleep closely next to him. More shocking they were both still in wolf form.

He nudged and shook her to wake up. She got up and stretched her limbs.

"So... we're still wolves," Lizzy said worriedly.

"We should get going," Joe said changing the subject.

"What...Joseph? What happened last night?"

Joe investigated the space with confusion, "All I recall was that we killed that Anthony guy."

Upon finding the red snow with small bone fragments, they were convinced they had to eat him. And though they've gained their human intelligence, both felt sick that they've devoured human flesh and decided to move on, Lizzy once again wrapped Joseph's wound, grabbed their clothing bag and walked off.

"I think these are Tasha's tracks," Joe said scanning the trail, "hopefully she's not far…."

"Joseph? Did we…uh…um mate?"

He shockingly stared at her but was strained to recall what had happened after killing Anthony and didn't wheater to say yes or no.

And just answered with a weak, "I don't know…"

"Are… are we turning into monsters?"

"Lizzy, this won't help…"

"We might kill your brother!"

"No, we won't!" he growled.

"Open your eyes, Joseph, how are we going to help Nathan? Can you speak human?! And do you think your brother won't shoot us on sight?!"

"Will you stop?!"

"Will you just listen to me?!" she yelled up, echoing a bark through the woods catching the hearing of the Clyde.

"Whoa, steady boy, they're still out there," Nathan said calmly. The giant horse whimpered and jump back a hove. The hunter looked around the surroundings, listening and watching before hearing familiar barking.

"Tasha!"

He saw his hound alive, and joyfully running towards them when trying to dismount Clyde, Nathan accidentally stuck his injured leg on a skinny tree. The pain made him fall in the snow and scream like a child.

"Listen, did you hear that!" Lizzy cut in; both heard the screaming from a distance that Joe recognized as a human in pain.

"That's Nathan!" he ran off.

"Joseph waits"

Laying in the snow with his leg's pint snapped in two, Tasha rushed to her master and began licking his face, Nathan picked himself up by the trend cover of Clyde's saddle.

"God damn it!" he cursed from the pain in his leg bones. He sat on the horse to cut the rope and thigh and ankle. To his surprise, he could move his toes and maneuver his foot with the boot on, but still felt the hard pain from his busted fibula. Casually he got off the horse with one crutch and walked over to leash Tasha.

Before he tied her collar, the hound wagged her tail, and he saw from out of a thicket two large wolves, with one standing on his back legs and long arms out.

The horror stormed his mind, heart pounding like inner thunder, and like a mad gunslinger he wretched out his .357 magnum. The beast's eyes grew wider with fright.

Nathan fired three loud shots and the female werewolf shoved him aside the last minute and the pair took off running disappearing in the forest.

Tasha barked at her master and took off in the wolves' direction.

"Tasha Wait!"

The hound left her master once again to help the brother and his mate.

The werewolf couple ran and ran faster than a race car.

They rush through the woods, over frozen rivers and empty highways Northward, with as much strength their wolves' legs can take them.

Miles and miles past the U.S. border deep within the Canadian wilderness and into the province of Ontario, upon stopping Lizzy collapsed from exhaustion and began eating the snow to stay hydrated.

 Feeling terrible for what he'd put her through, Joseph came across a cave where a black bear is hibernating. Wanting to get shelter from the coming snowstorm, Joe killed the bear in his sleep cutting its throat with his claws and teeth. After dragging the carcass out, he ran back to find Lizzy passed out with Tasha sitting by her. Joseph took the duffle bag off her neck, picked her up with his long-bloodstained arms and carried her inside the cave.

In late in the day before sun settled down, Lizzy awoke with on top a pile of warm leaves and straw.

"Glad you're awake," Joe said watching her getting up.

"You found us a cave?" she said walking out to find a bear corpse.

"No, stole one… are you hungry?"

"Starving," she answered, Liz began eating the cold flesh of the bear, with Joseph watching out in the woods with a depressed look, when she finished, she walked next to him.

"You were right Liz; sorry I didn't listen to you."

She said placing her paw on his. Tapping it real gently, she understood Joe's deep concerns with his brother, and both knew trapped in a wolf body would be all too dangerous to get near Nathan.

"We're trapped in this form, but we still gotta help him," she said. "With that… bitch Wendigo out there."

The two left the cave to go out and search for Nathan again, leaving her behind their duffle bag. The rushed through the snow lead by Tasha, until they came across Lake Abitibi near the town of La Sarre where they help the hound catch food at a nearby sheep farm. The trio killed a half dozen Suffolk sheep and ran off again in the woods.

Deeper into Canada, Nathan and Clyde came across another cabin. He saw the lights shining from the windows and smoke coming from the chimney, with his stomach rumbling with hunger and the deep desire to get inside from the cold the man road up, hoping the owners will help him.

He dismounted the horse left his firearms on the saddle, took out the crutches and made his way to the front door.

He knocked.

"Qu'est-ce?" the owner asked in French.

"S'il vous plait, I need help...please?" Nathan replied in a shivering voice. The door opened slowly with a middle-aged woman.

"Qui es-tu?" she asked.

"My name is Nathan, and I'm lost."

"You speak English?" the lady asked, and he replied nodding. The woman opened the door wider where Nathan could see her child standing behind her.

"What are you doing out here?" she asked suspiciously.

"Look I'm sorry to bother you, but I have a bad leg, I don't know where I am, and I'm lost..."

She stared at him a little unsure, turned to her son behind her. "Okay, forgive me but I'm not letting you in, would you like me to call for help?" asked the woman.

"I just need to know where I am, can you tell me?" he asked.

"You're on my property," she answered.

"I know that...look...listen to I sorry for trespassing, it's just that I was... traveling on horseback and lost my way, is there a town near me?"

"Where did you come from?"

"I'm from Graytown, a small place 60 miles north of Utica New York," he answered, and the woman's shroud face turned concerned. "Now, where am I?"

"You're 5 miles east of Hawkesbury, a long way from New York."

"La Tuque? Which way do I get there?" The lady told him she was going to fetch her cell phone and told him to wait out on the porch, making the man wait on the snow-covered wood, she returned to the doorway with two hot steaming mugs.

"Here, I just made some stew and cocoa," she handed out and he graciously took them.

"Merci Beaucoup, madam," he said downing both the cups. When finishing his warm meal, she showed him the GPS on her phone that showed him the way that'll take him straight to town. He gave her back her phone shook her hand and left for his horse. He arrived at the town late in the day around the hour 7:45 pm, riding on the plowed road.

He first stopped in front of a restaurant/hotel, but he only had the last 40 Canadian bucks in his wallet, even worse he realized he had left his bank card back in his house. The frustration grew with pain kicking in his shoulder urging him to lay down on a soft pillow.

The first thing he did was down more pills and walked into a restaurant, the place had less than a half dozen customers and all turned to look at the strange man, dressed in camouflage clothes with crutches. As he limped to the counter with the sounds of his growling stomach, music from the radio and the people chatting.

He dropped on a seat of the counter and waited for service. After a large bowl of hot soup and coffee, Nathan paid the bill and was out the door where he found a town deputy observing his horse.

"Excuse me, officer?"

"Is this your horse?!" the man asked.

"Yes…"

"Why are you riding a horse in town? Don't you have a car?" the officer interrupted.

"I have no car," said Nathan packing his crouches in the saddlebags.

"What happened to your legs?"

"I sprained my fibula."

"So, you're riding a horse out in the cold with a sprained leg, why?"

"I'm traveling," he replied. Nathan grabbed Clyde's head collar before the cop grabbed the other side.

"Traveling to where? Answer my question," demanded the deputy.

"Going to Ontario," Nathan lied.

"All the way up here, and not taking a bus or a plane?"

"Yes, can I go now pleased?"

"And these firearms, they're loaded and don't have a lock on them," the cop stated.

"I have the right to bear arms."

"That's the U.S. this is Canada, and we have regulation," the cop said.

"So, what are you gonna do?" he asked.

"First I'm gonna call for backup and you're coming with me to the station," the deputy walked to his car to call for back and Nathan came up from behind holding his 357 to his head.

"What are…"

"Shut up deputy!" Nathan whispered really angry, "If you wanna live to see your loved one again, you'll do what I'll tell you."

So the cop walked with Nathan into the ally and followed his demands, to remove his gear belt and toss him the handcuffs, he ordered the cop to turn around where cuffed the cop and walked to his cruiser, he laid the young deputy in the back seats and destroyed his cell phone and car's radio.

"Now I didn't want to do this, I have no choice, I have important manners to attend, I'll leave the car on for you, so you'll stay warm, someone we'll find you," Nathan said closing the unlocked car doors.

The cop didn't reply and just gave the man and pissed off face.

Quickly he limped to Clyde and road out of town, crossing the frozen Ottawa river and into the Quebec region. Stressed out by what had happened, realizing he made himself a criminal and cops we now hunt for him, all Nathan did was ride on with an empty head, when from out of nowhere came a call.

"Nathan!"

Clyde felt his the pulled to his halter, the master looked around to whoever was calling him out.

"Nathan! Nathan Scotfield?" he heard in a young male voice.

"Joseph?" he said kicking his spurs in the horse's side. He followed the call where he found a roaring campfire.

"Joseph, hello?" Nathan asked after dismounting the horse, where Clyde began to build up in a panic and the man tied him to a tree. "Steady pail, take it easy."

Nathan walked up to the fire with tracks all around it, he called out again but got no answer in reply. With only the sparks of the fire as the noise and light in the dark forest, Nathan heard Clyde beginning to whimper, there was something watching them, he limped back to the horse and took out his shotgun.

"Joseph? Is there anyone out here?!" he yelled, slowly walking back to the fire, hearing the sound of snow ruffling and breaking branch, he shook in worry, pumping in a shell and flicked off the safety.

"Nathan!"

He jumped in the snow and turned around. Standing nine feet tall with a form of most disgusting appearances.

Wendigo Edith had a naked boney form with saggy breast, hanging skin from her exposed muscle and her abdomen was opened, with intestines sticking out and steam smoking out of it. Only her human head remained normal with a disturbing grin as she imitated his brother's voice.

"It works every time," she said laughing so god awful in the mix of a hyena and a dolphin. The sound rang in the ears of the master and his horses, so loud and painful it made Clyde fall off his long legs.

 Nathan tried to crawl back, but Edith stepped her hooves on his bad leg.

The woods echoed with the loud blood-curdling scream of Nathan, as the Wendigo grind to the pain, while turning from the human face to a long wolf like skull with large red eyes and deer antlers.

Nathan took up his shotgun with one arm and shot the monster in the stomach, it yelped and lifted its hooves off his leg.

Pulling himself up while grabbing a burning branch Edith let out a light laugh.

"Clever to use silvertip bullets and buckshot, but that can't kill me!"

Nathan fired another shot but missed and swung out a torch in front of its face.

Edith swung her long arm missing Nathan by a single inch, he stood back up and set fire to the monster's shoulder fur.

Letting out a piercing scream, loud enough to make the man drop the gun to cover his ears.

The blaze built upon the Wendigo's face making the monster pounce and jump in the snow.

It kicked Nathan and claimed up to a tree, he got back up with the shotgun, ran over to the horse and tied it loose.

"Go and run!" yelled, standing Edith on top a leafless oak tree, back into her old human body.

"I'm not running, I'm gonna kill you for the Kess family!"

"Aah so you've been talking with the spirits, yet I thought you were stupid like all white farmers!"

"Where is my brother?!" Nathan yelled shaking with boiling anger.

"Killing people, eating them, humping legs like the monster I'd turned him in," she said chuckling. She shot her again with the pump action which made her annoyed.

"Scotfield you don't know what's your getting into, I can rip you in limb by limb, just like that," she said breaking a heavy branch off, but the man didn't get intimidated and fired at her again, she through the branch at him and he kicked Clyde to run.

"I'm not afraid!" he yelled.

She leaped over a few trees and down to the hunter and grabbed Nathan off Clyde.

"You underestimate the power of unholy nature," she snarled, only to get spat on by the angry farmer. He watched as Edith's face stretch and twist with her eyes sinking back and the skeleton snout grew out of her mouth.

He took out his pistol and fire up its chin making it let go of him and fall to the ground.

The injured monster screamed again, but Nathan didn't budge and fired two more shots at her.

"Catch me if you can farmer loser!"

The Wendigo got on its four legs and ran into the thickets, the angry man rushed to Clyde.

"Yah!" he yelled as they chased after the monster.

Chapter 24. Symptoms.

Coming upon a thicket, housing a sleeping deer came in the two werewolves and hound, Lizzy took the unsuspecting buck by the leg, it woke in horror as it was dragged out of its bedding area and met its end as the predators gorged down on him.

The trio made their way south where they continued to feed off farm animals, sleeping in burrows, under trees, bridges, and under house porches.

On cold night late in December Joe, Lizzy and Tasha took shelter in a tool shed somewhere near Lake Temiskaming, the night was so cold the two werewolves snuggled closer to each other draping their arms over their bodies.

Upon waking up early in the morning, Tasha was gone again, and he tugged Lizzy's ear to wake her.

"So, she ran off again huh?" she asked stretching.

"Looks like it yeah, are you okay?"

"Just hungry," Liz answered, when the two exited the shed, she felt something as if she was kicked in the ribs and she dropped with a grunt. Joe came to her and asked if she was alright.

"I'm fine, why? notice something different?" she asked, and Joseph gave her an odd look of worry.

"Yeah… um… you're… your chest," he said.

"What?!" she said walking off, shrugging off what he said, Joe felt stupid, but he wasn't lying while the two wondered on Lizzy took a stop and placed her padded hand/paw on her chest and could feel bumps in two rows.

"What? What… what the fuck?!" she said feeling the swelling of her six nipples, the she-wolf nearly screamed after feeling her stomach. Joseph came up with a look of regret.

"I can't be!" she said sadden while shaking her head in denial. Joseph and vet recognized the signs right away from the minute they walked off, he placed his hands on her shoulders calming her down.

"It's gonna be okay Lizzy."

"How do you know?"

"I'm a vet Liz, I tended hundreds of animal mothers giving birth…"

"We're not in a doctor's office! Where in the fucking woods! And have you forgot we're trapped in the bodies of wolves…"

"Elizabeth! I helped many dogs and animals have pups out of the office before, I did house calls, I even helped breed horses…don't panic, we're gonna be fine."

"You got me pregnant," she sniffed before pulling Joseph in a hug, "do you love me?"

He hugged her back, then looked into her eye and asked, "do you."

"Yes," both answered and gave each other smirks and kisses on the jaws.

With a new burden to bear, Joseph and Elizabeth came across another cave inhabited by a small pack of gray wolves; Joseph approached with three adult males coming out growling. Even though he was much tall and stronger than regular wolves, he tried to show he and Liz meant no warm to them. And when Joe walked closer to the entrance the Alpha charged and lunged at his neck.

Joseph howled and shoved the wolf down, it pounced again this time on his rib wound, the pain made him swat the alpha to the ground. It retreated to the cave but the other two stood their grounds ordering them to leave. Lizzy walked up.

"Are you alright?!"

"Ahh...yeah..." Joe dropped to his knees, but Liz picked him up as they walked away. "Well, that wasn't smart."

Joe laid down to rest against a tree, with nowhere to go, the two decided to wait awhile before going off to search for food. Joe was still down with the broken rib, so Lizzy decided to go out and hunt alone.

Joe opposed the idea to let his mate going out by herself but fearing that running will cause more damage he decided to let her go.

That evening while sleeping in a snow cave Lizzy returned with a large chunk a calf.

"Where do you get this?" he asked harking down the raw beef.

"There's a couple of farms not far from here," answered Lizzy, "and I tried to take down an older one, but I couldn't take it down, so I went for the small one."

"Don't be ashamed."

"I'm not… Joseph… we're wolves… were probably trapped as wolves…maybe forever."

"Liz, don't think like that, we're going to figure this out, we're going to be fine, you, me and our babies."

"And Nathan?" she asked. Joe gasped in horror and nearly clawed himself for not remembering his brother, yet again with his wound, a pregnant mate he couldn't think of any alternative but to just care for Lizzy and himself first and he knew Nathan's a smart man.

Early in the morning, the couple were awoken by a gunshot.

"Joseph?" she said when he got on his feet.

"Stay here Liz," he said storming off to find the source of the gunfire, Lizzy rolled her eyes and followed him anyway.

Joe ran faster ahead, she tried to catch up with him, worried for his safety.

"Joseph, wait!" she yelled.

Another shot fired and Liz ducked in behind a thick oak tree, Joe kept running think it was his brother, but he was wrong.

Joe ran out of her sight and she heard three more shots and a frightening scream.

"Oh no," she repeated as she followed her mate's tracks. She sprinted out of a bush to discover a dead gray wolf with two gunshot wounds in its side. She lifted her nose, smelling blood in the air, human blood.

Panic rushed through her body, tingling the fetus she carried. Running in total worry she looked out to an open area where Joseph stood over a man that he killed.

Lizzy sighed in relief and marched up furious, Joe turned his bloodied face to her where he met a smack on his side.

"OW hey!"

"Don't ever do that again!" she cried, "You could've been killed!"

"Oh babe, I'm sorry, I thought it was my brother...I saw him kill one our... I mean I couldn't remember."

"Joe, don't leave me like that again."

As she licked the blood off his face the two looked to the hunter, it wasn't Nathan, the man looked to be an old man from the farm Lizzy found last night. Both felt sorry for the death and realized that they are slowly losing control in the human minds and are becoming more wolf.

Snow came flurrying down, and Lizzy heard a noise, both stopped in their tracks and scanned their surroundings, believing it to be a hunter, Joe ordered Lizzy to duck down, but from the distance came a trio of gray wolves, two males and one female that looked much older.

Joe recognized it from the cave they've crossed, the one that looked to be the Gamma gave the two a grateful grin, wagged her tail and gave the two a bow.

"They want us to follow them," he said when the three walked off. They followed the whole way back to cave from before, the pack allowed the werewolves in the cave, since they've killed the hunter who shot one of the alpha's mates and they allowed them in the shelter in a way to thank them. Both couldn't be more happy to be out of the cold, in a place to relax with the wrath of more wolves, in their first night with the pack, when the snow died down, they followed the gray backs up on an open hill where the full moon broke through the clouds and howled with excitement, before running off for a hunt.

Chapter 25. Sanctuary.

A month past into a new year, the winter
continued and so did Nathan's hunt for the Wendigo. But
now lost in the forest, lost his way around, lost track of the
time, not knowing where to go or what to do, the man
crashed with exhaustion off Clyde. Out of food, short on
medicine, with his leg turning from pale white to swollen
pink. Nathan started a campfire and draped the blankets
over his horse, with the short fire blazing the two sat
miserably through a small blizzard nipping of Nathan's lips,
nose, ears, and fingertips.

On a Sunday evening after Church serves Father Benedict
closed his chapel in Cobalt for the night to go home.
Driving down the plowed road pulling in his driveway to
his house. He went in and fixed himself a kettle of hot
water for tea on the stove when he caught a glow of a fire
in his woods. Off with his stove and back on with his coat
he went out to investigate, first crossing a whimpering
horse, and a sick man laying by the fire.

Slowly opening his eyes, Nathan found himself on a warm
bed, in covers inside a heated room with snow outside a
window.

Dumbstruck and in denial of where he is.

"This can't be," he said getting up and discovering he's wearing clean pajamas. He walked out of the room where he found the old priest cooking.

"Oh, you're awake," Benedict said.

"Who are you and how did I get here?" Nathan said rubbing his head.

"My names Franklin, Franklin Benedict," he answered sitting the man down. "Found you outside, passed out on my land."

"And you changed me in these PJs?"

"Young man, it's 30 below 0 outside all week, what in the name of God were you doing out there?" Benedict said cross armed.

"I was... hunting and I lost my way."

"You foolish American nit-wit you could've frozen to death!"

"I was lost and... wait how do you know I'm American?"

"I read your license, and your clothes were all wet. What were you doing out there?"

"I told you I was out hunting, and I got lost," Nathan answered.

"All the way up here? On a horse, alone?" Benedict said, "Sir, are you in some sort of trouble?"

Nathan looked around nervously, trying to avoid shaking, "Sir, I thank you for your help, I wish I had the cash to pay you but I..."

"Son, I want no money, I'm a priest I help people," Benedict said, reside yourself and tell me, are your running from the law? Are you homeless? You can tell me and perhaps we can work this out."

The priest placed a hand on his shoulder and Nathan cracked a tear, for the kindness giving to him he decided to tell him everything, his divorce, burning down his own home, the werewolves, the Wendigo. He told in detail of his story, how he trapped them how he lived outside in snow shelters, the loss of his brother and his present hunt for the Wendigo.

The preacher was shaken and weirded out by the werewolf part, yet he continued to listen.

Nathan felt completely stupid telling him all this, he couldn't have believed him, yet he saw how the old man kept his eyes to his and was paying attention to all his details and emotions.

The thought of embarrassment disappeared as Nathan began to wrap up his story.

"...And though I lost track of the monster responsible for all this I must find it and kill it. I know it all sound crazy, I think I've lost my mind myself, not knowing what else to do but to kill this thing... I really have nothing else in life, alone, broke and tormented by a Shapeshifting, Satan-worshipping bitch, weeks probably months now leading me North, always north threw snow, woods seem to be driving me into internal anger. Now here I am... I thank you for taking me in."

When Nathan finished his story, Benedict sat quietly and heard the bubbles boiling on his stove.

"Soups ready," he said, "also your clothes are dry, they're hanging in the laundry room down the hallway. When he walked in the room to dress, Nathan notices his bad leg was newly wrapped up elastic ankle-leg support. It was warm and soothing. When the man got all his hunting clothes on, he thought he should just leave, thank the man and be on his way, but there was also a part of him to just go back to New York and just try to find his brother.

"Mr. Scotfield?" Benedict said at the door.

"Yes, I'll be right out sir."

"No hurry, I also wanted to tell you, that your horse is resting in my garage." Nathan for almost forgetting Clyde.

"Thank you, sir."

After getting his coat on, Nathan walked out and found the giant horse lying on a heavy blanket, well fed with an electric blanket, he walked up and gave his trusted steed and few pats on the head.

"A good horse you got there, and he's huge," said the priest.

"Yeah, I love gentle giants. Thank you for feeding him, father," said Nathan.

"My pleasure sir, he's a good horse. Now come inside and have something to eat."

At the table Father Benedict watched Nathan eat.

Though the man was hungry but for some strange reason, he ate real slow like a sloth. Nathan stared into space with the thoughts of his brother and Officer Wallstone, the thought of them dead.

"Nathan?"

"Ehh oh, sorry, what?" he said.

"Are you alright?"

The man stared out the window as the snow was fluttering, before shaking his head. "I'm fine to thank you."

"Are you sure?"

He saw that the Priest had a look of suspicion in his eyes.

"It's my story was it?" asked Nathan. "I knew you wouldn't have believed me."

The old man sighed, "well it's, it sounds strange, to be honest, but I don't think you're crazy..."

"That's good reassurance."

"Look, Nathan... to be honest I don't believe werewolves or wendigos but as a Man of blood, I do believe there is evil in this world. But I think it would be best and wise... for you to go back home," Benedict stated.

"I can't."

"Nathan, you're not well, it's the middle of winter, it's not safe for you to go out there."

"Father, I have to go."

"Nathan... you need help, go back to New York and..."

Nathan pounded the table, "Damn it I can't! Were you even listening to my story, I have no home, my brother is missing and there are some hells pounded skinwalker bitch out there!"

"Running out in the cold woods alone? You'll die out there!"

"I got nothing else to lose anymore... I'm not scared."

Nathan walked out of the preachers dining room and back to the garage to saddle Clyde.

"You should at least wait until the Spring."

"I can't wait, look thank you for all your help," Nathan took out the last of his money."

"No, I don't want your money, I want to help you."

"Father, you helped me than anyone else I've known in my life, you saved my life and I thank you If my brother wasn't danger, I would return... but I have to go."

The Priest looked concerned but shrugged his shoulders. "Let's finish lunch and then you can be on your way."

Benedict poured Nathan a second bowl of hot soup and Nathan finished the whole thing and sipped down his last warm tea.

"Before you leave, I have something for you," Benedict said walking from the table, the priest returned with a small foot-sized box he handed to his guest.

Nathan opened it and inside was a dozen cans of chowder, beans and vegetables, five boxes of 12 gage slugs, a book of waterproof matches, two outdoor candles, an old Holy Bible and a small metal snow shovel.

"Awe Father…"

"Just take, I have no further use for it."

Nathan took out the old Bible, on the first page before the Genesis, were the signatures of Albert, Edward, John and Franklin Benedict.

He looked up to the Priest in shock, "This is your family bible."

"Yeah, past down by my Great Grandfather, it's over 120 years old."

"And you want me to have it?"

"I have no child to pass it on, I'm a man of God with hundreds of Bibles at my church, "besides, I think you need it more than I do."

"Thank you," Nathan said shaking his hand, though he knew he was never a believer he took it as an honor and shook the kind man's hand.

Nathan packed up his guns and belonging and walked Clyde outside.

"So, do you know where to go?"

"I'll find it, I'll hunt for this bitch if I have to go up to the North Pole," he replied claiming over the giant. "Thank you again, Benedict, farewell."

"Godspeed to your son."

Hearing that as the road off touched Nathan, as though he heard his own father Patrick.

Now deep into the woods again, on the hunt for Edith Ester, the man and horse crossed open snow-covered field with a herd of deer scouring for grass, a perfect spot for an ambush.

Chapter 26. Weaknesses.

That evening back at Benedict's house, the old Preacher knelt by his bedside for prayer, only to be interrupted by a knock at his front door.

"Ha, I knew he would come back," the Priest said getting up, he walked to the door where the knocking continued. "Well, it took a bit longer than expected though."

"Yes, coming!"

He opened the door and there was no one.

"Hello?" he called out in the snowy darkness, but got no replied, he looked to the snow where there were footprints, bare footprints that lead around his house.

"Hello? Is there anyone out there?" the priest called feeling suspicious, and he walked off his front step, "Nathan? Is that you?"

Before the priest could follow the tracks around the corner, he heard growls. The man paused and leaned against the wall. The growling mixed the sound of footsteps and wheezing screeches, it almost sounded like laughter.

Father Benedict felt a sickness to his gut he ran back into the house and locked the door.

"Lord watch over me, by Kingdom come," father said as he went for his shotgun in his bedroom. As he looked for his boxes of shells he heard knocking again. He placed two buck shots in the barrels and walked to the living room where the knocking continued.

"Who...who is that?! Whoever it is I just called the cops...get off my land!" the preacher yelled shaking with his double barrel.

The knocking stopped and there was silence, Benedict ran to the phone to call help, but the line was dead.

"Lord protect and watch over me," he said aloud feeling sore pain in his heart. The priest walked to his room where the power went out. In his darkroom, he took a battery lantern illuminating his room. He saw the holy water on the bed set next to his heart medications and alarm clock.

He placed the lantern on his bed and looked to his window and though the father kept his faith strong his felt weakness in his hands, believing his home wasn't being stalked by a human or a bear.

While pulling down the blinds of his window, he heard something from the living room.

"Hello? Is anybody home?" he heard; it was the voice of a child. The Priest walked to his bedroom door but hesitated to open it.

"Hello, are you in there I need help?"

Benedict backed up to grab his gun and yelled, "Get out of my house!"

"But I need help!" the child said tapping at the door, from tapping to jerking at the doorknob, while backing away into his closet a sudden smell hit the priest's nose, a reeking smell so back it made blood ooze out of the nostrils.

"God keep us keep us safe."

"Your God can't help you," he heard.

Breaking from the walls of the closet shoved the man to the foot of his bed, from the closet outstretched the long bony limbs crowned by a human head of a woman, smiling with long yellow sharp teeth with blood dripping off the chin.

Benedict's eyes grew wide, unable to close them as he stared at the disturbing misshapen form of the monster with the face of a toddler for a head.

The face of the Wendigo changed from a young girl to an old lady, the man of God was looking into a supernatural beast for the first time he was horrified and amazed at the same time.

"God Keep us safe, I..." he whispered a prayer. The long fingers of the monster's hand wrapped around Benedict's neck.

He clawed the rotten flesh with his fingertips as Edith raised him off the floor hitting his head on his ceiling fixture.

"So, my God-fearing shill fuck, all alone are we?" The Wendigo said in the vice of the toddler.

It licked the preacher's face; he kicked the creature it's wrinkled stomach. It through the man out his bedroom and into his hallway.

Benedict crawled to the living room, where it was lit by the flames of his fireplace, he graded a log where he felt a pain in his tibial on his left leg.

He screamed as the monster pulled him back, he turned and struck Edith in the face. The Wendigo let out a scream, the erupted the man's hearing aids, making all his windows shatter, it echoed far out in the woods. Clyde whipped followed by the attestation of Nathan.

"Franklin, no…" that moment Nathan dropped the trap he was building, grabbed his gun and rode off in the dark woods.

After striking the demon, Benedict clawed back to the fire where his cross fell from then mantel The Wendigo grabbed the priest by his legs, tightening the muscles and squeezing the blood out of his flesh wound.

The injured man took the cross and sat up in a single touch of the cross Edith felt a shocking burn run through her veins. Realizing she had touched an object associated with the Holy Spirit, the Wendigo screamed louder throwing the old man in his kitchen and retreated to the woods, leaving the injured priest cold, and frightened.

As he tried to crawl to safety, but the old man couldn't feel his left arm, with the inability to move Benedict just curled in the corner of his kitchen. In the living room, the fire sparked out of the chimney and set the rug a blaze.

Nathan arrived at the fractured house, he put the fire out with snow and found the injured priest.

"Christ Frank, are you hurt?"

"Nathan?" Benedict kept in joyful tears.

"Are you hurt? Can you move."

"No, I'm afraid I can't…"

Nathan scooped the priest in his arms and laid him on the couch near the broken window where Edith escaped, he saw the monster's footprints in the snow, but Nathan had to help the priest.

"Do you have a cell phone? I'll call an ambulance." Benedict said his cell was in the bedroom, while the hunter left to find it the priest looked over the couch to the outside woods.

Nathan searches through the dark room with a small flashlight when he's startled by the old man screaming.

He rushed back out with his gun drawn and found Benedict on the floor shaking.

"What? What happened?"

"It's out there! I saw it!" the old man replied, Nathan, stood and looked to the opening to the dark forest, outside he heard Clyde whine. And before he knew the

Wendigo crashed through the ceiling, grading Nathan by his bad leg.

Edith stood over him, snarling and drooling on his face.

"Time to die, Scotfield," Nathan pinned to the floor tried stabbing the monster' with his knife, but it didn't stop the Wendigo slowly coming down to bit off his face, and before the jaws touched his cheeks, father Benedict threw a liquid on Edith's face.

The wendigo screamed steam lines some off her head and blood from her right eye, splattering on Nathan's face.

 The Wendigo ran off again into the darkness, Nathan sat up. And rushed to Benedict.

Laying the matted man on the mattress of his bed lit by candles, after calling for police and paramedics, Nathan stood by the old man's bedside.

"You have to go," the priest said.

"I can't leave you alone."

"That… the beast is out there… you have to kill it."

"What did you use, that made it flee?" Nathan asked.

"Holy water, crosses, and my clergy stole, those will hurt that demon…"

The priest wheezed and coughed and pointed to where they were.

Nathan found the devotional items and walked back to the old man.

"I'm sorry I didn't…"

"No father, please don't apologize," Nathan cut off kneeling by his side. "I'm sorry I left you alone… don't worry help is coming, you'll be okay…"

"Nathan, you have to go!"

"I'm not leaving you again!"

"That beast is out there; it's getting away and it will kill again! Go, son, I'll be fine."

At that point, Nathan thought about his brother and realized he knows the wendigo's true weakness, so he agreed. He laid another warm blanket over the old man and left him his shotgun to defend himself.

"You'll be okay?"

"God is with us, son…go."

Nathan took the preacher's supplies and mounted his horse again, back on the chase.

Chapter 27. Form bound.

After Nathan left, police and paramedics arrived, they took the wounded priest by helicopter to the hospital in Sudbury. Benedict was doped with medicine, now on the verge of a long sleep the priest did small prayer on his bed while looking to his window. Though he never met his brother the man of God said a prayer for Joseph Scotfield.

Nathan still after Edith armed with a cross and a priest choir around his neck like a scarf. The cold night froze his lips dry, fingertips turning black and exhaling a cloud of breath. With his eyes glued on the darkness. He could hear her laughing and tormenting him at mind. But he knew deep down she was scared and frightened of him. The monster is now the hunted, and the broke man who lost everything was now the hunter.

While this was going on, police were tracking down Nathan, ever since the disappearance of Elizabeth Wallstone. Investigators led by detective Matt Geyer discovered the skeletal remains of Captain Francis, officer Merv, the Kess family as well as several other dead locals from Graytown who were killed by gunshot wounds to the head and side. They suspected Nathan Scotfield to be the killer. Nathan was on the FBI most wanted list, in both the U.S. and Canada. That winter, a squad of Canadian mounted troops picked up Nathan's trail at Father Benedict's house.

Far off in a cave, sleeping with a pack of wolves next to his month pregnant mate, though pitch black in the cave, he could tell Lizzy was awake.

He tapped her and whispered.

"Are you okay?"

"I'm fine. You okay?"

"Well… I… I don't know," he said stutteringly.

"What's the matter?"

Joseph signed and answered with his brother's names.

"He's alive, Joseph, I know he's alive."

The then cuddled up close to one another and listened to the whistling winds, then the growling in the stomachs. Due to the cold weather, the game wasn't easy to find lately. So, tomorrow Joe plans to hunt alone to catch food for the pack. As they both drifted back to sleep in the cave of wolves.

The next morning Elizabeth awoke in the cave, Joseph was gone to go out hunting, accompanied only by the pack elder and 6 puppies of one of the females.

The fury babies waddled up to her, yelping and began licking at her. She smiled and chuckled at his little friends as the claimed all over her and began sniffing her baby bump. She laughed at the awkward yelping when two puppy siblings wrestled around, she separated the fighters by picking the two up in both hands. After some playing around, she decided to stretch her legs by walking with the pups outside. Poppies pouncing and rolling around in the snow was fun to watch, really put a smile to the shewolf's heart. Snow began to build up, so she decided to take all the cubs inside.

Before she crawled in, she heard a whisper, she stopped and looked around but thought of it nothing but a wisp of the wind.

That evening Joseph and the pack returned empty-handed.

"Did you find anything at all?"

"Nothing," replied Joseph. "I gotta go back out, we need food."

"Be careful, Joe," she said. Joe left and Elizabeth said in front of the cave, where she heard the whisper again. She looked around and she heard her name called out quietly.

"Lizzy?"

She stared into the snowy woods when came the spirit of her sister.

"Lidia."

The werewolf stood and the glowing spirit walked closer, Lidia knelt down, with a depressed face.

"Oh Elizabeth...I'm so sorry," the ghost said.

"Oh Lidia, I would've helped if you had told me," said Lizzy.

"I was afraid, she made us monsters, now you...oh sorry sis," Lidia said weeping, she wrapped her arms around the she-wolf.

From behind Lizzy saw the spirits of her nephew and niece both of whom equally sad.

"Don't worry about me, Lidia...you...what about you sis?"

"Until the Wendigo is killed, hopefully, Nathan can stop her," explained Lydia, "until then we are trapped."

"Nathan will kill her, if not then Joseph and I will. She'll never get away from what she had done to you," growled Lizzy.

"Oh Lizzy, you're expecting!" Lidia said smiling.

"I am..."

"I'm sorry I won't be around to see you become a mother..." Lidia said as she began to fade.

"Don't leave me, Lidia."

"I will always watch over you, Liz," Lidia said as the wind blew her and the kids away. "You and your children."

Lizzy stood alone in the dark crying.

Sometime later, dawn came, Lizzy awoke to some echoing barks, she looked up, seeing Joseph pull something in the cave.

"You found something?" she asked, Joseph turned around and, in his paw, /hands was a dying dog.

"It's Tasha, I found here on the side of a road," said Joseph laying her down in the corner. The mixed hound shivered, but the fear of the wolves was gone since she had Joe and Lizzy by her side, and she slept warm and safe that night.

The next morning Joe left early to hunt, while most of the pack stayed, most of whom wanted to kill and eat the dog, guarded by Lizzy.

When Joe returns again with no kill, the pack grew hungrier and more aggressive, snapping at the two werewolves, and nipping at their tails.

Lizzy woke up when Joe was going out again, most of the adult wolves left to find food, but the alpha stayed behind, the Gamma left as well leaving Liz, Tasha and the pups alone in the cold cave.

The six pups wondered outside, and it crossed Liz's mind to keep an eye on them, but she feared the alpha would attack Tasha. She was unable to move her since the poor mixed dog was freezing and starving too weak to move alone or fight back so leaving her with a hungry alpha was a no go.

The Gray Alpha stared at the she-wolf, though she was taller the alpha was large enough to make a good fight. He stood and stretched his limbs and slowly walked towards her.

"Get back!" she barked, he paused. She stood over Tasha; the Alpha took a step back eyeing the weak ridgeback hound underneath her. He moaned, growled and snarled violently before walking outside.

The pregnant she-wolf exhaled with relief until she heard a puppy yelp. She ran out and saw the alpha jerking one of the little pups in his jaws, he was killing one for food.

After watching the poor young creature die, enraged, Elizabeth sprinted from the cave entrance, and she was on top of the alpha. She crushed his back, breaking its spine before biting off its right ear, she crawls punctured its lungs before she bit his neck, the old alpha was dead. She picked the pup out of the dead wolf's jaws and tried to wake it, but the pup was long gone. Tears jerked out of her eyes she gathered the remaining 5 pups. When all went inside, she turned back to bury the pup and tore into the alpha's corps that use gave to the starving Tasha.

The pack returned late that night with, all sad for the wolf mother that lost one pup. Joseph though had returned with a kill. He dragged in a mauled caribou in the cave and gave his mate a severed leg piece as the rest of the pack gorged down on the meat.

"So, you killed the alpha, to save the babies...you make a good mother," Joe said.

Chapter 28. Sick Riding.

It was another cold dawn, with Clyde still jogging through the woods, he had lost another horseshoe, his long hair tail was frozen stiff from the snow and mug he kicked up, that his master neglected to brush. Nathan was equally in bad shape. He had lost his rifle, just when he thought they had caught up with Edith, Nathan took aim but missed, when the Wendigo took up to the trees again, he thought he had placed the rifle securely in the saddle holster but it slipped out and after a sprinting gallop chase he realized he no longer had his Savage model 99. And he literally punished himself by giving his face a punch with his own fist.

The determined, vengeful soul didn't turn back and just kept chasing the demon monster.

Edith could hear the man was still after her, she kept luring the human farther out into the deep Canadian winter, to let nature kill Nathan, but then new sense caught her smell.

Nathan came across a frozen lake, where he dismounted Clyde. He nailed in the last spare horseshoe and decided to make camp. Clyde laid down to rest while his master gathered firewood, Nathan's lips were as dry as stale as rotten fruit, pink with frozen blood in his brunette bead. He now had long thick hair covering the back of his neck, his fingertips were purple, and he felt a little lightheaded.

He piled a stack of twigs and while light a match he sneezed and coughed really violent, blowing out the match. He lit another and he coughed again, no mystery he had caught himself a cold.

He lit a fire, sat on some dry bark, next to his horse, the man rocked back and forth, coughing mist and blooded flem.

His sickness made difficult to think straight, and the soreness to his throat made it hard to swallow and talk. Clouds in the sky were turning dark, but a warm breeze was in the air and rain began to drip down. The rain poured like a sprinkler and slowly began to douche the flames of his campfire.

Fearing it'll get cold again and turn the slush snow into ice, poor Clyde and Nathan had to move on again to find shelter. The man and horse walked across the frozen lake, at the middle of opening Nathan heard a hail of gunfire.

The shots were the sound of a shotgun loading as thunder, with a semi-auto deployment between firing.

When the man pulled his horse, Nathan slipped on the ice, landing on his buttocks. "Shit!" he hissed. He dropped the reins and straighten himself out, the gunshots continued in a long off distance, Nathan felt a bad feeling that some poor soul has crossed the path of Edith, yet he and his steed were too, cold, sick and tired to move rapidly. They really needed a dry place to sleep.

Off the lake, they found a hiking trail with old snow tracks belonging to a human. Nathan decided to go the opposite direction, in hopes, it would lead them to a road, a cabin, someplace better for his horse to walk on.

What felt like a horse with rain dripping on them the two found a public parking lot, connected to a plowed road, Nathan sighed in relief and followed the quiet road until they crossed a sign. Titled both in French and English, "Karby's Country peace lodge."

The man and horse continued down the road and found the lodge lobby building, the driveway wasn't plowed, a van was parked outside of the garage and no sign of light in the windows. However, the man notice smoke was steaming out of the chimney...someone had to be home.

As the man walked closer to the building, Clyde began to build up feeling some threat to this place.

Nathan tugged and pulled at his giant's reins and stopped next to the frost covered van where he tied them around the outside mirror.

"Don't have any money, just hope they'll show me charity," Nathan thought to himself.

At the door, a schedule dual notice was on the door's window, "lobby hours open Mon-Friday from 6am-8pm and Sat-Sunday from 6am-7pm."

Nathan took a deep breath, and struggled to clear his sore throat, and knocked at the door. No reply.

The man looked to the front windows of the porch and saw they were barricaded

"Damn it," he whispered and knocked numerous times.

"Can anybody hear me? I need help! I'm sick and I'm lost!"

Leaning his head to the solid oak door with a peephole, he could hear footsteps.

"Who's out there?!" yelled the person from the inside.

"I need help..." Nathan answered in his deep voice.

"Who is it?"

"Nathan!" he spat before coughing.

"Back away from the door!"

The man reversed to the steps and the door opened, in the dark opening, he saw a young

woman holding a shotgun with an injured man in a red uniform jacket.

They stared at one another before the girl broke the silence.

"Who are you?" asked

"I'm Nathan," he coughed, the heel of his boot fell down the edge of the step and the man fell back first in the snow.

The young lady rushed out, "You okay?"

The man in the Red mounted uniform grabbed her, "Come on back inside!"

"No, stop!"

"Please I need help," Nathan begged as he sat up.

"We need help too, but there's no electric here, we can't call anybody!"

"He doesn't look so good, officer," said the girl, "We should take him inside."

"No!" he replied.

"Please, sir…"

"How do we know he's not some…demon?!"

"The young girl sighed and looked at Nathan still sitting cold and wet in the snow, she stuck her hand out and helped him on his feet.

"Come inside."

"No!" Garzio tried to touch the girl but she shoved him away, "This is my family's house, you may be a cop, but my property my rules!"

The two walked in leaving the injured mounted cop on the porch.

Inside the dark house, the wood stove was burning with a pot of something boiling, and a fire lighting the living room, with a child sitting near it holding a cat.

Nathan knelt near the warmth hearth, removed his gloves then he placed his blacked tipped hands to the heat. After five minutes of warming up, he notices the kid was staring at him, and the girl was still arguing with the man named Garzio in the kitchen.

He walked in to ask the girl some questions.

"Might I ask who you guys are, miss?" asked Nathan.

"I'm Laurie, Laurie DeAnya and the kid is my little brother Ben," she answered, "why were you out with a horse?"

"I've been out for days…"

"I know who he is!" Garzio cut in, "He's a wanted criminal, we've been after you for weeks since Hawkesbury."

"He's a criminal?! What did he do?"

"Let me explain…"

"He's a murderer," Garzio answered, and Nathan's eyes almost sprung out like bubble gum.

"No, it wasn't like that!"

"You shut your mouth bastard! You got a lot of trouble on you!"

Without thinking, Nathan drew his .357 and cocked the hammer.

"Now listen here! I know what this is really about, about that cop in Hawkesbury, and I murdered no one in cold blood!"

Hearing crying the little boy ran to the teenage girl holding up her shotgun.

"You're still in trouble…"

"Shut up! Both of you!" Laurie cut in, "Sir, put down your gun."

"I...I... I can't there's some creature out there, I've been chasing it since New York... if you want my gun shoot me!"

"Creature!" Laurie said surprised, "You've seen it too!"

The girl turned to the mounted cop, and Nathan could see that something has happened with these people.

All enter the living room with Ben staying near his sister and Garzio by the back door. Nathan sat on the couch to the other side of the room.

Neither knew where to start so Nathan shared his story with the kids and cop. After his story that letter the trio shocked, Garizo then spoke.

"We picked up your trail, 30 miles south of here just outside of Timmins. Sergeant Jordan divided half of our troop and try and cut you off to the north.

We camped out on the other side of this lake, where...where..."

"What happened? Nathan asked.

"A... uh...what...it looked at first, looked to be a... woman..."

"Edith," Nathan whispered while gripping his sidearm.

"And just in a blink of an eye, killed our horse, and ripped my friend to pieces. I ran across the lake and slipped on the ice...that's how I sprained my arm, I found Jordan's camp I told him what happened, but he didn't believe, and

I desperately tried to get him to leave.... It was the night before she slaughtered Jordan and I had to run through the snow again, that's where I came across this lodge...Laurie's parent brought me inside."

The man turned Laurie where she spoke in.

"We lost power to the storm a couple of nights ago, our van's shot and then here came officer Garzio we saw how to hurt he was, I tried contacting help, but I couldn't get signal to my phone..."

"What happened to your mom and dad?"

As soon as he said that little Ben began to sib and his sister held him tighter.

"I... I don't know, mom and dad left for help yesterday," Laurie said. "They haven't been back since."

"Where's the nearest town?"

"Ollda airfield is 15 miles from here," Garzio answered, "we're on our own until somebody drives by here."

Chapter 29. Under siege.

That evening the trio excepted Nathan's trust, and Garzio helped him bring Clyde the horse inside the garage. They laid the poor horse down on a sleeping mattress Laurie brought down from the guest room.

All set and ate soup near the fireplace, the two kids fell asleep, Nathan drapes a blanket over them and stood watch with Garzio.

"So, is your arm hurt bad?"

"I think it's broken," the officer answered.

"Look, sir, I know... I'm in trouble but I'll help you if you help me."

"First we gotta get out of this place."

"Not with that... the thing outside," Nathan replied.

"Let us just hope Mr. and Mrs. DeAyna will get back here soon," the office saw Nathan had unfeasible expression, and he began to shake his head.

"Don't tell the kids...but I fear they won't be coming back."

Morning came with a bright sun, gleaming through the cracks of the boarded windows. Nathan awoke to the smell of coffee, he walked to find Laurie brewing it up in a tin can.

"Morning," she said.

"Hi, where's Garizo and Ben?"

"He went to the latrine out back and Ben's with your horse," she answered.

"Thank you for letting me in Laurie, I really appreciate that."

She just nodded and poured him a mug.

"Thanks, so is there any other guns in the house?" Nathan asked.

"Just my dad's shotgun, we had another one, but out folks left they took it with them," looking at the man's face he had watery eyes of panic.

"Maybe I'll make some tea later…"

"Thank you," Nathan took the black coffee and went into the garage where Ben was petting Clyde.

"I like your horse," the kid said.

"Thinks he's a Shire Draft."

"How big is he?"

"7'9" in length, 6' in height and weighs near a ton," said Nathan next to the kid. "He's a real giant."

"He doesn't look so good," Ben said.

"I know, we've been traveling in the snow forever… do you guys have any hay?"

"What?"

"Hay, straw, something I could feed him with?" he asked.

Ben replied, "No, but we have cheerios and some carrots!"

The kid got up ran to the kitchen and back with four carrots. Ben brought one up to the giant's mouth and Clyde took with great pleasure.

"Thanks, Ben," Nathan said.

"I like horses, can I ride him?"

"Not now, perhaps another time," Nathan said patting the kid's shoulder.

Nathan slowing sipped the hot cafe, that helped soothed his windpipe, Garzio walked inside, trying to tighten his self-made arm sling.

"Here, let me help," Nathan offered, and sat the cop down and adjusted his support into a cast, and took a bandage giving by Laurie to make as the new support around the neck, "Thanks," said the officer.

"Now, this might be a dumb question, but where's your radio?" Nathan asked.

"Back at the campsite. But I ain't going back there!"

"Never mind then… but you believe it right? … you know… the Wendigo?"

"Well, you've seen it, so I guess so unless we're both crazy, and if the parents don't come back, guess that proves the case…" Nathan shushed him fearing the kids might have heard that.

The men walked in the dining room where Ben was playing with action figures, and Laurie gnawing on a granola bar.

He watched the three people sit around the dining table and Nathan began to think... what if Garzio was right? He sat next to the Canadian cop and told everyone his proposition.

"All of the leave?"

"Yes," said Nathan, "I... I... don't think it's a good idea to stay here. Ollda airfield is our only safe haven."

"Well, do we get there?"

"You kids will ride on my horse, while Garzio and I can walk."

"For 30 miles?" said Garzio.

"And Mom and dad went for help, we should give them some time," said Ben.

Nathan glanced at the cop, "I know son, but if the weather gets bad again, more snow means no rescuing, we gotta get away from here."

"Why, we have a weeks' worth of food, firewood, the windows are sealed, I think we can manage," Laurie said.

"That not the point girl," Garzio said. "It's that... monster."

"Guns can kill it," Nathan stated and all three stared at the man.

"Wh... what?"

"No strong weapon can kill this...Wendigo, that's why we gotta get as far from here as possible we're sitting pray here."

"We can't leave at we should at least wait for our parents to return…"

"Laurie your parents are dead!"

"Hey!" Nathan yelled. Little Ben sat horrified and Laurie was stunned, she stormed upstairs holding her brother who began to sniff in tears.

"Shh, Ben, it's okay." after she left him in bed, she comforted to two adults arguing downstairs.

"Alright, out!"

"What? Garzio said, seeing Laurie holding the shotgun.

"Out! Both of you leave!" the girl demanded.

"You can't be…"

"Laurie, Garzio didn't mean to…"

"Shut up! Get your horse ride on and leave us!" Laurie said pointing the double barrel at him.

"Laurie, I can't leave you and little Ben here alone, come with us to Ollda," said Nathan. "Please, put the gun down."

She lowered the gun and when Garzio tried to walk up she ordered him to back off.

"We're not going anywhere," she said, "If you two wanna leave for the airfield go right ahead, but Benny and I are waiting here for mom and dad to bring help."

"Okay, fine… I not leaving you two here…we'll wait," Nathan said reluctantly.

"So, we're stuck here?" Garzio said.

"If you hadn't opened your big mouth," said Nathan.

"Don't talk back to an officer!"

"Worry not about my words, pal, worry about what's out there that killed your friends...we'll probably not get out of this place alive."

When nightfall came, Laurie was preparing another pot of soup, Garzio sat in the dining room, and

Nathan brought in his supply of Religious materials. While the two were in the kitchen they watched Nathan walk around with a bible and a stainless-steel flask.

"What the hell is he doing? Thought Garzio, he stood and asked the man.

"I'm cleaning the house," he answered.

"Cleansing the house?" asked Garzio.

"Yes, blessing it."

"Are you fucking kidding me?!"

"No. I know these things weakness..."

"A book? And a bottle of water?!"

"Holy Water," Nathan replied irritated.

"Oh, and what else? Build a shrine? Call and pray for a second coming?"

"Leave him alone," said Laurie.

"How the fuck is this going to help?"

"I told you! I know this monster's weakness, it's a demon that can't stand the relics of Christ," Nathan said.

"Really?" said Laurie.

"As I said, no bullet can kill this creature, but this could."

"Such bullshit!" Garzio said walking off. Laurie stepped up.

"Are you a priest?"

No, but I got this stuff from one, there's a spare Cross in my bag, you can have it, might protect you."

"If, bullets can't kill...that thing... Mom and Dad..." Laurie became worried and rushed towards Nathan's bag where she took out all the other equipment pieces. She found two cross necklaces and ran upstairs to give one to Ben. Garzio just sat on the couch annoyed. When Nathan walked in to bless the living room and place the second cross up on the fire mantel, the mounted trooper just staged.
"Wasting time here..."

Nathan stumped his foot and turned, "Look here! I'm trying to help, I only knew you for one night and so far, I'm the only man trying to do something to protect us, while you a police officer just lick your wound and complain like a baby."

"I'm gonna enjoy it when we arrest you Scotfield."

"Whatever!" Nathan replied.

Chapter 30. Panic scare.

A week past and it was near the end of February, after a series of snow, covered the road, with no signs of plows, or rescue. No phone signal and food supplies in the DeAyna pantry were going empty. Nathan and Ben would go out to stretch Clyde's legs to the frozen lake.

"You know, if we run out of the food, we could always icefish," Ben said.

"Good Thinking kid."

"Do you like fishing?"

"Oh yeah...used to have my own private charter," answered Nathan.

"Wow, I hope to get my own boat one day," Ben said patting Clyde's neck.

"I hope you will too...what would you like to be when you grow up?"

"I love animals...I think I wanna be a veterinarian when I grow up." When he said that Nathan paused and stared into space.

"Um, are you okay? Mr. Scotfield?"

"Huh? Oh yeah... veterinarian, that's a great job, let's go check the dock out." He said changing the topic, the old wooden dock was built near an old metal shanty with a canoe leaning against it and an upside-down flatboat.

"Do you guys come up to this lodge every winter?" he asked the kid.

"No, usually we stay here during our summer vacations, dad had a job up here to fix some airplanes since he was going to work all through Christmas, he decided to bring us all up here."

Nathan stared at the boy for a bit and looked back to the lake.

"Nathan? It's not true is it?" Ben asked.

"What?"

"Mom and Dad? They're okay...you think?"

The man had a worried look, with a mix of guilt and sadness. Then only answered, "I... I don't know son."

Nathan took the boy and mounted him on top of Clyde's saddle, which placed a smile on the poor boy's face. Unknown to both humans and horse, the monster was watching them just across the ice-bound lake.

Night came with a snowfall, it was peaceful, and calm, with only the sound of snoring coming from the living room of the DeAnya's cabin, with their fire nearly burned out.

The siblings slept next to each other with Laurie gripping little Ben's hand, Garzio was asleep on their father's chair and Nathan who was supposed to be on watch fell asleep in the garage with Clyde.

"Little Ben."

He opened his eyes, and sat up, he thought it was Laurie up she was sound asleep, he pulled his hand away and walked to the toilet, when he heard a sound.

He walked to the front window an heard the sound of foot crunching in the snow, he walked to the garage to get Nathan but heard a voice cry out.

"Benny?!" the boy heard the voice of a woman, a voice whom he had immediately recognized.

"Mom?" he said, walking towards the door, he stopped to peek through the boarded window but the ice on the glass blurred out the face, but she saw someone out there.

"Mom? Is that you?"

"Yes, Ben it's me let me in!" answered from the outside. Slowly the boy began to unlock the door. And just as he was to unlock the knob, he was graded from behind by his sweater.

He yelped and before his mouth was palmed by Nathan.

"Shh, quiet," whispered Nathan wrapping his right arm around him, lifting him off the floor.

"Ben? Honey?" the woman said knocking on the door while turning the knob.

"Laurie, Garzio wake up."

"What the hell?" Garzio said.

"What is it?" Laurie said trying to pull her brother away from Nathan.

"It's mom, she's outside!" said Ben.

"No, no it's not her!" yelled Nathan, the four heard the continuing knocking and the lady yelling both for both kids.

"How do you know?" Laurie asked.

"It's the monster, it shapeshifts!" said Nathan, Garzio felt scared and grabbed the fire poker.

"Alright upstairs, now," before Laurie could object, Garzio shoved her, and Nathan carried her brother upstairs, she followed. As she walked upstairs, she listened to the continuous knocking and crying from outside.

"Laurie! Ben! Please let me in!"

The girl paused, 'what if he's wrong' she thought.

"That's mom."

"Laurie come on!" Nathan took her hand.

All went into the master bedroom where they kept the priest supplies and the shotgun, lit only with two lanterns.

"Nathan, that's my mom," Ben said, the man turned to the child with a sad glance.

"No son, that what it wants you to think...your mom is gone," Nathan went downstairs.

"Where the hell are you going?!" Garzio said. He watched Nathan rush to the garage. He closed and locked the door.

"Give me the shotgun."

The two kids and cop stood in the far corner of the bedroom, away from the door and window, they could hear a noise in the distance, sounds of, footsteps, whimpering and crying. The woman got in the cabin.

"Laurie? Ben? Where are you?" their mother called.

Laurie wanted to answer, but Garzio ordered her to shut up. To the bedroom door, the lady began jerking at the knob, followed by loud banging.

"Laurie? Please, it's mom!"

Laurie stood feeling worried, "Mom?"

"Yes, let me in, please! I need help!"

Laurie walked over the bed, towards the door, Garzio tried to stop her but the pain of his arm prevented him from grabbing her.

"Mom? Where's a dad?" she asked standing, against the door.

"He went for the airfield, and I'm hurt, please let me in!"

Laurie turned towards her brother… then unlocked the door.

Their mother was plumped on the floor, sniffing in tears. Ben claimed on top the bed, with excitement in seeing his mother again. She was wearing the same clothes, coat and sweater she wore when she left. Laurie helped her on her feet her mother was white, with a red bleeding nose, where the blood was frozen to her lips and her hair was frozen like ice sickles.

"Oh, Christ mom what happened?!" she asked.

"Get back!" Nathan yelled, as he entered the bedroom, with one hand wielding the cross, and a torch in the other.

"Who are you?" their mother asked.

Nathan turned to the girl, "Laurie back away!"

"It's my mom!" she yelled.

"No… it's her… Edith," Nathan said, as he walked closer to the woman, he held the cross to her face making her step back to the bed.

 "Will you stop it!" the infuriated Laurie cried.

He saw the woman get on the bed and wrapped her arms around the little Ben, in panic waved Nathan flew into a rage.

"Ben no!" he shoved Laurie to the floor, dropped the cross and pulled the boy away by his arm, "Shoot it Garzio!" He demanded.

The cop hesitated and the woman stared blankly at him like a puppy, and Ben began to cry, When the mother tried to stand and reach out for the child, Nathan drew his side arm, then the room was deafened by a loud bang.

Garzio stood def and disoriented, as he stared down at the woman bleeding from the head, with her bleed oozing all over the wall and sheets.

The officer then looked to Nathan who stood pointing his pistol with steam smoking from the barrel.

The room was again deafened by the screams of the two children, after witnessing the murder of the mom.

Garzio was stunned, feeling the blood splatter on his face. He saw both Ben and Laurie crying together on the floor, with Nathan standing expressionless. He killed their mother.

"What have you done?!" Garzio said.

Nathan just looked at the man as he lowered his weapon, he then looked down at the kids crying near his boots, under the light of his torch.

Before he could explain, Nathan heard Garzio pump his shot gun, he looked, and the officer was aiming at him. In a flash, Nathan turned and ran for the stairs, Garzio fired a round with a buckshot piercing his shoulder.

The man jumped downstairs, and ran out of the house, in the cold snowy forest. He paused against a tree, dropping to his knees, weeping in guilt.

As the man sat in the snow, wrapped with the guilt he began to think… "Am I crazy…have I gone mad? Yes, I'm evil…I'm a killer… there was no Wendigo… there were no werewolves and it was me I killed my brother… I'm the killer!"

He said all this aloud fearing he had lost his mind the entire time he'd wondered the wilderness. That moment Nathan gave up, as he laid back, hoping to die in the cold, his life flashed with all his happy times. Through his life from a millionaire to a simple farmer, now a cold killer, Nathan was ready to die.

He blacked out in the snow as he sat agaist the tree, just waiting for it to end.

Chapter 31. A cold immoral surprise.

Dawn came with Garzio sitting on top of the staircase, fearing that Nathan might return he stood alert, ready to shoot the man on a sight. He left the two kids to have some mourning in the room where he draped a sheet over their dead mother's corps.

Ben had stopped crying and just knelt in silence, but Laurie continued to weep despair, for such in appalling sight for a son and daughter to witness the shooting death of their mom.

The cop peeked through the bedroom door and watched the poor children kneeling at the foot of the bed, he then walked downstairs where he'd blocked the door with a heavy deck table. Outside the sun broke through over the mountains reflecting from the shiny snow, the Canadian trooper made for the garage where the horse stood.

The man thought a while, since they now had the horse, he and the kids could now ride their wat to Ollda, but with Nathan still be out there, the fear once again clouded the officer's mind and so he decided that he and kids should stay and again wait it out, maybe Mr. DeAnya did make to the airport.

Meanwhile outside in the woods not far from the house, Nathan had survived the night, he awoke and was covered head to toe with snow and was soaked like a washcloth. As he stood to brush the frost off his coat, the man felt a strange bump on his lower shoulder, where Garzio shot him, upon retching behind he could feel the lump of frozen blood from the buckshot wound.

Nathan dumbstruck and guilt-ridden, for not dying from his wound or the freezing cold, the man drew his pistol, cocked back the hammer and was ready to up and end his pathetic life once and for all. As he slowly brought the gun to his skull something from afar caught his eye. He lowered his weapon and decided to look. In the snow, he found patch of frozen blood in a trail of snow prints. And upon closer examination the slightly buried in footprints were not in the shape of human feet all too familiar to Nathan's memory.

And that wasn't all, for the trail that led from the house, Nathan discovered more blood and the remains of a grown man, tattered clothes, blood and body parts were all over snow. And from the trunk of a dead tree he found a frozen body of a woman. The disgruntled man shivered and trembled as he stared at the face of the lady who had the same face of the woman, he'd shot dead last night. It was Mrs. DeAnya, the poor woman was stripped naked, her throat was slashed out, with flesh tissue ripped her, arms, legs, and backsides. Both her and her husband were eaten alive.

"OH shit! Laurie!" Nathan then realized that he was right, and that it was Edith last night all along. He turned and hurried his way back to the house.

Back inside up in the bedroom Garzio walked in and kneeled next to the kids.

"'I'm sorry kids… really I am," none of the two replied and just snuggled closely together, still mourning to their loss, As Garzio lowered his head for a moments silence, the dead woman arise from the bed.

The three looked up, horrified as the dead body sat up on the mattress. The corps of Mrs. DeAnya grew into a strange tall form, pulling down the sheet, exposing something the three could only imagine in their worst nightmares. From their mother transformed into a face of an old woman with the body of a partly covered skeleton with stretched mangled like arms covered in decaying pale flesh. The face of the creature smiled to the trio as they stared and slowly stepped away.

"Awe, come now little ones, is that any way to behave to your mother?" Edith mocked in the voice of Mrs. DeAnya.

"Run," Garzio told the kids. Laurie and Ben fled from the room, and ran downstairs, Garzio stood no chance as he stayed to protect the kids, he raised the shot gun, but the wendigo snatched it out of his hands. Now defenseless, the officer stared into the dead eyes of the grinning man-eater and began to cry.

Since the front and back entrances were blocked, Laurie and Ben made for the cellar, as the kids made their way downstairs, they heard the cries of screams of the policemen being dismembered by Edith.

When they realized there was no other way out of the cabin's basement, Laurie slapped herself in self-guilt, realizing she'd gotten Ben and herself cornered.

"Oh, Benny? Laurie? Where are you?" Edith called in their mother's voice; it was an echoing voice that scared the crapped out of both kids.

"I know you're down there," Edith taunted sadistically, "I'm coming for you two and I'm hungry."

 The kids were deafened by a pitch whizzing screeches, from atop the Wendigo broke through the floor and crawled into the basement. Laurie and Ben retreated to the corner near the furnace, cut off from the stairs.

Climbing off the ceiling with her long appendages, topped with disfigured finger with hook like claws, the monster, dropped to te floor and clawed up to the kids with the head of officer Garzio between its jaws.

Slowly she bit down at the skull, blood squirted on Laurie and Ben, both crawled far against the wall, as the thing swallowed the crushed skull. Ben began sobbed so helpless with his sister holding tightly. As they sat holding one another Laurie equally scared and helpless, was staring deep into the beast's deviled eyes, and that moment she could hear the cries and screams of her

parents and imagining the horrid fate she and little Ben
will share with them.

The Wendigo's head shapeshifted back to the old woman's
face, she smiles with blood on her chin and laughed
hysterically.

"Oh, just lovely...the cries of children...brings such joy to
me," Edith stated coming closer. "Time to die meat."

She took Ben from his sister's arms, the boy screamed,
Laurie tried to fight it but the monster pinned her to the
corner with her long skeletal arm. Edith brought Ben closer
to her mouth and began to lick the boy with her long lizard
tongue, her human mouth soon grew into long deer
shaped snout wit crooked sharp fangs. Slowly it opened
up, and Ben just saw a dark hole of its throat, which was
hike a whole with rows of yellow sharp teeth. The kid
closed his eyes, with his final hope for it to be a quick
death.

Suddenly Nathan stormed in the cabin, he followed the
blood trail of Garzio, leading to the basement, with his gun
and cross he found on the floor the man ran down and
found Edith, and the two kids. To his horror poor Ben was
about to be chomped to death he placed aside his pistol
and took out his flask of blessed liquid.

"Hey Bitch Demon!"

Before Edith placed the child in her mouth, she felt
something burning. The monster paused and felt her back
was burning with skin melting off her spin, she let out an
agonizing howl, dropped Ben and releasing Laurie.

Before the beast knew it, Nathan jumped on top splashing more Holy water on her face resulting her right eye melting from its sockets.

"Looks like you can feel pain after all?!" spat Nathan, has he held the monster by her ears. "Kids run, get out of here, save yourselves!" Nathan yelled to the kids, Laurie scooped her brother on her arms and ran upstairs where they fled on the road. And began to run the entire way to Ollda.

As the children escaped the man and Wendigo wrestled around the basement, crashing into tables, shelves, chairs, and tools, it backs into the walls and ceiling, trying get the human off its back, but Nathan held with all his might. When the man used the last of the Holy water, he reached for the cross he had on his belt. Then like a dagger he plunged the True Cross of Christ into the man-eater's back.

It boiled its blood, sizzled its skin and made the monster scream with a woman's voice. Edith reached back and grabbed Nathan's boot and pulled him off. She took Nathan by his coat and placed his head into her mouth, but the stole vestment that Nathan scarfed around his neck protected him from the Wendigo's mouth. Wrapped all the pain Edith threw Nathan toward the Furnace and ran off upstairs with the cross sticking out of her back.

It made a break for it; but Nathan ran after it. Upon running upstairs, he watched the beast run for the lake in broad daylight, he made for the garage where Clyde stood

ready for his master, after opening the door, he mounted his steed.

"Giddy-up!" he commanded and Nathan road off, in pursuit. From road, still running, Laurie saw Nathan and Clyde chasing after the monster on the ice. After a brief moment she hoped the best for Mr. Scotfiled and continued her was to the airfield with her brother.

Ridding on the lake not far behind the fleeing demon, Nathan could see the smoke steaming off the monster's hide.

"Scared of me now huh bitch!" he yelled. "yah!"

The horse galloped casually, and his master rode him onto the water bank where he can run more faster and avoid slipping on the ice.

He followed and followed down the lake trail and past the sign the read 'Minshika creek falls.'

The Wendigo struggled to run any faster since it was now half blinded, and was burning on the right shoulder, rendering her limb useless. The cross in her body felt like a hive of hornets stinging all over her but now she was more afraid of the hunter than anything. It just limped down the ice-covered lake. Unaware of the dead end ahead.

Chapter 32. Death Falls.

Edith kept to the ice limping in pain until it stopped at the frozen edge of a waterfall, atop a 70-foot drop, and before the monster knew it. Nathan and his horse came from the woods.

The man dismounted the giant, where the two cut the monster off any chance of fleeing in the forest. Thus, the Wendigo must fight her way.

"Where you gonna go now Bitch?!" Nathan taunted, "Come on! Fight! kill me! Finished what you've started…. Let's end this."

The man drew his bowie knife and the monster charged, whacking Nathan off his feet. She lifted him by the legs and body slammed him down on the ice.

After being slammed, Nathan stuck his knife in Edith's deformed hove-like foot, nailing her in the ice surface.

The pain made the wendigo squeeze his leg, once again breaking his right tibia, Nathan let out a scream, he took out the half-empty flask of blessed water and splashed the hove. Setting it ablaze.

In a painful rage, she picked Nathan up again and was about to throw him off the cliff, but Clyde charge and shoved the Wendigo on its side, knocking it down. Nathan crawled to safety as his horse stumped on the beast with his heavy horseshoes. After a struggle, Edith slashed the horse with her claws, cutting Clyde's throat open.

It stunned Nathan to the heart after his horse made a final whine, Clyde turned and gave the Wendigo a strong back kick before retreating into the woods.

Natan watches as his companion Clyde disappear, he then turned to the injured monster struggling to pick itself up. In the snow he saw the True cross of Christ, the man sprinted with his injured leg, grabbed it and claimed over the monster.

Nathan was over the monster, held the cross over his head and down he stabbed the wooden remnant into its chest piercing its small heart. Edith dug her claws into Nathan's back as she rolled tumbled over the ledge. Over the side and down the icy waterfall the man and beast fall hard on boulder where Nathan broke his neck.

The monster next to him sat up with the cross burning into its heart, with steam lines rolling off her body simmered of the burning flesh. It let out the cries and screams as Edith's entire body began burn off the bones. The wind blows the ash into the mist, leaving the skeleton sitting bare and lifeless, the beast is dead. And then in a flash the skeleton shattered like glass into the cracks between the rocks and ice. After watching the decay of the monster, Nathan felt so relieved and triumph but suddenly realized he was unable to move.

He was paralyzed.

Chapter 33. Hospitalized.

Joey was shaken by the shoulder, and the exact moment he opened his eyes in the dark cave lit by moonlight from the entrance, he realized that he was human again.

"Joseph." he heard her voice and turned.

He looked to Lizzy, who was kneeling next to him and could barely see the shape of her pregnant human form. They had no more fur, no long snout with sharp teeth, no black paw pads, or tails. They were now free from their giant werewolf bodies. When the couple stumped and walked over the sleeping pack, some wolves awoke followed the two humans out of the cave but didn't attack them along with Tasha.

"Okay… Where do we go? What do we do?" she asked in a panicked tone since she was concerned about their situation, being stuck cold, naked and lost in the snow-covered forest.

And the man just answered, dumbfoundedly, "I don't know...oh wait!" He just remembered the farmstead that was not far from their cave, and that was their best and pretty much only bet into getting help.

They began their way through the woods, leaving the pack howling goodbye to them, Tasha took the lead as they wondered barefooting in knee high snow. The sub-freezing temperature quickly got onto their exposed bodies, they could barely feel their feet and movement of their toes.

As they marched along a hunting trail, Joe quickly grabbed Liz from tripping down in the front, he picked her up and carried her the whole way to the farm buildings.

It took two miserable hours with the sun rising in the east, but they finally made it across a road with Joe's feet bleeding and burning from the rock salt on the pavement. Fearing what might come all he thought that moment was getting his mate and baby to safety.

A farmer's wife in the kitchen was preparing breakfast when she notices someone was coming. She pushed back the curtains and notice the two strangers approaching, shocked and puzzled she called her husband and showed him the coming nude couple followed by a dog.

"What the hell? Should I grab my gun?" he asked.

"No... somethings up," his wife answered, and she made her way to the front door.

"Maude what are you doing?!" her husband yelled, "I'm calling the police." the wife did not object as she slowly opened the door and saw the naked man holding the pregnant woman stop.

"Hello, uh bonjour... who are you?" the lady asked peeking out the door. The naked man holding a naked woman stopped in his path they were both trembling and shaking in cold and embarrassment. The Ridgeback hound also stopped and let out a light bark followed by pleading moans.

"Oh, Ma'am please... we need help," Lizzy said seeing how Joseph was out of breath, she had him put her down and she took a few steps forward with both her hands covering her baby belly, then said, "We were kidnapped."

"What in world are you two doing out here?!" Maude asked opening the door the whole way, "come inside."

The husband walked in the living room, "Okay darling, I called the cops... he paused in surprise as the naked couple standing idle in the front entrance of his house, with his wife giving them fresh wool blankets from their laundry basket.

"Maude what are you doing!"

"Oh goodness Edwin, these two-need help look at her, she's pregnant!" realizing how sick and poor they looked, Edwin went back to the phone to request an ambulance.

"Come now please, sit down," said Maude, she sat to the two down in the warm living room where a fire roared in the chimney. Liz laid on the couch as Joe just crashed on Edwin's recliner, he signed in relieved, finally off his bleeding plants.

"Oh my, you need a doctor young man..." Maude said before Edwin interrupted.

"Don't stress I just called an ambulance, now tell me who are you two? And what were you two doing out there?" the old man said placing his wrists on his waist.

Joe and Liz looked to one another unsure what to say. Joe took a moment and right before he said anything Liz answered first.

"I'm Elizabeth Wallstone of the Utica police department," Lizzy answered, "and this is my boyfriend Joseph Scotfield, we were kidnapped."

"Kidnapped?! Oh my!" said Maude. "oh God... please come inside."

It wasn't long when the police and EMS arrived, seeing the bad condition of Joe's feet that was now swollen.

They rushed the couple to the hospital, and all the cops got from the two were their names and so they immediately got in contact with the Canadian Security Intelligence Service in Ottawa. The Canadian authorities then got into contact with American detective Matt Geyer, the investigator from the New York Police department in Albany.

Three days in hospital care in the same room together, they were washed, warmed up, dressed, well fed, with the assurance that their baby is safe. Detective Geyer and two Canadian cops were led in by the doctor.

"Joseph Scotfield? Corporal Elizabeth Wallstone?" the New York cop asked.

"Yes." both answered.

"I'm sergeant Matt Geyer, New York Police department, and this here is Wayne Wardell from Toronto and Pier

Durant from Ottawa, both from the CSIS." the three men shook the couple's hands and sat down.

"Did… you find my brother?" Joseph asked.

"No, but we've been looking for him," Wardell answered. "He's a wanted man."

"What?!" Joe said frightened.

"We're all here because we've been investigating the suspected cross-country murders of your brother, Nathan," Geyer said.

"What? Murder?" Joseph asked." no you got it…it can't be…"

"We've also been trying to track you two down since the disappearance of police Capitan Francis and murdered locals of Graytown."

"My brother didn't murder anyone."

"Well that still needs to be proven in a court of law, but we have a good reason, Dr. Scotfield," Geyer replied.

"Nathan was just trying to save us!" Elizabeth said.

"Look, son, we're sorry to share such sad news, but both of you shouldn't panic, you're not the ones in trouble, you two are victims. It's been months and now we have a lead, we need answers," Wardell said. "Now you two are here and alive, you're our only lead into finding Nathan."

"We don't know where he is," said Elizabeth. Geyer looked to Durant.

"Okay… well we're not just here to find Nathan," said Geyer sipping on his cup of coffee, "but we also wanna know what has happened with you two since your disappearance."

"The doctors and the old farm couple informed us that you said that you two were kidnapped," said Durant.

"Yea…uh yeah, we were," stuttered Joseph.

"Well, in any case. We need to know because we're not only looking for your brother, but we also need to locate an old woman," Geyer said, "A Graytown deli own named Edith Ester."

After seeing the last known photograph of the villainess who started this whole chaos, the two stared at the investigators for a minute before Joe felt Liz nudged his arm.

"Joseph?" Lizzy said, "let's tell them." Joe nodded his head; they were ready to answer their questions. Since the time of their recovery both suspected they would be questioned by the police eventually, so they were prepared to answer questions only in a half-truth. Knowing they would never believe the werewolf and wendigo parts; they were ready to stir up some lies.

"It's been over three months since I last saw Nathan and you guys still haven't found him yet?" said Joe.

"We've had a lot of reports of sightings, from Hawkesbury Quebec where a cop said he was handcuffed by your brother and far past to Lake Timiskaming Ontario, where police found an old priest's house destroyed," Durant said. "The mounted police have been on the hunt for him, since then and they picked up his trail North East of Timmins, it's amazing that he survived so long through the winter."

"So, we hope they'll find him eventually, and I'm afraid he has to be apprehended because he's got a lot to answer for, "Geyer added, "but in the meantime, you have to tell us what you know."

"Very well, "Joseph said.

Chapter 34. Police Interview.

Joseph was taken to a private room to be questioned first. All sat in a round table with hot cups of coffee.

"Alright Joseph, this is Detective Wayne Wardell of the Toronto Police department, investigating the manhunt for suspected murderer Nathan Scotfield. With New York Detective Matthew J. Geyer and Ontario inspector Pier Durant.

Today is February 28th, 2019. In Suebury hospital, Ontario Canada.

Here to question Joseph Scotfield, brother of Nathan Scotfield."

Wardell said in his recorder.

"Now please tell us, Joe, what happened that night back in November, when it all began?"

"It... It began when three Graytown residences abducted me," Joseph started. "I came to Graytown to help my brother around the farm since his leg was injured."

"You were kidnapped?"

"Yes."

"We were informed that when you were taken to the hospital you told the cops that you two were kidnapped, kidnapped by who and where exactly?"

"I was outside behind my brother's barn and three men, just pounced me, I never learned their names."

"You never learned their names?" Geyer asked looking to the other investigators, "okay well... maybe when we're done with this, I have photographs and portrait of the other victims, the people of Graytown...We'll show them to you see if you recognize them, okay?"

"Okay. So like I said... it was three locals from town they took me to the deli, the 'Bloody rose deli.' Where they locked me in a cage in the basement."

"Can you describe what this basement looked like?" Geyer said, "because we have photos of that place as well."

"It was like a dungeon. Horrible," answered Joe, "they dragged me down in the room where they cut up the meat, there were Satanic markings on the walls, pentagram that I believe was written in blood, there were chains drilled into the concrete walls, chains and meat hooks hanging from the ceiling and small animal cages where they locked me into one them."

"They latterly locked you in one of those cages?" Geyer said.

"Yes," Joe said.

"What were they planning on doing to you? Did you know?" the NY detective asked.

"I kept asking, I tried to talk to these crazy people, but they would only beat me, they threatened me, and said they were going to make me one of them," Joseph said, "What I believe the whole thing was a Satanic cult."

"So, you think they've kidnapped you to make you become a member?"

"I think so yeah," Joe said keeping good eye contact with the man, he knew Geyer was reading him, watching for any sign of a lie.

"How long did they keep you in the cage?"

"Hours I believe, I had no watch and there was no clock, I was just like in like a circus animal cramped in a tiny cage. They left me alone for a while then two men came, one I think was an employee of the deli and they told me they were planning to kill my brother."

"Why would they want to kill your brother?" Durant asked.

"Since my brother moved to Graytown, he told me most of the residents weren't the very welcoming type, and they treated my brother like an outcast. I kept trying to talk him into moving back to the city or move to Vermont with me…. he just wouldn't listen."

"All right so, back in this basement in the animal cage, what else happened that night?" Wardell said.

"The same two men and woman, Edith Ester, came down with a dead policeman…"

"Dead policemen?" Wardell interrupted.

"Yes, it was one of the guys from Elizabeth's station. Wasn't Francis though.

"Was it Merv?" Geyer asked.

"Yeah! Yeah, that's it Oliver Merv."

"What happened to him?"

"He was stabbed multiple times by the cultist, they laid him on a cutting table and stabbed him in the stomach, chest, and back. When they left us again, I discovered, Merv was still alive."

"He...He was still alive?"

"Yes, there was nothing I could do, and I tried, yelling and calling for help, and Ester came down where she had her followers beat me again."

"So, you were beaten and then what?" asked Geyer.

"I don't know how long, maybe hours, I was trapped and Merv died from the stab wounds. Elizabeth came down, she got me out."

Joseph paused.

"Go on?" said Durant."

"I think it's time you talk to Liz and hear her part of it."

"Why? What happened? You can go on," Durant said in a demanding voice.

"Actually boys, let's stop for a second," Geyer said, he took the two Canadian detectives out in the main hallway.

"So, what do you make of it?" Durant asked.

"Well I believe he has no clue where his brother might be and I don't think he had anything to do with the Graytown murders," Geyer replied, "let's finish this up and we'll talk with officer Wallstone."

The three men sat around Joe, to hear what else he had.

"Well like I said, Elizabeth came down, to save me, and when we claimed the stairs to get out. Ester and the butcher had her sister."

"Sister?"

"Yeah, Lidia. Liz pulled out her gun and demanded that they let us go. The butcher drew a knife and held it to her sister's neck throat."

"So, they kidnapped her sister?" Wardell asked.

"So, we thought," Joe stated.

"Ester ordered Liz to drop the gun, she did so, but it turned out Lidia was part of the colt all along. And they locked us back in the basement."

"Christ," said Wardell turning to Durant.

"And naturally we tried to break out, but the door was made of heavy metal, we were both trapped downstairs."

"So, you two are locked down there, how exactly did you get out?"

"Well, it was Erin…Lizzy's niece…."

"Was she a cult member too?" Durant interrupted.

"I suppose, we didn't ask any questions, she unlocked the door and we snuck out. Erin stayed behind to buy us time, we never saw her again."

When Joseph paused a minute, Wardell and Durant were stunned, and Geyer was still trying to put all the pieces in his head, looking at the young man he felt that he was lying, but his tone, demeanor, and eye contact. He decided to question Elizabeth now.

She was brought in on a wheelchair in the same room, Joseph requested to stay with her, but they wanted just her to talk with. So, after Durant walked Joe out Geyer questioned.

"So, officer Wallstone looks like you and Dr. Scotfield had some rough time."

"You have no idea," she replied rubbing her belly.

"Hard to imagine the horror and torment you both had to go through," Wardell said, "Describe what happened that November night when you and your two colleagues were dispatched."

"Well, Joseph…I mean Nathan called and told that his brother had been kidnapped. So, we arrived at his farm, I can't remember the exact time, but it was late and ark.

Captain Francis sent us Merv and I out to go look around, it was a real cold night with of snow on the ground.

We followed the tracks leading from the back of Scotfield's barn using our flashlights because it was pitch black. We kept on going until we realized the snow prints were leading us right into town."

"Did you know what happened with Francis and Merv?" Wardell cut in.

"I never learned what had happened to Francis.do you?"

"He's dead," Geyer said.

A tear dropped out from Lizzy's eye socket, "What happened? She asked after a moment of silence.

"The decorated police captain...was torn to pieces," said Geyer. "Mutilated."

"You may continue Officer Wallstone," said Durant.

"Well...it's only going to get worst... the story."

"Tell us, please," pleated Geyer.

"As we made our way to the town, some men from the town ambushed us, I lost my flashlight and Merv and I got separated," Lizzy said, speaking only in a half-truth. "I heard my friend calling out, but he was already gone, I chased after them blindly through the woods, where I saw them take my friend down into 'Bloody Rose deli."

"And that's where and how you've found Joseph," Durant stated.

"Yes."

"So, is it true? What your sister and niece being members of that… Satanic cult thing?"

"I afraid it is," Liz replied.

"And you never knew?" said Wardell.

"No. Ever since Lidia married Brad and moved to that awful town, I saw less and less of her."

"Do you know what probably motivated these cult members in kidnapping Dr. Scotfield."

"I don't know why… That night… it was all horrible, what they did o Merv, Joe, and my sister being involved it was a nightmare." said Lizzy concealing her crying.

"When… you enter the deli, found Joseph, what happened?" Geyer said.

"Come on did Joe tell you that part?!" she yelled.

"Can you please answer us?" Geyer asked.

Wardell whispered, "Maybe we should stop…." when all the sudden Liz interrupted.

"I had my gun, I entered the building followed the bloodstained stairs down to the basement, where I found both Merv and Joseph!" she yelled. "Merv was dead and as I tried to get Joseph out, we were trapped by my own sister and that bitch Ester. Long story short they tricked me into dropping my gun, we were locked down there for God knows how long until my niece Erin came. She unlocked the door and helped us escape!"

"So, your niece helps you out of basement chamber thing, what happened when you both got out of the deli?" Geyer asked.

"We went out the back exit. I told Erin to come with us, and I tried taking her hand, but she pushed me away and just told us to run..."

Geyer looked to the other detectives.

"Elizabeth... I'm afraid your niece is dead," Geyer said regrettably, the woman dropped her head, and began to cry. The New York Detective decided to stop and let the young woman recuperate when the three men left the room, Joseph approached them.

"Is Lizzy okay?" Two of the men tried to shoo him away but Geyer leads him in to comfort the woman. When Joe knelt next to Liz the man turned and saw Geyer standing in the doorway.

When the man closed the door behind him, he sat on the other side of the table, "Look. Dr. Scotfield, Officer Wallstone, I don't mean to pry, I know you both had it rough. But I feel unsatisfied. I need to learn more."

"Well, what the hell else do you want from us?!" Lizzy raised her voice.

"I want to know what else happened that night, where you two have been, and... uh why were you both found ... um naked in the snow," Geyer explained, determined to get somewhere.

Both look to one another and decided to finish their half-truth story together, "That evening when we ran from the deli, we were just trying to get away from the cult, as far as we could." Lizzy said.

"We were lost in the woods, until the following morning, we found our way back to Nathan's house where we found in on fire."

"Did you know who caused the fire?" Geyer said.

The couple turned to each other, Joe shrugged his shoulders, "No, do you know?"

"We have reason to believe that it was your brother who did it," Geyer said. Joe was stunned. The detective looked to Liz then said, "Sadder still, we recovered the remains of Brad Kess ... and his son Josiah Kess, both were shot dead by a 308 Winchester bullet. The same caliber used to kill the rest of the people of Graytown."

Liz broke down crying, Joseph sheds tears from his eyes, "and my brother had a 99. Savage rifle. He really did kill those people."

"I'm really sorry Elizabeth," Geyer said. "Would you like us to leave and come back another day?"

"No… let's finish the story. And get through with this," Said Liz. With that Geyer called back the two other detectives, who sat back down with the recorder.

"After searching around Nathan's house, we tried calling for help on the police car radio, but all were severely busted," said Liz. "With no other option, we decided get out of Graytown and go for help."

"And when we took to the street that evening, we ended up getting caught by Ester's follower, and that's how we got kidnapped," Joseph lied, "Ester held us at gunpoint and sent her men out to hunt for Nathan."

"So, she sent out all her followers, being the one we found dead, after your brother," Geyer said taking out some photographs of the identified victims. "Was it just Ester holding you two captives?"

"Yes, sir," Said Elizabeth. Geyer showed the couple copies of the pictures.

"At gunpoint?" said the investigator.

"Yes," answered Joseph.

"And you think all of these towns folks were some sort of cult?" Said Wardell.

"Yes, I believe so, this guy here was the deli butcher," Joe said with the picture of Anthony. "He was one of the men who gave me a beaten and locked me in the dog cage. And your saying Nathan killed him?"

"And a whole lot more, we found at least 10 other bodies, all the folks from Graytown, found miles in the woods, all shot with the same rifle caliber, stripped naked and burned."

"I could never imagine. Nathan doing such things like that," Joe said nervously.

"It's tragic, but anyone is capable of committing murder," Geyer said, "so back with the story with the leader Miss Ester where did she take you two?"

"She drove us up to the mountains, to my brother in law's hunting cabin," Lizzy lied.

"In the snow?" Wardell asked.

"Yep," said Joey. "she held us up there for over two months."

"Where is this cabin, exactly?" Geyer asked curiously.

"It's a place in the Apica hunting acres, west of Woodgate," Lizzy answered, "I use to live there with Lidia and Brad before I entered the Police academy."

"And how long exactly where you guys held there?"

Joe and Liz look at each other and shrugged their shoulders, "Like I said at least two months, she wouldn't talk to us or give us any information. She would always have us in her sight, keep us tied up in bed and would barley feed us."

"What would she feed you? And how did you two get to Canada?" Durant asked.

"She would feed us raw meat, and uncooked food she took from the deli," answered Joe.

"The place had no electric or running water, and she didn't want to leave us to go outside for firewood because," added Lizzy.

 "And when food was out and Edith heard no word or sign for any of her followers, she became more and more paranoid. And I told her that Nathan was gonna come after her," Joe said. "So perhaps around Early or in the middle of December, she forced us in her vehicle, and drove back to Graytown to a house owned by one of her followers."

"And what happened there?" Wardell asked Joseph.

"We didn't stay long, perhaps a week or less, when the roads were plowed, we left by car again. She had Elizabeth tied in the back seats and made me drive us across the Canadian border."

"Now in Canada, where did she take you?"

"To the middle of nowhere," Joseph replied. "She made keep driving and driving until dark, where she told me to stop and get Elizabeth out of the trunk."

"She marched us far away from the road to an isolated area, "added Liz, "and made us remove our clothes."

"She... so she literally, left you both out naked in the cold?" Wardell asked stunned, the couple nodded.

"She left us to die, we hike through the snow and that's where and how we came across the old farmer couple. We made it out alive."

After a minute of silence, Geyer felt they had more to share and the two other detectives had more questions, but everyone was just quiet.

"So… that's all?" Geyer broke the silence.

"Pretty much," Joe and Liz said together.

The story for the investigators seemed considerable, realistic, traumatizing and tragic. They couldn't get any more out of the couple and

decided to leave them be, Geyer was more satisfied, mostly due to the fact that it had nothing to do in finding Nathan Scotfield or Edith Ester and secondly now that Nathan is somewhere in Canada he had no authority in participating in the manhunt of his suspect.

Returning to their hospital room, Liz had Joe lie in bed with her, the next morning the hospital gave Liz her obstetric ultrasound, where she and Joe and finally see their baby. But it turns when the visual images appeared, they along with the nurses were shocked to a big surprise.

Chapter 35. The Greenarrow cabin

Late in the month of March, old man Hal Greenarrow and his grandson Rick road along a trail on their four-wheeler to collect their tap buckets from the maple trees, followed by their shaggy Greyhound Kiba.

After riding a mile down the trail, they made it to their maple trees, the two offboarded the terrain vehicle to collect full buckets of maple sap. Hal packed the last bucket and Rick called out for the dog.

"KIBA!" he yelled followed by a whistle.

"Couldn't leave him alone for one minute, can we?" Hal rolled his eyes; the pair walk searched all over woods while following the loud barking in the distance.

"Kiba!" Rick called out again.

"Stupid mut," Hal stated as they followed.

"I think he's up at the falls, Grandpa." Rick said sprinting out. The old man followed behind with his walking stick, the two hiked up the hill where they found Kiba barking at a group of ravens circling over some dead carcass.

"Kiba!" Rick ran up and took the dog by the collar, "Oh my god, Grandpa come over here!"

"Damn it Kiba! What are you doing?!" Hal said as Rick struggled to keep him still. The boy then pointed to the dead mass lying on the ground.

"Holy shit. It's a horse," Hal said.

"Looks like it's been dead for weeks, what do you think happened?" Risk asked as he wrangled a rope around their dog's collar. Kiba jumps and hauled the boy along the riverbank.

"I have no idea, never seen a horse around these parts in ages. But wherever he came from he's certainly not a wild horse, see? It has a saddle."

"Should we call a ranger?" the boy asked.

"Yeah, we should notify the rangers, let get back to the cabin."

Hal led the way towards the lake trail, while his grandson hauled Kiba by leash, upon crossing the waterfall, the dog was again barking into a crazed frenzy.

"Jesus Christ Kiba what now?!" Hal said.

"He must've smelled something," Rick replied.

"No way, a dog can't smell something in the water," he said, but the Dog pulled the kid down the trail near the rocky ledge next tot e falls. Ricky pulled and tugged at his dog, before noticing something strange lying down at the bottom of the drop.

"Oh God, grandpa look!"

Hal walked up, and the two men saw a man lying motionless on a rock.

"Rick go, take Kiba home and, get your father down here now!" the man ordered. When the kid and dog left for the cabin, Hal hiked down to the rocks and stood over the man who he thought was dead. The man was pale white Caucasian, with wet dark brown hair, and a short scraggly beard, wearing dark brown winter clothes, had a leather holster belt with a pistol on his side. Hal examined the surroundings and discovered a fractured stained piece of wood, he picked it up and that discovered it was a cross with a silver form of Christ. He also notices that the handle was stained in blood, more curious and confused, Hal looked back to the man and realized something terrible must've happened.

When Hal knelt again, to check for pulse, after placing his fingers on the person's neck, the man let out a scream.

"Holy shit!" Hal yelped almost falling into the water. He claimed back on the rock and found the man was still alive, breathing, and crying.

"You're alive," said Hal, "Are you hurt, what happened?!"

"Help me, I can't move… I fell off the falls…I think… I think I'm paralyzed." Answered the man. Rick arrived at the riverbank with his father Jimmy, the three took the injured man to their isolated cabin.

"Okay let's put him in your room, Jim," Said Hal as he and Rick carried the man in a stretcher. "Now Jim go contact Ollda and call for a medevac.

"Sooner this man gets a doctor the better, he's hurt pretty bad," said Hal, laying the stranger on on the bed. "Rick fetch us some dry clothes, in the dresser."

The man gains conscious again, only able to move his mouth, after some heavy breathing and sobbing, the man huffed.

"Where am I?"

"It's ok, friend your safe..."

"Where am I?!" the man asked again.

"You're in our cabin about 10 miles south of Ollda and 60 miles north of Dubreuil Ville, my name is Hal Greenarrow," the old answered, "and who are you?"

"I'm Nathan... from New York... I can't move," he said weeping.

"Don't worry, Nathan we have a radio we'll get a helicopter here to you to a hospital as soon as possible," Hal said, his grandson enters the room with new clothes and a buffalo hide blanket.

After introducing the boy, he ordered Rick to go cook dinner as he began to cut away his cold wet hunting clothes, getting a glance of the wounds and scars on the white man's body, all his toes were frostbitten, they notice his right shin was badly fractured, and has his of collar bone protruding through the skin.

Both Hal and Jim quickly and carefully dressed the man in sweatpants, a sweater and placed one pillow underneath Nathan's head. Laying head up so he could breathe more clearly.

"Sorry I had to cut away from your pants son, but your near ice...Christ, you're lucky you haven't frozen solid."

"Thank you," sniffed Nathan.

"Okay, I'm gonna check on something, be right back..."

"No, no please don't go!" Nathan plead.

"It'll only take a second," Jim and Hal walked out and found his dad talking with the operator.

"Yes, ma'am the man is hurt pretty bad, must have slipped off the cliff and snapped his spine, we need help here right away. Over."

"Copy that, Mr. Greenarrow, remain indoors and we'll send help, eta 24 hours. Over."

Jim took the phone, "any chance you can come sooner? Over."

"Negative, we need to refuel since we made over a dozen flying trips over Akagami Lake because the mounted troops are hunting a dangerous criminal in the area. Over."

Hal looked to his son, "Dangerous criminal?"

"Yes, a criminal might be around the area, a murderer from America. Like I said just remain indoor and you must wait until tomorrow, we'll get there as fast as we can. Over and out."

Jim hesitated, but replied the same, "over and out."

"Dad?"

"Yeah," Hal answered.

"I think we have this criminal... the man says he's from New York," Jim explained. "That's probably him."

Nathan laid motionless, crying, with mixed feelings of relief with the memories of the monster he had killed. The Native Canadian trio enters the bedroom.

"Here Nathan, take these painkillers, think it'll help," offered Jim.

"It's okay... I don't feel no pain,"

"You should just take one in case," Jim put the pill on Nathan's tongue, as Rick carefully poured warm tea in his mouth.

After feeding him some Turkey rice, soup. Hal sat near the guest with the other two standing behind him.

"You're in trouble, aren't you? Mr. Scotfield," said Hal.

"Dad we shouldn't...." then Jim got interrupted.

"More than you could imaging," Nathan replied. "You would never believe all I have been through."

"How did you end on the rocks?" asked Rick.

"I fell."

"And how did you fall?" asked Jim.

The Man with only his face to move stared at the three and saw that they wanted to know his story.

"If I tell you what you want to know, can I make a request?" said Nathan.

"What that?" The trio said together.

"Write a letter to my brother Joey... please?"

"Okay deal."

The night rolled over with as the Greenarrow's listened to the horrid tale told by the man they've rescued. Nathan confessed everything to them, from the burning of his own house to killing the Wendigo Edith off the Waterfall.

"... all that I've done.... never have I thought I was destined to commit such terrible things, hunting, killing men, women and a child. I helped them escape their curse. They were not the monsters though; those poor souls were enslaved by a devil. The world we live in is filled with so much evil, that we're too moral to dream of, the Wendigo had many chances to tear me apart and kill me, but it found my emotional pain more appetizing. My poor horse Clyde and I chased it north until I finally cornered it and with God by my side, I killed it."

Nathan inhaled and began to cry again in joy, "I have done it, the Kess family, the people of Graytown and my brother are all free. Now I'm here paralyzed, and will soon be locked up for murder, at least... but at least I rid the world of some evil...my only regret is that the fall did not kill me. I won't blame you guys if you believe not a single word I've said, I know it's too much to take in. But it's over now...

bless you, for finding me and taking me in, giving me this warm hospitality. And that is my story."

Jim had tear steam from his eye, Hal felt his heart skip a few beats, and young Rick trembled in fear. Before any more questions could be asked, Mr. Scotfield passed out.

"Come, boys, he needs to rest," Hal stood and lead the two out.

The evening the three stayed, only Rick falling asleep on his father's side.

"What do you make of it grandpa?" Rick asked Hal, the old man took his pipe and calmly puffed it.

"Well…. No doubt the man suffered…perhaps suffered too much. I honest to God hope he's not the man their…."

"He is," Jim cut in, "He's the one the mounted troops have been hunting for."

"You don't think they would lock up a paralyzed man?" Hal said concernedly.

"Maybe, I'm no lawyer… and I know nothing about America's justice system… personally though, I really hope not." Jim rubbed his son's back. "but we'll find out soon."

The next morning Rick awoke on the couch, with the bright sun melting the snow outside. He walked in the kitchen where his dad and grandpa were having breakfast.

"Come, Rick, we're having your favorite raspberry flapjacks," said Hal.

"Can we give some to Mr. Scotfield?" asked the boy.

"He's still sleeping, we shouldn't disturb him."

While eating the trio heard the radio buzzing, Jim approached and picked up the transceiver.

"Greenarrow? Greenarrow, do you read? Over?"

"Copy we hear you over?"

"We nearly finished with fueling up the evac chopper, ETA 4 hours."

"Thank you, now before you come, I think I should inform we've learned the name of this man we've found, over," said Jim.

"Okay, who is he? Over."

"The man says he's Nathan Scotfield from New York, does that name mean anything? Over."

The radio went silent for a couple of seconds.

"Hello? Do you read? Over." Jim asked, no reply.

"Yes, yes, we copy, over. Nathan Scotfield is the man the police are searching for... he's a murderer."

"Murder?... I assume you're sending the police? over," Jim said regrettably.

"We'll send out a mounted party to arrive before the helicopter, keep you and your family safe until then. Over and out."

"Well, the man is paralyzed I don't think…" But the radio went silent again, and the station disconnected them.

"Way to go, son, have an injured man arrested," Hal said.

"It's not like I pressed charges, besides they were gonna know sooner or later."

Hal stared for a moment and made for the bedroom. He saw, the poor Scotfield laying like a rock, he was stiff as a log and when touching his hand, it was cold as frozen beef. Hal then placed his hand on Nathan's forehead, and he opened his eyes.

"Oh, it's you, morning."

"Good morning… Jim called the airfield, they'll be here around 10, and…" Hal paused.

"And what?"

"The police are coming too," Hal answered.

"Matters not anymore, I don't care."

"Wish it wouldn't end like this," Hal said sadly.

"It would've been better if I'd died in the fall along with the Wendigo."

"Ever since my years as a youngling, my granddad horrified me with tales of Werewolves, Wendigos and Skinwalkers, but never heard one of a man slaying one. Anyway, would you like me to write this letter to your brother, Nathan?"

"Thank You."

Hal finished writing Joey's letter and could hear the chuffs of a helicopter blade. Rick peeked his head in and said the police are here.

"Hal could I make one final request?"

"Sure Nathan, what is it?"

"Now… you don't have to do it if you don't wish to. But my revolver, do you have it?"

"Yes," Hal walked to the dresser and took out Scotfield's .357. "And you got one bullet left."

"Well Hal. I can't live this way… either locked away in prison or a secured hospital the rest of my life and I don't want that…"

"You want to end it all together now do you?" Hal said.

Nathan look at the old man, "Would you please?" Hal nodded yes.

"Thank you, Hal… for everything."

"You're not a bad person Nathan, I could tell your no murder even if we can't prove it." Hal stepped up to his bedside. "I wish we could've known one another someplace else."

"Now listen Hal, I don't want you to get in trouble and locked up because of me." Nathan said.

"Don't worry about nothing, Jimmy and Rick will be fine, and besides I'm 75 years old now, I've lived a good life, what more could they do to an old dupe like me? Is there any other request you would like to make?"

Nathan thought a moment, and all he could think of id his brother. "No sir, I'm ready and thank you."

Standing outside infront of their cabin, Rick was with his father as four Candian police walked up.

"Is he in there?" one of the cops asked, and before Jim could answer a gun went off.

The policemen drew their side arms, and told the father and son to remain outside, after searching the living room and Kitchen the trooper went to the bedroom where they found the Hal had shot Nathan dead.

Chapter 36. News media.

The month of April, spring melted all the snow on the ground and warm air breezed on through the land. Tending his work in his office in Albany New York, Matthew Geyer heard his phone ringing.

He answered phone. "Detective Geyer, NYPD?"

"Hello sir, it's Wayne Wardell from Toronto."

"Ah hello Wardell, what's going on?"

 "Well sir, we've found your killer, Mr. Scotfield… He's dead."

The man sprung from his chair stunned, knocking his office chair down.

"Dead?!" yelped Geyer.

"Yes sir, Nathan Scotfield was found by some native locals near lake Akagami in the Algoma district," said Wardell.

"What happened?"

"Well the three locals are the Greenarrow family, they're local syrup tappers, and they discovered Scotfield severely injured on their property, he'd broken his neck and right before we could take him into our custody Harold Greenarrow the grandfather, shot Scotfield in the head with his own revolver."

"He killed him? No way," Geyer said dropping down in his chair.

"Well, it was more of a euthanasia," Wardell replied.

"Euthanasia. You mean like a mercy killing?" Geyer said.

"Yes, we're arranging the body to get back to the states. Scotfield's family should be informed."

"Oh, you didn't inform his brother yet?"

"Nope, my sources said, he and his girlfriend check out of the hospital the other day and just took a plane back to New York."

"Oh… Okay then, I'll…I'll let him know, thank you for calling, goodbye."

"Wait!" Wardell spoke up, "I was also informed when they took in Harold Greenarrow, he gave the police a written letter from Nathan, and said he'd wanted it to be sent directly to his brother Joey. Now I don't have his address, would you take it and give it to him?"

"Of course, I will."

Miles in the sky on a plane, Joseph and Elizabeth sat in couch, it was late in the day Joseph awoke on his seat to the captain informing the passengers they'll be landing in their destination within the hour and found Lizzy's with her forehead against the window.

"Are you okay?"

"I'm fine…" Lizzy said.

"Are you sure?"

"Yes, just thinking." Joe placed his hand over her shoulder.

"What about?" he asked.

"Just about how the hell is we gonna care for six kids," Liz said rubbing her growing abdomen.

"It's gonna be hard, but we can't fell apart now," said Joe, "right now, let's just get home and put our heads together."

"What about Nathan?"

"I... well... If they don't find him soon, I'll go out and look for him," he replied.

The airplane arrived at the International Airport in Rome, As the couple walked out of the airport, they were greeted by three Utica policemen, one of which Liz recognized.

"Elizabeth Wallstone, welcome home," said the police chief, before shaking her hand. They gave her and Joe a police escort to the station to a pleasant surprise.

The Utica police greeted the couples. They were brought to the HQ station where they received a loving welcome home from Lizzy's police friends along with the congratulations on their coming babies.

They also met with the families of Lizzy's fallen colleagues of Francis and Merv, when the welcome celebration ended that afternoon, with Liz awarded the NYPD Medal of Valor for bravery, the two decided to drive to the cemetery to pay her deceased family a final farewell.

They found headstones of the Kess family, after a long while grieving on her knees in front of her sister's grave,

Joe helped his mate back up and walked out of the cemetery.

The next day, Liz awoke on her bed with Tasha laying near her legs. Still not used to being back into her old house, she washed up, dressed and walked out of her room where she found Joe in front of her tv with a face of despair.

"Are you okay?" she asked grabbing his shoulders, and Joe just shook his head.

"Oh hey, Liz, the airport dropped Tasha off an hour ago…," Joe said while crying.

"What's the matter? why are you crying?"

"I just saw my brother's image on the news, Nathan's a serial killer."

"What?"

"And take a look outside," he replied, Liz walked to her front window and saw a group of people, a mix of reporters, a crew of cameramen talking with some of Lizzy's neighbors.

"When I woke up, they were banging on the front door, when I answered them, they asked me the most disgusting questions anyone can ask me.

"How does it feel having the blood of murderer?"

"What the hell is that supposed to mean? I asked. They also asked if I've defied my brother for his crimes, asking what our childhood was like, saying our father had beat us, saying we were attics, lie after lie! And now I just watched Nathan's ex on tv, she was interviewed by NY Times. Most sickening slanderous words I heard; I now have a headache after watching it."

Joe began to cry and cup his face like a little boy, Liz turned to him and took his hands. "Joe don't listen to them, they no nothing," said Liz closing the window curtains. "Just sit down and don't let these losers get you down."

"I slammed the door in their faces…. They told me, Nathan…they told me that he's dead!"

"What?" she said stunned. Liz shook her head in deficiencies, she didn't believe it she couldn't believe it she thought. When Joe took her hand and pulled her on the couch, he switched the new channel after channel. When they found NY crime daily, it was their news anchors and journalist marked Nathan as a monster and a cool-blooded killer who targeted his neighbors, innocent men, women, and children. Photos of the victims were shown on the screen along with Liz's sister Lidia and the rest of the Kess family.

Clips were shown from the interview of Nathan's ex-wife. Candace Powers along with her attorney and a psychologist were interviewed on national television.

"Being married to that monster was pure hell on earth, she said on camera, "he would beat me, threaten me, I lived in fear every night I slept with Scotfield," she stated.

"How did get out of that horrid marriage?"

"I decided to go from scared crying girl, to a strong woman and I up and left him, but it didn't end there…"

"He threatened you again?" the news anchor said.

"Yes, when I realized it would get worse, I contacted Mr. Powers, and we taught that monster a lesson."

"Do you think the divorce motivated Scotfield to do these murders?"

"I suppose so, but there might have been other things in his past that made become a serial killer, like his father…."

"Oh my God! turn it off!" yelled Liz, unable to stand what they were watching. Joe switched the channel and cried alongside his girl.

"I also heard on the news that… Nathan's dead…."

Chapter 37. Letters & Forgiveness.

   Making his way to Utica after a 95-mile drive, Geyer parked in front of Wallstone's house, walked up and knocked on the door.

"Good Morning Officer Wallstone," he said, "may I come in?"

The woman only resounded with a nod, as he walked inside the living room was packed with boxes, and he saw a grieving Joey morning in the dining room.

"Hello Joseph," said Geyer.

"Oh, you again."

"I take it you've heard about Nathan," Geyer looked to Liz who robbed the sobbing man's back. "May I sit down?"

"Yes, you may," said Liz.

"Uh... Dr. Scotfield, Wardell has sent Nathan's body back here to America. Nathan's in a morgue in Albany, " Geyer said to Joe who barely looked at him, "and maybe... not now but when you are ready, I'll take you to see your brother one last time... if you wish it."

"Really?" asked Joe, "You take me to see him? and pay my last goodbye to him?"

"Of course," replied Geyer, "Now or whenever you wish."

After some competitive bickering, Joe and Liz agreed to go to Albany now, and follow the man to the morgue all the way back to the state capital.

The investigator brought Joe in the corner building where Wardell, Durant, the Utica police chief met them. The emotional couple was walked into the lab with the Diener standing over an operating table.

When seeing the black covered mass on the medal table, Liz told Joey that she couldn't stand it any longer and decided to wait back in the lobby with her police chief comforting her.

"Well Joseph, here we are," Geyer said patting Joe's back, "Are you ready?"

The man nodded his head and the surgeon pulled off the black plastic body bag.

Joe stood and stared down at his brother, pale gray, with dark brown hair, his neck, and eye sockets were eggplant purple. He had buckshot holes in his upper shoulder and a bullet hole in his forehead.

The other men switched their eyes to the little brother, who to their shock did not cry and was just as motionless as Nathan laid.

"That's him," Joe said plainly. After a moment of silent Wardell spoke first.

"Um… we…uh… the man who shot him Harold Greenarrow told us your brother requested a mercy killing.

It is legal in our country to provide a authorization, but if you wish to press charges, maybe…"

"I refuse to press charges," Joe interrupted. "He did Nathan a favor. Let him go, leave Mr. Greenarrow alone. If I was there, I've done the same thing, even I'd rather die than live paralyzed the rest of my days."

"Very well, that's that. Case closed," Durant said to Geyer signing a document. The two Canadian detectives left to give the order to release and dismiss all charges against Harold Greenarrow. Geyer stayed with Joe in the room, with him still staring at his deceased brother.

Tears streamed down Joey's eyes as he stared, Geyer placed his hand on his shoulder, and Joe nudge it off.

"Please…just leave me for a moment."

Geyer wanted to say something, but he realized the man was in deep mourning, so he left the room with the denier.

After some crying, a small prayer and a hug, Joe pulled body bag back over his brother's face, then "So long brother."

Joe came out of the room and inform the denying Geyer that he was done, he walked into the lobby to find that Geyer had left, and Liz was holding a paper.

The pregnant woman stood and walked to him, they stared into each other's eyes for a moment.

"Well, come on Elizabeth, let's go home to Vermont."

"Okay, I'll drive," she replied. When they made it back to her home in Utica with dozens of boxes of her belonging packed up for moving, Liz had something for Joe.

"Joseph? detective Geyer, when he left the officer… he told me to give you this," she gave him the paper the turned out to be a letter.

"What is it?" he asked.

"He told me he got it from Wardell, who said it's a message Nathan wanted you to have before he'd died."

Joe glanced to the paper and took it out of the envelope and read aloud.

"Joey, if you're reading this, it means you're alive and you're human again. You may not recognize this handwriting but because I'm unable to grab a pen, no am I able to move my arms to write, I'm paralyzed, I've broken my neck and thought I was going to die in the pool of a waterfall.

A family of good souls had found me, they took me in, cared for me, placed me into a warm bed and fed me. I've had one of them write down my last letter to you. I'm deeply sorry that I had lost you, I promised myself I'd go out and find you, but I cannot move, I've lost my strength, lost my home, my horse, I just pray that I have not lost you.

I can't live like this. Sorry that it must end without me personally saying goodbye to you. I hope you understand, I just can't bear the life in a wheelchair, or never being able to move again. I hope you'll forgive me like God and Christ, may they have mercy on me. Farewell Brother, I love you. Also, if and I hope they've made it, please tell officer Wallstone and Merv that I said thank you for helping me.

Nathan."

The man's eyes watered, and he nearly dropped to the floor in grieve, Liz caught him and sat him down on her couch. Joe cried on her shoulder, as she followed along with the grief.

After a couple more days of packing, the former police officer and soon to be a mother had her things sent to Joseph's home in Burlington, as she accompanied her lover to her brother's funeral.

At the Catholic church where Nathan's coffin was open for people to pay a final farewell. Joe sent dozens of invitations to Nathan's old friends from his golden years, but no one showed up.

The day passed by, with only three people at the funeral being held at Staten Island. Lizzy and the priest tended the weeping Joseph. They stood alone with hundreds of photos of Nathan, depicting good and positive events that had happened in the past. It was then Lizzy notice three strangers enter the cathedral. A middle-aged couple and an older man wearing a similar outfit of the preacher's, slowly they came walking from the front doors and up the aisle to the first row.

"May I help you?" the church pastor said.

"Uh, yes, this is the funeral of Nathan Scotfield?" the middle-aged man asked.

"Were you invited?" stood Liz, Joey looked back and reconsider the couple.

"Mrs. Gracer?" he said to the lady.

Upon hearing that, the memory pop in Liz's mind. Joe seized the crying and looked to the other priest.

"Hello Dr. Scotfield," Mrs. Gracer said.

"What… why are you?"

"We came to say…" Mrs. Gracer cracked down in tears when her husband spoke up.

"We both came because… Well, there are many people who hate your brother and think he's an evil serial killer…" Mr. Gracer said emotionally, "but Rebecca and I…we're not one of them… it was hard to stop hating him when he shot our son… but hate solved nothing and made our pain worse, so we came to make peace with Nathan and his family."

"Thank you," Joe said silently.

Rebecca walked to the casket having one glimpse of the dead man who shot and killed her son, over a year ago and placed a single rose on his chest. The woman began to dry and retreated into the arms of her husband, they then just fell and wished Joey and Liz well.

The young couple then looked to the old visitor.

"And you are?" asked Joe.

"My name is Father Franklin Benedict from Cobalt. I didn't mean to intrude on this sad occasion, but I too have come to pay my respects, to the very man who saved my life."

"Safed your life?" Joe said.

When the Canadian preacher nodded, he allowed the man to go approach his brother. Joe then asked the church pastor to leave them, so he can speak with Benedict.

"So, you're that old preacher, detective Wardell told me about?" said Joe. "I've read a copy of your report when you were in the hospital."

"Oh yes, the man called me two days ago and informed where you'd have Nathan's funeral. When I told him what had happened, I saved Nathan from freezing to death and he saved me from being torn to pieces… naturally no one, even Wardell didn't believe me and thought I was just a crazy old bible thumper."

"Bible? Oh hey!" Lizzy said with excitement, she reached into her purse and took out the Holy book Benedict had given to Nathan. "I think this is yours."

"It was sent to us from the Greenarrow family, said they found it on him," Joe added.

"My God… I gave it to him for good luck, guess luck just wasn't on his side."

"Do you think God was on his side? And forgave him for ordering his own suicide?" Joe asked with a sniff.

"My son, the Bible, and church are against killing and suicide… but as such God forgives if a sinner, if they ask for it." Said Benedict. "You know on TV and the news they call your brother a murderer… I think… and believe that is not true, though none of us can prove what've really had happened…at least some people know."

Joey cried again, but this time in joyful tears.

"Well, I must be going."

"Now? but you just got here," said Lizzy.

"I would love to stay, my dear," Benedict said, "but I have a plane to catch, for I'm going on a missionary with my church to Latin America. Before I leave, Joseph I have one last thing for you."

The priest handed the man a folded paper.

"Another letter?"

"Yes, a thank you letter, it seems I wasn't the life Nathan saved from a Wendigo. Farewell and God Bless you all." As Joseph began to read Benedict to one glimpse back to Nathan's stained casket, crossed his heart and left.

"Dear Dr. Joseph Scotfield. Your brother Nathan came to our aide after our mother and father were taken from us. We were almost killed, and he saved our lives, because of him me and my brother our alive to send you this letter of appreciation. We're very sorry he died, we wish to come to his funeral and personally give you our gratitude and pay him our respect, but our uncle adopted us and we're now moving to Nova Scotia real soon. We wish you well."

Take care. Laurie and Ben DeAnya of Karby's Country peace lodge, Ontario Canada." Liz burst into tears and kissed Joseph.

Chapter 38. Sextuplet.

Five months past, since Joe laid his brother to rest down in St. Paul Cemetery in Staten Island NY, right next to their father Patrick. Lizzy now heavily pregnant moved in and settled with Joe at his home in Burlington. The future mother of six worked endlessly preparing for her babies. She spent her time exercising, room decorating in the nursery made up in Joe's only guest bedroom, and care for Tasha.

Since the funeral, Tasha has been down with depression, no longer the joyful, pouncing, energic dog she once was and a few times a day both Liz and Joe would find her staring out the front window near the door as if she's waiting for Nathan.

Joseph was happy to be back to his job helping sick animals, especially the thoughts of being a father, however, he had deep concerns, he and his girl were still wolves. Since after they've returned to New York, they discovered they can turn into their wolf forms. Unlike before when the moon rises or bounded in a single form, they both had the ability to shapeshift from wolf to human at will. So, in a way, the werewolf curse was still upon them...perhaps for the remainder of their lives, but neither of them was afraid of hurting people since they can control their wolf form. The main worry of the couple was the safety of their children, they'll be having six kids and will have their hands full, in a small house in an urban neighborhood.

Joe tried to think about how and where they should have their babies, Liz wanted to have a natural childbirth.

On a hot summer morning in August Joe woke up with Liz next to him she pushed off the blanket and slept only in a shirt and underwear. He kissed her on the cheek and went to dress for work. He left for work early that morning but after leaving his love interest a warm breakfast of bacon and eggs on the table. He arrived at the vet around 6:30 am until he heard his cell phone ringing and it was Liz.

"What is it, babe?" he asked.

"Joey, my water just broke!" he answered cheeringly, "come home we're having babies!"

Immediately Joe restarted his car and drove back home, leaving the secretary and note that he can't come to work today, he arrived home, entered his house, and found Liz in the portal birth pool.

"Liz are you alright?"

"I am wonderful, I'm so excited," she said, when Joe walked to her, he gave her a kiss, "I've been having a lot of contractions, I think this is the day!"

"Did you call the midwives?" he asked.

"No..."

"Why?"

"Honey there's a full moon this evening... if our babies come out as wolves, what's gonna happen to us?"

"Oh shit! I never thought of that," he said stupidly, seems after all the time of preparing for the birth they didn't have a backup plane. Then suddenly Lizzy stepped out of the tub.

"Well honey, minus well put your veterinarian birthing skills to the task," she dropped on all fours, and shapeshifted into her wolf form.

Joseph quickly gathered the things they would need for this situation, he pulled out the spare mattress from the guest bedroom single-handedly, and laid down some old blankets on it, to make Lizzy an nesting area.

Liz laid on the mattress, breathing, grunting and wheezing heavily on and off, her claws scratched the sheets when she gets a contraction. Joe came from the kitchen with leftover food from the kitchen, feeling this would be very long, perhaps all throughout the night and she'll be hungry later.

Lizzy laid back, and turned on her left side, moaning in pain with Joseph kneeling next to her, patting her face.

"You're gonna be fine sweetie, we're having a family tonight," said Joseph with gloves on.

As the day rolled on with Liz making wolf sounds and light howls, Joe kept every door and window locks, and all curtains down shielding the windows, in case of any suspicious neighbors.

Liz struggled to bear with the pain as much as possible, and around the afternoon, literally several hours past and she began to worry. Joe sat, Liz's head on his laps and stroked her belly, while looking into her eyes, telling her to hang in there, our babies are almost here.'

Joe left her a minute to get her water, all she could think about how much longer this was going to take.

"This is so painful," she said to herself, I just want to meet my babies!" He gasped with a bark.

"It's going to be okay sis," she heard a whisper, the she-wolf looked up in the lamp-lit room and saw no one, Joe came in with two water bottles.

He felt a strange presence in his house but saw no sign of life. He kept back next to Liz how stood up on her front legs, she was now entering the latest stage of giving birth. She gasped and moaned and could feel that they were coming.

"Oh, their crowning, here we go Liz," Joe said, and within the hour all six other litter came out. Their six fraternal sextuplets, four girls and two boys. They named each after a loved one, Patrick Nathan the first who came out, Lidia, Erin, Josiah, Thora, and Silvia the small one.

All six were in their wolf pup forms, Joseph transformed into his werewolf and laid right next to his mate with their litter lying in between them.

As the first month past both Joe and Liz had to care for six kids, who were loud, crying humans' babies during the day and, howling cubs at night. It was hard and exhausting for both of them, but they loved their children, nonetheless. It wasn't long though when the neighborhood grew concern and began knocking on Joey's door, wondering about the loud howls and things got worse when one annoyed neighbor called animal patrol to investigate.

 They managed to avoid any trouble with the patrol and told them lies that it was just coyotes prowling in their backyard.

One night while nurturing the litter, Joe came home after a long shift. Liz waited for her kids to finish their meal, and when they were all asleep, she carried them to their cribs and sat next to Joseph in the living room.

"So, how was work?"

"Good," he said plainly and turned on the tv.

"Are you okay, you look sad," said Liz.

"I'm not sad babe, just concerned," Joe said with a sighed, "I got this notice in the mail, the neighbor threatened to get a search warrant to remove any negative animal we have on the premises."

"What makes him think, he can do that?!" Liz said with disgust, "such assholes, and I thought New York was bad."

"Well… let's not worry about that now, as long as they don't come in the evening, we'll be okay." Joe said, "So how about you? How were the kids?"

"Oh, just little angels and they seem to like each other, which is good, and they were eating well. But I just don't get it how come we can change from wolf to man and the kids only change at night."

"Well… I've been doing a bit of studying and I guess in some species of werewolves can shapeshift at random at a certain age, probably when they're in their adolescence, they'll learn to change in and out of a wolf in time." Joe explained, "I'm starting to like my wolf form, for some reason."

"Yeah, me too," Liz replied, then from the nursery, they heard one of the cubs began to yell, Joe, signed and got up to care for it.

In the kid's bedroom packed with toys and baby supplies, two of the cubs somehow claimed over the crib and played tug of war with a sock, Joe picked them up and placed them back in bed.

"Here we go babies, go back to sleep, okay?" he patted the two pubs and rubbed one of them as they drifted into their slumber.

As Joe looked down to his children Liz came and hugged him.

"You're a good daddy," she said.

"And you're a great mommy," he replied.

The couple shifted into their wolf form and decided to bring their cubs into their bed to sleep with, in the middle of that evening the wolf parents awoke to the whimpering light howls of their kids.

"Oh Jeez," said Joe.

"Welcome to my world," Liz said in irony.

After a minute of the pubs howling, Joe finally quit all six down to go back to sleep again. Hours later Joe woke again to the alarm clock followed by the cries of his six kids.

"Good morning," Lizzy said.

"Good morning family," he said giving each a kiss. He got up and made his lover breakfast and spent the morning feeding kids. Throughout his day off, he and Lizzy began to chat about how they plan to raise six little werewolves, and the first subject came was Lizzy's idea to move.

Chapter 39. Blood on the Tombs.

The Scotfields decided moving to a new place out of state would be a good solution to raise a big family. Like what his brother had done, Joe and his new wife Lizzy use both their money to buy a ranch out west. They planned to buy a place out west in the country and someplace warm, surrounded by country land instead of urbanized towns like Burlington. Towards the end of summer and into the fall, Joe married Lizzy and they had their belongings ready to move, but before the Scotfields could leave the Mid-Atlantic region they had to say one last goodbye to someone.

On a late afternoon in November, the Mr. and Mrs. Scotfield with their kids drove all the way down to Staten Island in their new family van.

The family entered St. Paul Cemetery with a banquet of fresh flowers.

Joe pulled the stroller carrying three of his kids, with Lizzy following with the other three.

 They introduced their six kids to their late uncle and grandfather. After placing the flower beds on both Nathan and Patrick's gravestone, the newlywed couple held their babies and took a moment's silence.

"Say goodbye to your uncle, Patrick," Joe said quietly to his son as he held him near the stone. The kids became tired and fuzzy so Lizzy took all of them back to their van so they can take a nab and leave father alone to have a moment's peace with his father and brother.

Lizzy brought the babes into the vehicle and sat them inside on their seats, she then got her baby supply bag to take out pacifiers. But then from the sunset gleaming on the parking area, she saw a provocatively dressed lady walking past her van.

Joe stared at the two gravestones, crying in joy, knowing that Nathan and their father would be proud of him for having a family.

"Hey there!" Joe heard a voice; he turned and saw the woman who interrupted his moment.

"Candace?"

"Long time no see, Joey." She came walking up, in a revealing dress, and high heels, she stared at Joe as if she wanted him. But the man kept his distance.

"What are you doing here?" he said.

"Oh, just in the neighborhood, and though I pay my respect to my ex," she said, Candace took out her smartphone and snapped a photo of the Scotfield gravestones.

"What are doing?" he said disturbed, "What was that for?"

"Oh, just taking some pics for a book I'm writing," she said.

"A book? you're writing a book about my brother," Joe said.

"Well, my marriage to him actually, it's called 'Married to a Monster,' just accounting my experiences and how I survived being wedded to a killer."

"Nathan was no killer," Joe said silently.

"So, how's life since…" Candace turned, and Joe was already walking away to the cemetery gates.

When the man made it to the vehicle, he saw all the kids sound asleep.

"They're all milk drunk now, so they'll be napping for quite a while," Lizzy said.

"Good, best we get going, the sooner we're away from here the better." Joe crossed his arms.

"Who was that lady dressed like a Vegas hooker?"

"You don't remember? It's Nathan's ex."

"No!" she said, looking from the driver's window, and saw her up to the van smiling. "What the hell does she want."

Joe looked up and saw Candace approaching their van. Lizzy rolled down the window.

"What do you want?" she asked.

"Oh hi, you must be Joe's wife, I'm…"

"I know who you are, what do you want?" Lizzy said again.

"I just wanted to meet you," Candace glanced inside the van and saw all the sleeping babies.

"Holy cow, that's a lot of brats you got back there," Candace tease, "did you consider abortion before he planted the seeds?"

Lizzy was disturbed, if it weren't for the seat belt restraining her, she would've got out the van and kicked the shit out of that bitch. But instead, she rolled up the window and flipped her the middle finger.

The woman gasped and marched to her white Porsche, and when the two thought she'd just drive away, Candace deliberately, drove head on and smashed into the back of their van.

"Oh, Christ!" Joe yelled; in the back seat all their kids began to cry. Lizzy claimed off her seat and went to the back to calm their babies down.

"Are the kids okay?" he asked. Joe looked up and from the back window, Candace stood from her Porsche grinning like a mule. The man quickly unbuckled and got out of the vehicle.

After damaging the rear bumper of the van, Candace sat up waiting for Joe to confront her, but he never came to her car's side and he was nowhere in sight.

"Where is he?" she thought, peeking van's passenger side, Joseph wasn't there. But just a pair of jeans and boxers laying on the pavement.

Candace sat back in her seat to start her car, when suddenly to her driver's side, a huge wolf popped up growling dangerously, snarling and staring into her eyes.

The beast bit her in the left arm, dragging her out of her car, the woman cried, pleaded and yelled out for help, Lizzy watched from the van smiling sadistically as her mate dragged the gold digger into the cemetery.

Candace screamed, kicked and sobbed uncontrollably, when the dragging ceased, she laid on the grass, unaware that her arm had been torn completely off from her shoulder and blood began to spray on nearby gravestones.

The werewolf pounced on her, and the last thing she saw was the long snout jaws, biting into her head, taring her face off her skull.

Lizzy stared the van, Joe ran back to the dark parking lot, he turned back to his human form on dressed himself and enter the van. He started the vehicle and drove off after whipping the blood from his mouth.

"Are you okay?" she asked.

"Yes, I'm fine," he replied looking back to his children who'd transformed into little wolf pups. Lizzy drove the van back up to Vermont to gather the last of their belongings, they worked all night as their kids stayed snuggled in their crib.

All was ready. The following morning when New York City Police officials discovered the mutilated body of Candace Power, Joseph had signed the final papers of the documents in selling his house. And then the Scotfield family left for the warm state for Arizona, to follow in Nathan's footsteps in starting fresh with a new home out in the country on their own family ranch.

Chapter 40. New Home acres.

Six years went by, and the six cubs grew into, brave, loving, energetic, and playful younglings. The Scotfield family settled on a 36-acre ranch in Apache County Arizona.

The property consisted of a newly built, two stories log cabin that stood on top of a hill overlooking an open field near a fresh running creek. Joseph gave up his veterinarian practice and grew corn on the property. The family named their home Nathan's acres in honor of Joey's brother. As Joe would stay home to tend the fields, and the kids, Lizzy got a job back in law enforcement as a deputy in the local sheriff's office.

Life was rough at times, for a farm hand, and a cop raising six children, and an old mix hound dog, the couple did their best in protecting their kids. Rasing them with love, and guidance, teaching them to walk, to talk, to read, and write as a human. At nights when all kids turn into werewolves, the parents would teach them the basic concepts of a wolf, like how to hunt in a pack, track animals, and always remain on their family property lines.

Though mischievous and unpredictable at times, Patrick, Lidia, Erin, Josiah, Thora and Silvia loved life on the ranch. Times when they don't listen their parents, especially their mother kept a strict grip on all of them and they would remain obedient to the rules.

As the sextuplets grew up, they tended a small school, each were quiet and withdrawn from other kids, but they would look out for one another and fight off any bullies who would harass them.

Tasha grew to love, Lizzy and children, and her new life on the ranch. But as the years went by she grew older, and still awaits for Nathan to return to her. Every night she sleeps near the front door, and every dawn she gets up and stairs out the front window looking and waiting for him.

Lizzy was removed from the highway patrol and was given a desk job at the office, hours were long and boring, working as the sheriff's personal secretary.

And as for Joe, times were much harder for him than anyone else in the family, moving to a new state, starting a new job and a family was much harder for him than he could imagine.

After a hard day of work, Joe crashed to bed and his mind began to drift into the horrors from the past.

The dream haunted him with the thought of his brother's death, and sad depressing memories over his death of people of Graytown still runs in his mind. Lizzy awoke to her husband who was tossing and crying in his sleep.

"Joe? Joey, wake up!" she said shaking his shoulder.

"What! What?! What happened?" Joe sat up sweating.

"You were crying...you must've been dreaming," Lizzy kissed him, "was it a nightmare?"

"It was Nathan..." He replied sobbing. From the bedroom door, two of their little ones strolled in.

"Looks like you weren't the only one have night terrors," she said, "Come on up here babies." Lizzy took Josiah and Erin up on their bed, the two cubs snuggled in next to their parents and all went back to sleep.

The next night on a Friday evening, Lizzy returned home late, to a surprise she was greeted by all her kids in their wolf form.

 Joe allowed the kids to stay up so they can all have the night together and have a lovely wolf family dinner.

Lizzy and Joseph transformed into their werewolf bodies, and the Scotfield pack stormed out the cabin to hunt for a wild supper. As the eight werewolves ran through the cornfield, they crossed the creek and entered a pine forest, where the pack stalked a herd of Pronghorns, they chased the antelopes out of the woods and through an open plain.

        With the moon illuminating the wide-open terrain of the fields and hills, the creek and the mountains domes of the Southwest, it was a perfect night for a wolf hunt. The Scotfield pack pursued a straggling buck/ They chased it from the rest of the herd, forcing it to flee uphill alone and vulnerable. Lizzy and Joe flanked the pray on both sides while their six cubs, who were led by Tasha ran up from behind the buck. As they closed in on the pray the six young werewolves pounced on the pronghorn like a lion pride taking down a water buffalo.

The successful hunt ended with the family pack gorging themselves on the meat, with their stomach's all full they then ran together on top of a large rocky slope. As the Scotfields stared up into the beautiful sky to the alluring Luna. The night roared with their chanting howls, that can be heard out for miles, followed by other packs of wolves and coyotes. It was at that moment when the howling seized, Joseph looked towards his mate, then to their children sitting all around them, wrestling and playing together. Spending times like this with his family is what he had always dreamed of and wished it would last forever, but then again, he recalled that it was all a new beginning both for him and his whole werewolf family.